Table of Contents

Twenty Seconds

After The Bomb

True Love That Remains Later In Life

Bad From The Start

Evolution

Doctor Charm

Good Morning

He Was Only Ten Years Old

Fight To Death

TWENTY SECONDS

Twenty seconds...twenty seconds that makes the difference to the whole of a man's life.

Yuri had often thought about those twenty seconds, and sitting on his bunk in the prison camp he thought about them again.

Everyone knew what it meant when the men in the long black overcoats stepped alongside a person on the street, when you see the black Zil glide to a halt a few metres in front of you and a rear door is opened.

Should he have run? He didn't know whether they had weapons, it was most likely they did.
Could he have taken them on? Not then.

Yet he knew - as everyone then knew - what the set-up meant, where he would land up.

The men in the long black coats didn't touch him before they reached the car - they didn't have to. One nudged him into the car and followed him in while the other man went around to the other side and sat in beside Yuri, who was now wedged between the two of them.

He was deposited at the jail, taken in and briefly processed.

Name, Address, Identity Number, a quick search to ensure he had no concealed weapons or anything sharp or dangerous and he was pushed into a cell already holding three others.

It was simple, one chair, a pot that was obviously meant to be the toilet for the cell, and a jug that probably contained water.

One man sat on the chair, another was standing leaning against a wall, the third was sitting on the floor. Two of them were talking to each other, the third was quiet, he looked sullen.

They asked who he was, and why he had been arrested. He told them his name and said he had no idea why he had been taken to jail.

"You'll find out soon enough tomorrow morning."

"What happens then?"

"They take you to court and then you'll find out your sentence."

"My sentence for what?"

"For whatever you've done that got you in here?"

"I haven't done anything to be here."

The man laughed. "Of course you have. Otherwise you wouldn't be here."

"There must be some mistake."

"There's never a mistake. You're here and you'll be sentenced tomorrow."

"How do you know all this?"

"I've been through it twice before. This is my third time. First time they put me away for two years. Second time for six years. I reckon this time, I'll get at least ten."

"What did you do?"

"I rob. I'm a professional thief."

"But you get caught."

"Every few years they get lucky. In between I do very well. Much better than my schoolmates who became doctors or engineers in Siberia and are freezing in the dark in the middle of nowhere building power plants, or working in emergency rooms with old lousy equipment and none of the good medicines they have in the west."

The other two had said nothing.

The night had passed. Yuri had been relieved no-one had started a fight.

Next morning they were all taken into the court. It was an ugly old room, cold, old wood furnishings. The judge sat at a table with two clerks on both sides of him. The desktop was covered with papers.

He had to wait more than three hours until his name was called. He hadn't slept much during the night and he had been almost asleep when they called his name.

He stood and went in front of the judge's table. His name was read out and he was asked to confirm that he was the person.

Another man then stood and walked to the table and announced "I am his lawyer".

"Excuse me. I don't know you. I've never met you. You haven't talked with me. I don't even know what the charge is so, I can't have discussed it with you -"

The judge ignored him and continued.

"The charge is Public Dissent and Disturbing the Peace and Incitement to Riot."

"That's a load of nonsense."

"You are confirming the correctness of the charge with your behaviour," said the judge.

"Excuse me. You tell me about charges I have never heard of and certainly would deny. You tell me a person I have never met who has not asked me what my story is in regard to these charges I didn't even know existed is my lawyer, and then you tell me I am dissenting and inciting riot. Does it look as if there is anyone in this room who is starting to riot now?"

"Mr Goldberg. I suggest you sit down and let your lawyer speak for you. He is appointed by the court to handle these matters."

"Thank you, your honour. Mr Goldberg pleads guilty to the charges and requests leniency as these are his first offences."

Yuri rose in a rage. "I most definitely do not plead guilty. This may be the first time I have been put in front of a court but these are not my first offences because this is a load of nonsense. I haven't committed any offences."

"Defender Korogyn. Your client convicts himself every time he opens his mouth. I see him as more of a danger to the peaceful nature of our society than you do.

I think that ten years in a rehabilitation camp might help him change his thinking and see the error of his youthful ways. He will emerge a more careful citizen with more respect for his elders."

"What? You are convicting me of supposed crimes that I haven't committed. You have not offered any evidence - you certainly haven't shown me a shred of evidence that I have committed any of these crimes and you are already sentencing me. Is this the democracy that we want people in the west to believe we practice?"

"Mr Goldberg. You continue to make false accusations against our state and the democratic nature of our institutions such as this court.

You seem to be one of these young people who only thinks of himself and not of the common good. You do not realize that you are not the only person in this country. You think that everything revolves around you. You will have to learn what your parents and teachers evidently failed to inculcate in you which is that there is a communal good that outweighs your selfish interests. Ten years, Mr Goldberg."

"This is a mockery. In the west they must laugh at us. People like you bring us into disgrace in their eyes when they see and hear and read about such things. You may be determined to put me away and be rid of me, but eventually there will be more and more people who will see the falsehood of public institutions such as this and will demand change. Not because they want to 'rebel' as you call it, but because they want something genuinely honest and truthful."

They had taken him away. He had been driven in a closed van with fourteen others to a different prison where he had stayed for a month, and then been transported by train and ship and truck to this barren, cold island prison.

The temperatures on Vaygach Island rarely go above freezing. The conditions were miserable, work was hard, staying alive was a challenge, many died.

Most prisoners believed they were in a death camp, but some still had the fire within them to live. Some even hoped that there might be regime change one day. Some had worked towards that and hoped others were continuing the good work.

Four years later:

As he often did Yuri sat on his bunk at the end of another draining day, thinking about what had happened, and the twenty seconds when he might have kept his freedom - but had done nothing and lost it.

He wandered over to his closest friend Jerry. "I think we have to go tomorrow. I don't know how much longer I can last with this work and the starvation. I feel myself starting to weaken, and we can't be too weak otherwise we won't have a chance to make it."

"Stop talking back there. You know you are not allowed to talk after dark". It was Dimitry, the room guard. Yuri and Jerry ignored him and continued talking quietly.

Dimitry stormed over pointing his rifle at Yuri who casually lifted it up in one movement as he arose from the bed he had been sitting on, and punched Dimitry hard in his armpit, causing Dimitry to let go of the rifle.

"Take your coat off. Now take your shoes off. Now pull down your pants. Now take off your sweater."

Dimitry pulled his clothes off, his face contorting as he tried to avoid the tears that he felt flooding his eyes.

"Now go back to your bed."

"Tomorrow I shall report you and you'll be in the hut for a week."

The hut was just that. A small hut placed in the middle of the prisoner's wards. It was almost airless inside. A prisoner was left with a large jug of water and a loaf of stale bread to last a week. In the summer it was unbearably hot and in the winter excruciatingly cold. Unless a prisoner was rescued from it before the week ended most didn't survive, or came out so weakened that their survival after the ordeal was very short.

"And you know what happens if someone is put in the hut. Everyone here will stand outside yelling until I'm released, and then the life of the person who put me in won't be worth anything. So don't make such a silly threat."

"You'll see. I'll report you and you won't be in a position to fight."

"And if I hear one more word from you, I'll put *you* outside."

Dressed in only their underwear, no-one would survive more than an hour or two outside, the cold and wind were so bitter at night.

They were up at 4 a.m, they dressed. They lined up outside to be counted and then each was given a can of a warm liquid that was supposed to have been a soup, and then they started marching.

Their destination would be the quarry where all day they would work hewing out limestone that would be loaded on to trucks. They had no idea where it was taken to, or what use would eventually be made of it.

There were forty prisoners, two bunks of twenty men each, supervised by their room guard.

They trudged in the deep snow, it would be about two kilometers to the quarry.

Yuri deliberately lagged, walking more and more slowly until he was at the end of the pack. He was a little behind Dimitry who had been walking parallel with the prisoners, about three or four rows from the front.

Some trees, a cluster of bushes, came up ahead, and Yuri grabbed Dimitry and threw him into the bushes.

He quickly twisted Dimitry's neck, killing him before Dimitry could utter anything more than a stifled cry.

Yuri stripped off Dimitry's coat and boots and pulled off his own, putting Dimitry's on him. He put Dimitry's hat on his head, and made sure that Dimitry's wallet was in the inside coat pocket, picked up Dimitry's gun, and quickly caught up with the end of the prisoner group.

He trudged alongside them slowly, not looking at any of them, until he was closer to Jerry and just behind the other guard.

When they were at the next cluster of bushes Yuri passed his rifle to Jerry and hustled the guard off into the bushes, killing him in the same manner as he had killed Dimitry.

Jerry joined him and took the second guard's coat and hat and gun.

The other prisoners had started to realize that something was happening. They saw two guards coming out from the bushes, and as the guards came nearer the prisoners realized that the men wearing the guards' coats were Yuri and Jerry.

Yuri spoke to the other prisoners, "We are going to walk on as if we are walking to the quarry. In a few minutes a truck with young soldiers is going to come towards us. These are the new recruits who have come for two months to give the guards a break. These youngsters don't really want to be here, but they have to as part of their national service. So they are vulnerable and easily frightened."

"When the truck approaches - and we'll hear it soon - we have to congregate in the middle of the road so the driver has to stop. We'll make the driver and his company step down, and then we'll take it over and send them on to the base on foot, and we'll take the truck."

They trudged on, in the dark, the only sounds being those of their boots in the snow. Very few talked, they were used to working long exhausting days and even talking tired them.

About half an hour later they heard in the distance the sounds of a truck approaching them. As Yuri had instructed them, they spread out in the centre of the road and towards the high snowbanks on either side.

The truck had to stop.

Yuri went up to the driver's cabin, dressed in his guard uniform. "There's been an emergency. We have to take the men back, some of them are ill. So your recruits have to get out and walk to the camp, it's not far from here."

Yuri and Jerry went to the back of the truck and told the recruits who immediately jumped out. The driver wasn't so agreeable. He seemed to be suspicious. He asked Yuri some questions about who was ill, why was it an emergency, why could the prisoners not walk back?

Yuri ignored the questions and when the driver seemed to become stubborn and started refusing to leave the cabin Yuri reached in and pulled him out.

The driver started to bluster, "what the hell is going on, who do you think you're pushing round?"

Yuri dragged him around to the side of the truck and out of sight of everyone kicked him hard at the back of the knee breaking his fibula, and then smashing his head into the side of the truck a few times until the driver collapsed, with a bleeding face. Yuri threw him into the back of the truck, got into the driving cabin, and turned the truck round and drove towards the small harbour.

On the way to the harbour he stopped briefly to throw the driver out into the snow, and then continued the journey.

"Wait here," he told everyone.

Yuri walked up and down along the harbourfront until he saw a boat whose size he thought would be appropriate. He stepped on to it, looking for a captain or owner. He found the owner, but was not very impressed.

He continued looking, tried two others, before he came to what seemed to be a fishing trawler. The owner had the leathery face of a man who had been out in the open most of his life. He was a man of few words yet appeared friendly. Money was exchanged. He would take them across the straits.

The seaman asked them to wait for a few minutes while he collected a few belongings, and suggested they try to hide the truck so that it would not immediately be obvious which boat had been used for them to escape.

Jerry drove the truck away, and as he was returning, the captain and what seemed to be a younger person, a girl, were walking towards the boat, each carrying suitcases.

It was barely dawn and bitterly cold when the captain took off. Most of the men were already below deck, Yuri and Jerry remained on deck, watching the captain, assessing if they could trust him, and looking back at the receding shoreline of the island on which they had spent the last four miserable years.

"Let's go down, it's really cold up here." Jerry led the way. There was an air about the captain, an impression of integrity, that even after four years of disbelieving everyone, of developing the cynicism that they had both associated in the past with people in their sixties and seventies and hadn't imagined that they would develop it themselves so young - but that was what the system did to you - yet here again they both perceived a different quality. A man working hard, on his own, in difficult conditions, with primarily only his own conscience to answer to. They hoped their estimation was correct.

They found some space on the floor of the boat and settled back to rest. The escape had not only been physically challenging and fast, but working up to it and executing it had been emotionally draining. Yuri fell asleep.

He didn't know how long he had been asleep but he felt Jerry waking him urgently.

"Something is going on. I hear some noise above. We should take a look."

Yuri took the gun he had taken from the guard and joined Jerry. They went up the few steps and came into the main lounge deck, and were astonished to see Nikolai, the biggest man of the group, crouching over a young woman under him on a table. Nikolai seemed to be trying to pull the woman's clothes off and she was trying to push him away and shouting at him to stop and saying "no" "no" and "no" again and again.

Jerry pointed in the corner to Yuri where they could see that the captain was being pinned against the wall by three other of the escaped prisoners.

"Go on Nikolai, I'm next," laughed Boris, the second biggest prisoner.

"Leave her alone. She doesn't want you. She's telling you to stop." Yuri spoke quietly but firmly.

Nikolai looked up at Yuri and laughed. "I haven't had a woman in six years and you're telling me to stop. Go to hell."

Two of the men advanced towards Yuri. "You may have helped get us out, but we're free now, so don't tell us what to do."

Yuri gave the gun to Jerry, "shoot these two if they take one step closer to you, I'll deal with Nikolai."

Yuri walked to Nikolai who had resumed trying to pull the girl's jeans down, and Yuri swept Nikolai's right arm behind his back forcefully until everyone could hear the crack of ligaments being torn and Nikolai screamed.

Yuri walked to the other side of the table and rapidly repeated the same action with Nikolai's left arm. Nikolai fell forward onto the girl and Yuri pushed him off, Nikolai fell to the floor, unable to stop his fall with his useless arms.

"You wanted to be next Boris. Which arm shall I break first?"

Boris laughed, and Yuri caught the trace of hesitation in his laugh. But Boris wanted to act the tough hardened prisoner in front of the others and he had to respond belligerently. He moved to the table and started to climb on the girl who was just sitting up. Boris pushed her down, but suddenly found his shirt grabbed from behind and he was pulled right off the girl and the table and landed heavily on his back on the floor.

As he was about to get up Yuri took hold of Boris's forearm and using his thigh as a lever cracked Boris's forearm.

Yuri turned to the men holding the captain. "Let him go." The men complied immediately. They had seen what the smaller and lightly built Yuri could do to the two biggest thugs Nikolai and Boris, and they weren't going to risk their survival.

Yuri asked the captain, "Is this your daughter?" "Yes," he answered.

"I'm sorry that these men abused your hospitality, and that they treated you so badly, young lady. I want you to put on some warm things and come up on the deck with me."

Yuri grabbed Nikolai and pulled him up the stairs to the open deck. He then pulled off Nikolai's trousers and underpants, and with some rope that he saw on the deck tied Nikolai's arms and legs to the nearest solid structure on the deck that he saw.

He took the belt off Nikolai's pants and gave it to the girl. "I want you to beat him with this. I don't want you to have nightmares about this experience for the rest of your life, and if you give him a beating instead of him raping you, it will help the trauma go away."

"I've never done anything like this."

"You've probably also never come close to being raped."

"No. That's true."

"Do it. You may not like it now, but it will make a lot of difference over the next twenty and thirty years of your life."

The girl took the belt and lashed Nikolai's buttocks for a while. She was reluctant at first but gradually the fear she had experienced and her anger at the memory and the thought of what that man had been doing to her overcame her and she hit him with more force and determination.

Nikolai's buttocks were covered in bruises and welts when she finished, and Yuri asked her father to take her back to the lower deck and give her a warm drink.

When they had gone, Yuri told the other escaped prisoners to go down. "The show is over. None of you is going to do anything so stupid again, are you?"

Yuri and Jerry untied Nikolai's hands, and leaving his legs tied together but no longer tied to any part of the boat they picked him up and threw him overboard.

"When those animals attacked my daughter and stopped me helping her I thought I had made the biggest mistake of my life. I have thought of myself as a good judge of character. We usually stay away from the prisoners, we think of them as scum. But when you approached me I had thought I saw a good man. I am relieved that I wasn't wrong. Thank you."

Yuri thought that might have been the longest speech the captain had ever given.

"Your daughter is a brave girl. I hope she will be alright. Will you get into any trouble for taking us?"

'We're not going to go back. There is nothing really for us there, and my daughter needs to get a proper education. She is very good in her schoolwork and there is nothing more for her here. She needs to be in a bigger place with proper schools. I'll leave you off at a place where there aren't any guards so it will give you a little time to disappear, though I don't think that all of your people will get away. Some will be caught, many because they will make big mistakes as they made just now. Then we'll move on and find somewhere else where we can go ashore and start looking to build a new life."

"What happened to her mother?" Yuri asked.

"It was very sad. She was a fine woman. She also came from a fishing family and so she knew the life I led. When my daughter Elena was eleven my wife went out shopping and a drunk driver killed her as she was crossing a road with her shopping bags. Elena has really been wonderful since then. I was quite a good cook, simple but tasty, and Elena quickly learnt herself, and very soon after her mother died she was already sharing the cooking with me as well as keeping up with her schoolwork. And although as you can see she is very pretty she wasn't going out much with the boys because she said that she has to look after me. In fact I was starting to get a bit worried. She's only sixteen and I didn't want her to become an old maid just looking after her father who can look after himself, you know."

The boat docked. They could see the lights of a town not too far in the distance but the cove they had pulled in to was quiet. Yuri and Jerry thanked the captain and gave him some of the money they had collected, and then they told the escaped prisoners still left that each had to go his own way now.

Yuri and Jerry walked away from the others, towards the centre of the town, Severodvinsk.

"You know where I am going to go now, Yuri. I want to start a new life away from this madness. Are you going to come with me?"

"No. I am going to stay in this miserable country and try to make something better of it."

"Remember, if there is anything you should ever need you can contact me. I am sure that you will find some way. You remember my uncle's name?"

"Yes. I wish you all the best. I know that you'll make it Jerry, wherever you land up."

Yuri said that he would walk for a while before deciding where to stay, but first, it was essential for both of them to buy some good food, and some simple clothes. The captain of the boat had given them each a pair of trousers and a shirt and had refused any more money from them, but he apologized that he could not give them any shoes.

They found what seemed to be a cheap clothes store with a selection of men's wear and each bought two more shirts and pants and a pair of shoes that they could walk or travel in.

Jerry walked to the bus station with Yuri, they gave each other a huge bear hug, and parted.

Jerry took two buses, the first travelled over two hundred kilometers and the second nearly three hundred. It was early morning by the time he arrived in the city, Voronezh, from which he intended to take a train close to the Polish border.

The train journey took another eleven hours. He slept for much of the way, arriving late at night.

He continued his sleep in the waiting room of the station. The next morning, after washing his face in the simple washroom of the station, he walked to the outskirts of the small town, finding a truck stop near a large road.

With an appropriate bribe he found a farmer who transported sacks of potatoes in his truck across the border, to take him in the truck and drop him off at the nearest town close to the border.

Jerry then took another train, this time to Bratislava in Czechoslovakia, and from there was able to enter Austria without much difficulty.

He went by bus to Vienna. In Vienna he called his uncle, and was relieved to find that his uncle was still alive and seemed to hear, speak, and think clearly. His uncle understood Jerry's situation and told Jerry that he would be happy to sponsor him, and that he would contact the consulate in Vienna, and Jerry should go there and apply for asylum as a refugee.

Yuri walked around the harbour town for a while. It was a nice town, he thought, looked well-kept, it was busy, but he still thought that a newcomer like him would stand out too much and it would be better to move on.

Yuri took more train rides, often slept in railway stations, found or stole some food from carts in markets, and eventually after three weeks decided to stop at Novosibirsk, a large town.

He was not surprised to find that the house that he was looking for was in a poorer area. He hadn't expected that Dimitry would have been able to afford a really nice home.

He found the street, the house was towards the end. He knocked on the door. A woman opened it - and he found himself staring at a pair of beautiful eyes that seemed as if they were ready to burst out from an exquisite face.

"Can I help you?"
"You are Mrs Grovodny?"
"Yes, I am."
Yuri took the wallet out from his jacket pocket. "You don't quite look the woman in this picture."
He showed her a picture of Dimitry, a woman and two small children.

She laughed, "yes, that is me, some years ago. How is it that you have this picture? Please, come in and tell me."

"Thank you. I have some not very good news for you, I don't know if you have heard it yet. I was in the prison camp with Dimitry. There was a break-out and Dimitry was killed. I managed to leave, and wanted to bring this back to you, and also this money that was in the wallet."

He was surprised that she didn't cry. "Thank you for bringing it to me and for bringing me the money. I'm not surprised he was killed. He had a tendency to mess his life up. That's how he got into prison. I'm surprised anyone escaped. I thought nobody ever got out of those places. He was supposed to be in for six years, but I never really expected him back. Can you tell me what it was like there. We never got to hear anything. There was no mail, and it was too far to visit. I don't think they intended anyone to ever visit. But first, let me give you something to eat."
"You don't have to."

"I was going to sit down with the children and have supper anyway so please join us."

He told her about the prison camp, about the constant hard work every day in the most difficult conditions, the starvation, the deprivations, the immense emptiness of the landscape. He did not talk much about Dimitry. He said that people did not share much about each other in such a place. People often assumed that others might betray them for the privilege of a little extra food, or not having to do the same physical labour but be put in charge of a work group. He supposed that must have happened with Dimitry, but he didn't tell her that.

While he talked he also looked directly at her, because he was mesmerized by the beauty of her face and her eyes. He found pleasing to his ears her soft but clear voice and the way she expressed herself.

She told him that she had managed to support herself and the children because she was a teacher in a local school.

He wondered how she and Dimitry had come to marry, she seemed much more educated than he had been.

"It was a mistake from the start. I did not have a happy childhood. My grandfather was a dictator who abused his children, including my mother. She married my father who was an abusive alcoholic. I think they married because she was pregnant with my older brother. My father regularly beat my mother, I would see her face bruised and puffy, I would hear the hard slaps and her cries, and I just wanted to run away and escape from that. She told me many times that he forced himself on her sexually when she didn't want it, and she hated him when he did that.

My husband came along, he pretended to be a happy and successful traveling salesman, selling a variety of personal things such as perfumes and creams, and things for the home, and would bring my family presents of these to make them like him and suitable for me. I found out later that he had stolen all these things and was selling them, and that's what led to his going to prison. He got caught. But by then we were married and had the children.

I knew it was a mistake from very early on. I knew there was something odd about these things he was selling, and his stories about how he got them didn't sound right. I didn't feel a sense of love for him, or passion or excitement. I know now I didn't love him. But I became pregnant quickly, and after having my first child I decided that I liked having children and it also kept me away from him for most of the time so I decided to have another, and then he was caught and sent to prison.

So you see I don't really miss him, I have no sense of big loss, I didn't love him, he wasn't the love of my life. I only have to find the words to explain to my children as they get older year by year, who their father was and why they aren't seeing him, and now are never going to see him again.

Now tell me, why did you seem so surprised when I opened the door, that you had to ask me if I was Mrs Grovodny?"

"Because you are so much more beautiful than your picture shows. You have the most beautiful eyes I have ever seen and the most beautiful face."

She blushed, "Thank you. It is so nice of you to say that. My husband never said anything like that. He just complained that I was too fat. I haven't asked you, where are you staying?"

"I haven't decided yet. I was going to look for a small hotel."

"You mean you don't have a place to sleep tonight. Then you must stay here. My son will sleep on the sofa here, and you shall have his bed."

"You don't have to go to so much trouble," Yuri protested.

"It isn't a lot of trouble, and you have brought more money for me than I shall be able to spend in a year, and you have also told me about life in that place. So I think that it is very appropriate that you sleep here."

"Thank you."

The next morning she woke Yuri and asked him what he would like to eat for breakfast. No one had ever done that to him since he was a small child and his mother would wake him to get up for school.

"Do you have work?"

"I am going to look for work. When I was studying I also worked as a car mechanic. I liked it, and I found that I was good at it. So I am going to try to find work in a garage somewhere."

"If you do that you are not going to have much time to look for a place to stay, so I would like you to come back here tonight, even if you find a good job."

Yuri was pleased with the invitation. He liked this woman, he had noticed how clean the house was and how well she looked after it even though it was in a poorer neighbourhood. He had really liked talking with her and didn't mind at all spending another evening with her.

Yuri asked her where most of the garages were and she told him the area of the town where he would find them and how to get there. He walked for half an hour and then went into different garages.

He came to one garage, looked around for a few minutes and then asked to see the owner or manager.

"My name is Yuri. I'm a mechanic, and I am looking for work."

The person who met him responded, "how long have you worked as a mechanic?"

"For the past seven months."

The owner raised his eyebrows. "Just seven months. And what were you doing before that?"

"I was a guest very far away in one of our government facilities intended to kill off people."

"Because you are a thief, or a murderer, or what?"

"No. I think I was labelled a political dissident."

"Ah, a trouble maker. Or could it be because you are a zhid?"

The owner hadn't said that term with any particular hostility or disdain. It seemed to Yuri that he had just asked it as a factual question.

"I believe you are correct. I am indeed a zhid and that was probably the reason for my being sent away after a

mockery of what is called a trial. So no, I have never stolen, I am not a thief and certainly not a professional assassin."
"Is there a special area that you like to work in?"

"I am pretty good at judging what might be wrong with a car when a customer brings it in, and recommending what to do to repair it quickly and for the least cost."
"O'k, I'll give you a try, and we'll see if you know what you are doing.
Just get started and I'll hear from my people whether you are any good."

Yuri worked all day, and at the end of the day the owner told him that he appeared to be very capable and he could return the next day.

Yuri was getting ready to leave, most of the other mechanics had left already, and just then, a woman brought in a car, and jumped out of it agitated. "It's been making these funny noises all day. I couldn't get it started for a long time, and then when I got it started I just rushed here."
Yuri didn't wait. He lifted up the bonnet and put his ear to the engine. He asked the woman to go back into the car and put her foot on the accelerator. He turned to the owner and asked if he could have some tools and a replacement part. The owner called to one of the other workers who was still there to bring what Yuri had asked for.

Yuri asked the woman to switch off the engine. He spent a few minutes unscrewing some parts and removing them and then replacing them with the parts he had requested. He then asked the woman to sit in the car and turn on the engine again. She did, and it made a completely different noise this time, the soft gentle purring of an engine running smoothly.

He said something quietly to the owner who nodded his agreement and then told the woman to drive the car outside for two or three streets and then come back.

She did and said the car was now running very smoothly. She asked the cost and Yuri told her to speak with the owner.

The owner came back to Yuri a few minutes later, "you handled that very well. For new customers we use a rotation, each person waits their turn until the next car comes in."

Yuri went to work the next day. He borrowed overalls from the locker room, introduced himself briefly to the other front-line workers, and worked on a few cars.

About mid-day, the owner asked him to step into his office.

"I can see that you are very good. I'd like to hire you permanently. What were you being paid at your last place?"

Yuri told him what he thought was the usual rate of pay. "I'll increase that by 10%. Let me tell you that what I expect from my workers is honesty, and courtesy dealing with customers. We try to do good work and not cheat them and we have a good reputation that is very important to me. Some customers like to give tips or gifts. We have a rule that tips go into a big box and then are shared out among everyone, so that the people who are not front-line and don't meet customers still get the reward for the good work they do. Gifts you can keep for yourself. How many days do you usually work?"

"Sometimes six, sometimes five. When I am in a new city I like to have the chance to sometimes have two days at the weekend to explore the larger area."

"That is alright with me, just make sure you tell me if you intend to take a longer weekend."

Yuri finished his day of work at the garage. It had been a good day. He had serviced five customers and had repaired their cars quickly and efficiently. They had all taken the short drive around the nearby streets to test that their cars were running well, and had expressed their satisfaction. He went back to Mrs Grovodny's house and told her that he had found a good job and would look for a place to live the next day.

"You are very welcome to stay here. I shall ask you to help and pay me some rent, I think it will be cheaper for you than finding a place of your own, and my guess is that I am probably a better cook than you. Also, I think it might be good for my children to see a nice, hard-working man in the house for a while."

Yuri was touched by her invitation. He had found himself very attracted to her, and didn't think it was just because he had not had a relationship with a woman for so many years. And even those relationships were with students. He had proved to himself that his sexuality had come back with the many women that were available in the first few towns he had stopped at. But those were just paid encounters, brief, with no personal feeling or passion other than the simple physical lust.

"I'm very grateful to you, Mrs Grovodny…"
"Svetlana, please. You don't have to be so formal with me. At home I'm not a schoolteacher."
"No. You're not. You are a very lovely woman who looks after a home beautifully and who has two lovely children, and who is a pleasure to talk to."

Svetlana blushed deeply. No man had ever spoken to her with such words, and in truth she had never believed that anyone ever would. She had never thought of herself as beautiful.

"Thank you. You say such nice things to me."

She gave him one of the children's rooms. She said that the children were still young enough to sleep in the same room.

He went to work regularly. He was prompt. He was efficient. He was polite and friendly with customers and he tried to get along with the other workers. He was very careful to place his tips in the communal box, because he could see that the other workers were noticing that many of the customers were giving him good tips, and were starting to come in asking specifically for him. He made sure to stay in the rotation sequence, so that the other mechanics had their fair share of work. It was just that he was a lot quicker in diagnosing the problems and fixing them than the others, even some of the older mechanics who had many more years of experience than he had.

He would come to Svetlana's home at the end of the day. Even though he had worked hard he still first sat with the children for a while and looked over their homework and school lessons with them. Svetlana observed this. She was realizing more and more that though he was working as a car mechanic he appeared to be a highly intelligent and educated man. She wondered what had happened to him to not let him become a successful professional or academic man.

After he had been working at the garage for four months the owner called him into his office. Yuri was concerned. Had his work not been satisfactory? Had he upset a customer?

"I wanted to have a brief talk with you Yuri. Your work has been excellent. I keep hearing very positive comments from our customers, and more people seem to be coming to us because of you. I'm going to increase your salary by another 15% because you have been such an asset to the business. I would suggest you not tell all the other mechanics, they might become very jealous and resentful. And one more thing. My wife and I would like you to come to our home for dinner tomorrow night."

Yuri was astonished. "Thank you. Thank you for both, the invitation and the salary increase. Tomorrow is Friday, isn't it. Yes, I'd love to come."

The owner wrote the address and brief directions on a slip of paper and gave it to Yuri. "On Friday evening we usually eat at 7. Is that alright for you?"

"Yes, definitely. Thank you."

Yuri told Svetlana that he had been invited to his boss's home for dinner, and that he would be receiving a salary increase, "and therefore I am going to pay you more rent."

"You don't have to…"

"I insist. You have been so good to me that I want to show my appreciation to you. And there is one other thing. I would like to take you and the children for a weekend to the sea. We can leave next Friday afternoon and drive, it should take us about five hours, and we can stay at a nice hotel for two days, and then come back for work and school."

"Don't you usually work on Saturday?"

"Usually yes. But I had an agreement with the owner that if I wanted to see more of the area around here I could sometimes take a two-day weekend instead of one day."

"I've never been to the sea. Nor have the children."

"Even more reason to go."

"Do we need swimsuits? I don't have one and the children don't."

"Then we shall go to a store early next week and buy swimsuits for you and the children. One thing. Would you mind very much if we all stayed in one room together?"

"I've never even been to the sea before. You think I am going to mind sharing a room? I am already so excited about the idea, and I am sure the children will be. Do you really think that I would mind sharing a room with you?"

"You blush so beautifully," Yuri replied. "So it's agreed. I can make reservations for a hotel?"

"Yes. Thank you so much."

Igor Revekzin, the owner of the garage, lived in a nice neighbourhood. The houses were modern, there was a little space between them, they weren't all crowded on top of one another. Yuri saw some children, they seemed to be about ten or eleven years old, still playing on bicycles as he drove to the house and parked outside.

The door was opened by a tall, thin, gangling teenage boy.

"I'm Yuri."
"Come in. I'm Ivan. My parents...oh, here they are."
"Hello Yuri. This is my wife Miriam."
"Yuri shook hands with a woman who was in her forties but looked well, a little heavy but carrying it well, and with a pleasant smile."
"I'm pleased to meet you Yuri. I have heard so many good things about you. Please come in. You've met Ivan, and this is Natasha, our daughter. She is 11 and Ivan is 12."
Yuri shook hands with them. The daughter was also tall, but had both parent's sturdiness, unlike her brother who looked as if he had no interest in food. Yuri gave them a bottle of wine that he had bought. "Thank you. That is very thoughtful of you."

They went into the dining room where the table had been laid, and then Yuri was surprised to see Igor's wife take a match and light two candles that were in a silver candelabra on a credenza behind the dining room table.

Yuri watched as she took a scarf and put it over head, then waved her hands before the candles and then covered her eyes with her hands, and then said in a clear voice.

"Boruch ato adonai eloheinu melech hoeilom, asher kidshonu bemitzvoisov vetzivonu lehadlik neir shel shabbos."

Without thinking Yuri immediately uttered "Omein."

Igor said to Miriam. "You see. I told you he was Jewish." "You are both Jewish?" asked an astonished Yuri.

"No," replied Igor. "I am not but Miriam is.

Miriam turned to Yuri, "you have seen someone in your family light candles Friday night before?"

"Both my grandmothers did. My mother didn't. I think she was just too scared. Perhaps my being put in prison justified in her mind not showing her Jewishness in any way."

"So you were in prison because you were Jewish?"

Yuri laughed. "Yes, and no. I am sure I was sentenced with what was basically meant to be a death sentence because I was Jewish, but officially the excuse for my arrest and being put in prison was because I was a university dissident and trouble maker.

But the trial was such a farce. There was no detailed explanation of the reasons for my arrest, there was no evidence, I was not allowed to challenge or cross-examine even the prosecutor, and I was found guilty without any explanation of the charges and on what they were based.

So I owe you an extra thanks for hiring me. Now I understand your comments about my being a zhid when you interviewed me."

"Yes. You do look very Jewish, Yuri. I told Miriam about you, and I mentioned you again over the past few weeks when you have been working so well, and she said we must have you over for dinner. There are not many Jewish people around here, and certainly not in my work. Not even people who actually are Jewish but prefer to keep it hidden."

Yuri told them about the prison camp. He didn't give them much detail about the escape. He just said that there was a break-out and a number of prisoners escaped. He didn't know how many were recaptured or killed, but he was relieved that he was still alive, and that he was pretty sure that his friend Jerry - who was also Jewish, he told them - was also alive, and he hoped by now in the United States.

He asked Miriam about her Jewish background and asked Igor whether his family had given him a difficult time for marrying a Jewish woman.

Igor laughed. "For about five minutes they gave me a difficult time. Then I introduced Miriam to them and they have been falling all over themselves since wondering how I could have found such a wonderful woman, and then since the children came along it's as if I don't exist anymore, that I was just a sperm bank to give them grandchildren."

"Oh, Igor, you know they love you and think that you are a really great guy. That you work hard. You have built up on your own a good business and you have a very good name as a decent and honest person."

It was an enjoyable evening. Yuri liked the family. He was impressed with Igor choosing such a fine wife, he hoped he would be able to do the same.

"Do you want to go with a friend to choose a swimsuit?" Yuri asked Svetlana.

"You are the person who is going to see me in the swimsuit most of the time, so I think you should come. It will be fun for the children also."

It was fun. Svetlana eventually chose a light grey one-piece that had a diagonal yellow and blue stripe running across it from one shoulder to the opposite thigh.

They left Friday afternoon after the children came home from school. Svetlana had packed knapsacks for both the children the night before and had made some sandwiches for all of them.

The children were so excited on the drive, they had never been so long in a car. But being children they eventually became bored and tired and were sleeping by the time they arrived.

Yuri and Svetlana carried the children half-asleep into the hotel, and then in the elevator to their room on the fourth floor.

It was quite a big room. Svetlana saw that there were two large beds next to each other, and then in the opposite corner of the room a two-tier bunk bed. The washroom was small, with a shower, sink, and toilet, and some towels on a shelf in the bathroom.

The room looked out over the sea, Yuri had insisted on that in making the reservation.

"It's a lovely room," said Svetlana quietly.
"That's because you are in it," said Yuri, causing Svetlana to blush again.
The children had woken up by now, and they all decided that it was time to eat. They went to the dining room and had supper, and then they all went for a walk along the street by the sea.

"The air feels different, and it smells different here," said Svetlana. "There is a freshness, it feels cleaner. I suppose we have so much pollution in the cities we ignore it until we come to a place that has much less and we see or feel the difference."
As they walked it became darker and they returned to the hotel. The children had a shower and then they put them to bed.

They left the lights off, and Yuri and Svetlana lay on their bed next to each other. Quite soon they heard the sounds of the children fast asleep. Yuri turned to Svetlana and gently kissed her on the mouth.

She responded by putting her arms around his neck and kissing him in return.

They continued kissing and holding each other, caressing each other, still dressed.

Yuri unbuttoned his shirt and took it off, then did the same with Svetlana's blouse.

She reached behind her and unclasped her bra and he helped lift it off, and then took both her breasts in his hands, quietly telling her that they were beautiful.

He caressed them, caressed the nipples, and then took each breast into his mouth and sucked on it and on the nipple.

As he did so, she caressed his back and his neck and his face. She ran her fingers through his hair and whispered in his ear how much she enjoyed what he was doing.

He stood up, undid his belt and took off his trousers and she loosened her skirt and let it drop to the floor.

"Why don't we take a shower?" he suggested.

They did. Seeing her fully naked for the first time he told her that she had a really beautiful body. "Thank you, but I know I am fat."

"No. You are beautifully rounded in a way that I very much like. To me you are totally feminine. What you think of as fat I see as being curvaceous, voluptuous, very very feminine. And to me very exciting," which of course provoked more blushing from Svetlana that Yuri could see, even though it was quite dark now.

They caressed each other while showering, and continued kissing. Their love-making was quiet, it was gentle and yet passionate. Yuri repeatedly complimented Svetlana on the beauty of her body, the softness of her skin, the excitement he felt touching and kissing and caressing her.

Igor invited him again for dinner many times. One evening, they were enjoying themselves, as usual Miriam had cooked a wonderful meal, but they were interrupted by hard knocking at the door.

Igor went to open it, and found a heavy-set youngish man wearing a smart coat and gloves on the steps. As Igor opened the door the man pushed his way inside.

"Excuse me," said a surprised Igor, "who are you, and who do you think you are, pushing your way into my house?"

As a reply the man turned and punched Igor in the stomach. "Shut up, and listen to me."

Igor was having difficulty breathing. Miriam and Yuri had got up from the table to see what was happening. They had heard Igor's gasp of pain.

"You haven't been paying your tax. I am here to collect it. Get it now," said the intruder.

Yuri did not like the sound of this. Genuine tax collectors did not come around to people's houses in the evenings and punch them and demand immediate payment. "What tax is he talking about, Igor?" he asked.

"Who is this?" snarled the man, who then turned to Yuri, "shut your mouth young man and stay out of this."

Yuri was not deterred. He had seen his share of bullies in prison over the years. "What tax is he talking about, Igor?" he repeated.

The man walked over to Yuri and pushed his face inches away from Yuri. "I said shut up, or I'll start on you."

Yuri stared back at him. "What tax is he talking about, Igor?"

The man went to hit Yuri in the stomach, but as he pulled back his fist to do so Yuri pushed that arm back and used the momentum to turn the man's arm behind his back and push it up towards his shoulder, very painfully.

"These people want 15% of our income each month. They call it insurance, or tax, or whatever name they give it. It changes from week to week."

"And you have been paying them?"
"No. I haven't been paying them."
"Good."

The man who had burst into their home said, "Not good. Everyone has to pay the tax. Let me go or it will be a lot worse for you."

"Igor, is there any good reason at all you should pay these people? Do they do anything at all for your business?"

"They do nothing. They are parasites. They threaten and intimidate people and so people pay. I have had enough of paying."

Yuri let the man go. "You have heard what he said. I suggest you leave him alone, otherwise you will also have me to contend with."

The man didn't leave once Yuri released him, but walked into the dining room. He looked around and saw a nice vase. He casually picked it up and dropped it on the floor where it shattered. He then left.

Yuri went out after him. "You just broke something belonging to these good people. Now you have to pay for it."

The man laughed and continued walking to his car. Yuri took hold of his shoulder to spin him round. The man was expecting that and as he turned lashed out - hitting air. Yuri then hit him very hard in his abdomen and then in his face, and kicked him hard in his testicles. The man crumbled to the ground. Yuri kicked him again, and when the man seemed at least temporarily helpless, Yuri reached into his pockets until he found a wallet and many rolls of money.

The next day at the garage, two large burly men came in. They were not bringing in a car for repair. Yuri did not like the look of them. They were going towards Igor's office, Yuri stopped what he was doing and also made his way towards the office.

He waited outside, he could hear voices inside being raised, and then some thuds and what sounded like an expression of pain from Igor. Yuri went inside. One of the men was holding Igor from behind while the other was punching Igor in the face.

Yuri had brought in with him a large and heavy wrench and he hit the man who was punching Igor, hard on his shoulders, on both sides. They could all hear the bones cracking. Yuri then turned on the man who was holding Igor and hit him hard on the backs of both legs, again breaking the fibula bones. The man collapsed.

Yuri grabbed the man who had been doing the hitting, and tried to force him to admit who had hired them, who had sent them to extort and beat.

The man refused to say anything. He could not move his arms well because both clavicles had been broken, and Yuri took his hands and smashed both with the wrench. The man cried out in agony, and Yuri turned to the other man, who was also moaning on the floor.

The other man quickly gave up the information. They would bring the money to an accountant who was called "the treasurer", and he would pass it on to the syndicate that 'everyone' knew was run by the mayor and the chief of police. Yuri was a bit shocked - yet not so surprised by this news. Igor shrugged his shoulders. It was no surprise to him. "This is what you would find in any city, Yuri. It's not peculiar to us."

Yuri and one of the mechanics dragged the men behind the garage, put them in a truck, and dumped them outside the local hospital.

Three days later, two policemen came by and told Igor and Yuri that they were under arrest and that the garage was being closed because of various alleged violations.

Igor told them that the allegations were nonsense, the garage was busy, people were lining up to have their cars repaired and serviced. He said that they would fight any charge in court, and if they sensed that a court was biased they would ignore any dishonest judgment.

He also showed them his face with the bruises from the beating, added that he and Yuri would not accept being arrested. Igor knew that the police force was small, and they could not afford to send more officers to try to enforce an arrest against people who were unwilling, and who had shown that they could effectively resist thugs and bullies.

But Yuri also recognized that it was time for him to go. That he was in some way contributing to difficulty for Igor and Igor's family. It saddened him. He liked them. He had liked the work. He had become very popular and much admired, and he had developed a very close and loving relationship with Svetlana and her children.

He went to Igor's house that evening and said goodbye to them, thanking Miriam for being so kind to him. They asked him if they could keep in touch with him and he agreed, he took their telephone number.

Then he had to come back to Svetlana and tell her and the children that he was going to be leaving.

There was a lot of crying. He had become very fond of Svetlana, and she of him. They had found a true companionship and a very deep liking of each other.

But he had to leave. He had seen that those in power could be very vindictive. He didn't want Igor and his family to be hurt any more, and he certainly could not let Svetlana and the children be hurt in any way.

Yuri moved on. He drove away with a better and larger wardrobe than what he had started out with, but otherwise he had not acquired much extra baggage.

He travelled for another three days, eventually turning south. He decided to stop not too far from Odessa where he had grown up. He had still not contacted his parents. He was concerned that they should not be persecuted in any manner more than they had been when he had first been arrested and jailed.

He found a place to rent, and had no difficulty finding a place to work. As before, he quickly became popular at work as a very quick and highly efficient worker who was an expert diagnostician and very conscientious in his repairs. He always insisted on driving along a few streets with customers after finishing the repairs so that they could see that the car was running much better.

Within a few months he had saved enough money to buy himself a small house, and had decided to open his own garage.

Not surprisingly, his garage was successful. People heard about him from pleased and satisfied friends and neighbours, and he became very busy quite quickly. He hired new staff, choosing carefully, and also made some security modifications to the garage. Painful past experience had taught him a lot.

But a year after he had opened his garage, he started to receive visits, from the potential extortionists of this city.

He tried to make it clear to them that however successful they might have been in intimidating and taking money from some owners, he was not interested.

The attempts to bully him then started. This time it did not take him long to find who was the 'treasurer' of this syndicate, and to follow that accountant to the weekly poker game where the other members gathered.

He recognized the mayor and the police chief - same story as in every city, he thought - and addressed them, and asked if the other people around the table were also members of the city council.
Some had probably been instructed not to answer, but others did identify themselves.

Yuri tried to encourage them to speak out openly, but some seemed to freeze at the opportunity and hesitate to take advantage of it.

So he told them bluntly that the extortion had to stop. People worked hard and paid taxes. For a small group of people to take money from people that they had done nothing to deserve was no longer acceptable.

He said to them, "I know that you are thinking who is this man, and maybe you will laugh after I have left. But I want you to realize that you have been spoken to, and from now on you cannot say that no-one ever challenged you and told you it is unacceptable and has to stop, that no-one ever warned you."

The next day, two burly men - it was obvious to him that this also was the same pattern in every city - came to his garage and started to tell him that the 'committee' had decided that his contribution should be 20% of his gross intake, and they would be checking his work each week to see how much money he was generating. Yuri told them that they were wasting their time and his time, and that they were not welcome at his garage unless they had cars that needed repairing.

The following Monday morning the two men reappeared, and seeing them at the entrance to his garage Yuri strode to them and asked them if they had a car to repair. They did not, so he told them to leave.

They looked at each other, and then one turned towards Yuri intending to punch him in the stomach. The man's fist hit metal, and the man howled. Yuri had strapped a large metal shield to his waist.

Yuri then took from a table next to him one of his large wrenches and hit the other man on his elbow, cracking it.

"Do you want more?" asked Yuri. "Go back and tell your bosses that even if you come back with twenty people the answer is no."

The next day there were not twenty - but there were six, and they came with weapons. Yuri knew that because as soon as they approached an alarm went off, a new security feature Yuri had added.

As the alarm went off, three sturdy and armed men stepped out from a room near the front of the garage. They were security guards whom Yuri had hired.

They approached the would-be extortioners. "Put down your guns, and leave them there at the door. You can have them back when you leave, if you behave yourselves," ordered one of Yuri's security men, "and don't think of trying to fire. You won't survive."

But some thugs have no other purpose and no value, and if they cannot do this job then they see themselves as useless, and so even with poor odds they will try. Three of them did try to pull the triggers on their weapons - and they were shot.

The three left standing put their weapons down. Yuri asked them if they now wanted to come in and discuss anything. Their leader said they had nothing to discuss. The message was supposed to be in the intimidation and the taking of the money. As the intimidation had been unsuccessful and the leader was sure that Yuri was not going to give them money, they would have to return and convey that message to their boss.

Yuri asked who their bosses were, the leader responded, "You know perfectly well who they are, you met them a few nights ago."

Yuri decided that the matter still had to be dealt with in a very direct and blunt manner.

He went first to the office of the mayor and told the mayor that this greedy and exploitative behaviour had to stop. That it may have been fun for a while but the people could no longer tolerate it. People had to earn their money by honest hard work, not by bullying others. He suggested to the mayor that the mayor ask some of the thugs who had been sent in the past few days whether they had been successful.

Yuri also suggested that the mayor also ask the thugs whether their experience with Yuri had been pleasurable or painful. Yuri could see that the mayor, who had grown fat and slovenly with his abuse of power, was starting to think seriously.

Yuri did not have the same impression when he went to the Chief of Police. The Chief of Police was a leaner man, he appeared stiffer, more rigid, and unwilling to even think of giving up or sharing the money and privileges he had accumulated as Chief of Police.

Whereas the mayor had seemed shocked and was quieter in his responses, the Chief of Police took a very aggressive position, threatening Yuri with a variety of grave consequences.

As they were talking the door opened and an attractive woman, probably in her mid-thirties thought Yuri, came in. The Chief of Police looked at her and in an abrupt and brusque manner asked, "what do you want?"

The woman replied, "I got called from the school, Alina wasn't feeling well, they said I should take her to the hospital."

"So go," he said. "I have," the woman replied, "I came here to tell you because she was asking for you."

"Well, I'm too busy. That's your job, to look after the children. I've told you not to bother me at work."

Yuri was astonished at this exchange, by the rudeness of the Police Chief to the woman Yuri presumed was the Chief's wife.

As the woman left, Yuri walked after her. "Excuse me, my name is Yuri. May I ask how is your daughter?"
The woman appeared surprised that any man would be interested.

"She's seven years old. She was throwing up in her class. It's not like her."

"I presume you are the Chief's wife?"

"Yes, although not everyone would guess it from the way he behaves towards me." she smiled. "I'm Valentina."

"Do you have some other children, Valentina?"

"Yes, Stanislav is nine, and Pavel is four. Do you have any children?"

"No, I've never been married."

"Oh, so you're an eligible young man. There are many lovely single women here, I don't know how many you have met yet. Maybe such a charming man has met all of them?"

He laughed, "thank you for the compliment. No, I've only been here a short time and I haven't had much time yet to meet women. I have been setting up my own business and that has taken time and energy."

"What do you do?"

"I opened a garage for car repairs."

"Oh, Oh, are you the wonderful young man my friends have been telling me about who is so good, and quick and very reasonably priced."

"That sounds very nice. I am glad if some of your friends had really good service. That makes me feel very good, very proud."

They had been walking outside the building, towards her car. He saw that she had a larger and smarter car than most. He wondered if that was how her husband kept her loyalty, with lavish gifts?

"My husband bought me this car. He thought that it would make up for all the time he doesn't spend with me, for the shouting, for the insults, the putdowns, the criticisms, and more."

"And more?" he wondered. "Are you going back to the hospital now?"

"As a matter of fact that was my intention."

"May I accompany you?"

She was a bit taken aback at first. Why would he want to accompany her, he looked so young as if he had just finished college. She asked him if he had been much exposed to older married women. He told her he hadn't, but that she seemed to him to be needing some company and someone to talk to for a while.

They went to a nearby café and sat. Valentina told him about herself, about her marriage, and about her fears that some new business ventures that her husband invested in would be as useless as others the Chief had tried in the past.

Two nights later he heard a knock at his front door. He went to open it, and was surprised to see Valentina, with a bruised face, and surrounded by three young children, each carrying a small suitcase.

He stood aside and invited her to come in. She came in and told him that her face was the result of abuse by her husband, that the abuse had gone on for some years, she had felt frightened of leaving in the past, but it had become too much for her, and she didn't think it was good for the children to see and hear two unhappy parents always arguing and fighting.

Moving her children into his home had been like the seamless repair of a torn skirt or pants. Within a few days it was as if they had lived together as a family for years.

She seemed to know almost instinctively what he needed and what space he required from her and the children. He liked the children and they liked him, and she and he were instantly comfortable with each other. Neither saw the need to make great demands on the other.

She and the children were in one room together, he had brought in a portable bed for her that she assured him was comfortable enough for her.

He had intended it for one of the children and that she should take one of the two beds with more comfortable mattresses, but she seemed to insist that she wanted the children to feel comfortable and not miss their previous home too much.

Mealtimes flowed just as naturally. She bought some groceries and asked him what he preferred in terms of fish and meat and how he liked them cooked or boiled or roasted or grilled and he asked her what she and the children liked. His years of deprivation in the prison camp had given him now an enjoyment of any pleasantly cooked solid food, and he found everything that she made nourishing and tasty.

It was in the kitchen that the first signs of affection between them had appeared. He would put an arm around her shoulder and give her a hug and thank her for a meal, and she would turn and put her hand to his face and gently kiss him and thank him for giving her and her children a home and being warm and accepting to them.

She had been living at his house for four months when he made a suggestion at supper that they go away for a vacation. He remembered the vacation he had taken with Svetlana and how much of a boost it had been to her and her children, as well as to him.

"Do you think you can ask your place of work to let you miss Thursday and Friday next week, so we can go away for a few days, all of us together?"

She was surprised. "That's very nice. But I don't think I can afford to go anywhere."

"Don't worry about paying. I would pay for everything."

"I couldn't let you do that. You have been kind enough in letting us stay here."

"You do more than enough to make me feel very happy that you are here. You and the children make this into a real home. It wasn't a real home before. It was just the place where I lived. You've made it a real home. I can afford for all of us to go away for a few days."

She had tears in her eyes. "Where were you thinking of going."

"When was the last time you and the children were by the sea, at a beach"?"

"I think it was four years ago, when Pavel was 1."

"And not since?"

"No. The last few years my husband went away with the mistresses. A different one each year. His secretary, he called them. He thought I didn't know when he said he had a conference, or needed to do some work away from me and the children. I knew. I understood."

When she told the children they were very excited. She wondered if that was just because they would be missing a few days of school, but listening to them talk with each other and with their friends it seemed that the idea of being away by the sea was very appealing.

They drove. They packed the car with what they needed, and she made a lot of food for the journey. The drive was seven hours, but as they came nearer the children opened the car windows and claimed that the air already smelled different.

The dacha was in a forest but he told her that it was only a short drive to the sea. It was old, probably pre-revolution, but had been well kept inside. There were two bedrooms on the upper floor, and a kitchen and dining room and sitting room on the ground floor.

Yuri lifted the bags out of the car and brought them into the house. Valentina brought in the food as the children ran into the house examining all the rooms.

"Are we going to sleep in the bunk beds?" asked Stanislav. "I want the top one," Pavel called out.

"That leaves the large bed for you," Yuri turned to Valentina.

Valentina took Yuri's hand and guided him to the main bedroom. "I think it's time that we shared a room together. I want to be with you."

Yuri looked at her, and put his arms around her shoulders. "I would like that also."

Their time at the dacha and the sea went quickly, that's how they thought about it afterwards, but all of them enjoyed it. The children had loved the forest and the beach. They had run into and out of the ocean shrieking with delight each time. Yuri and Valentina cooked together, and when the children had gone to bed they made love as if they had known each other for many years and knew exactly what each liked.

Yuri asked her what had gone so wrong in their marriage. She seemed to him to be a very decent, sensible, level-headed intelligent woman, and a very lovely woman physically. He wondered why her husband would have treated her so badly.

She had told him that he had seemed to her at first to be a very nice man, a very strong man, but she had come to see that he didn't understand very much about women, and didn't seem to want to. Women, she said, are so often attracted to the 'bad guys', that there is something challenging and almost compelling about such men, even though something at the back of the woman's mind tells her from the beginning that this man will end up hurting her - hurting her badly.

She had seen this in women older than her, divorcees in their 50's and 60's, and of course in numerous young women in their twenties and thirties.

She admitted to him that she had seen the signs from the start that her husband was a very controlling and bullying person, but when she was younger she had mistaken that for love and ambition. She had initially admired his desire to become police chief and his conviction that he would, and she hadn't realized it was so that he could become rich, push people around, and be petty and vengeful towards anyone who disagreed with him or crossed him.

It was dark when they returned to their home. There were few lights from other houses in the street. Their house was dark. Yuri sensed something was wrong as he approached his house but he couldn't yet articulate it as a clear thought in his mind.

Turning her head back towards her daughter's request saved Valentina's life as the first bullet shattered the windscreen and just missed her head.

Yuri pulled hard on the steering wheel and turned the car sharply towards the trees at the side of the driveway.

"Down everyone," he shouted, "keep your heads down, lie on the floor."

Yuri opened the car door on his side and slid out. He then put his hand under his seat and took out his automatic rifle, and then opened the compartment he had made under the dashboard on the driver's side and took out his night goggles. They were a recent pair someone had brought from Israel. He knew they were not quite as good as the latest American models, but they were a pair that could be brought to the country and sold.

Yuri put on the goggles and waited a while for his eyes to adjust. He then slowly crawled to the front of the car on the driver's side and carefully looked.

He saw one, two, three men walking along the driveway towards the car. The three of them walked carrying weapons, automatic rifles. Yuri had no doubt that they were now advancing to make sure that no-one was left alive.

Which one to shoot at first? How would the others react? Would he have enough time to kill all three before one of them could shoot back?

Yuri decided to shoot at the man furthest away, hoping the others would instinctively look towards him and away from Yuri, giving him that precious extra time to shoot at them before they realized where the shot had come from.

It worked. He shot the man furthest from him, the two others turned to look at that man as he cried when the bullet hit him and Yuri shot them both.

He climbed back into the driver's seat, with his elbow punched out some of the shattered glass, and drove towards the house. He quietly asked Valentina to take the children into the house and told her he would be a little while clearing up.

Yuri went outside to where the shot men were laying on the scrub, and went through their pockets. He took their wallets with their identification, and found various keys which he then tried on the truck that he assumed they had come in.

He eventually found the keys that started the truck, and he piled the bodies into it.

Yuri drove off with the bodies to the large and very deep ravine on the outskirts of the town. No one else was around, the area was deserted.

He took the bodies one by one and placed them inside the passenger compartment of the truck. He pulled down the trousers of each of the men, and positioned them as if they might have been indulging in some sexual activity.

He drove the truck as near as he could to the edge of the ravine, removed whatever traces he could find of his own presence, put the driving shift into neutral gear, and climbed out.

He went to the back of the truck and started pushing. The truck gathered some speed and eventually went over the edge of the ravine.

Some seconds passed until he could hear a faint crashing noise from the ravine. Yuri carefully looked over the edge and could see the truck still bouncing off some rocks, making its way to the bottom. It was too dark to make out any details in terms of how much the truck had been damaged in the fall, but he doubted that the bodies would survive such a fall in such a small enclosed space intact.

He tried to brush away his footsteps as much as possible, knowing that some traces might still be visible, and then began the long walk back to town, trying to stay out of sight of any passing vehicles. Fortunately, there were very few.

It must have been nearly two hours later when he came into the room to Valentina, undressed and took a shower.

"They were police officers. I presume they were sent by your husband."

What are you going to do? He seems determined to kill us."

"I know you are right. We have to think very carefully how to deal with him."

"I'm not a person who hates, but I don't want to die myself and leave my children without their mother, and I don't want you to die. So I am prepared to accept anything that you need to do to stop him.”

“Thank you, Valentina. I hope that you are not sorry that coming to me has led to this.”

“What are you talking about? Being with you has made me the happiest I have been for as long as I can remember.”

He was at his garage the next morning when the chief of police stormed in.

“What have you done with my men?”

“What men?”

“The men I sent to arrest you.”

“You sent men to arrest me? When was this?”

“You know perfectly well. Where are they?”

“You mean that you have lost some of your men that you claim you sent to arrest me. Since no-one came here to arrest me, perhaps they realized what a stupid waste of their time and energy it is to work with you and they just left. Have you checked their homes to see, maybe they just packed up and went to look for a better life somewhere else.”

“Don’t try to play the idiot with me. I don’t have the time to waste on this nonsense. I’m arresting you myself.”

“Oh, and why do you want to arrest me?”

“I am charging you with resisting arrest and with causing my officers to disappear in some way.”

Yuri turned very quiet and spoke to the police chief firmly. “You are not arresting me. You don’t know where your own officers are, you are making up stories as you go along, and I’m not going to listen to any more of your nonsense. We have a lot of work to do here, the citizens of this area need our services, and you are just interfering and holding up things.

"So whether you resisted arrest before or not, you are resisting arrest now. Turn around and put your hands behind your back."

Yuri turned away from the police chief and continued working on the part of the car he had been examining.

The police chief screamed at him, "turn around and put your hands behind your back."

He started to pull his gun out of his holster to threaten Yuri with it. Yuri moved forward to the police chief and very abruptly brought the lead pipe he had been holding down on to the wrist of the police chief, breaking it. The police chief screamed in pain and dropped his gun. Yuri then hit him again with the lead pipe across the bridge of his nose, and then hit each knee hard.

The police chief collapsed to the floor, screaming in agony. Yuri moved over him and briskly shattered the other wrist, leaving the chief quite helpless.

Yuri left the police chief sitting on the floor. He told him and two of his workers nearby that the chief was to be fed when he requested some food, and a pot to be brought to him when he needed to urinate.

When it was dark, Yuri went out, locking the building after him but reassuring the police chief he would be back. He went deep into the woods that were behind the concert hall and the police station. He chopped down two trees and chopped those into smaller logs.

He built a small enclosure that when he had finished had the appearance of a small cage. He dragged the cage to the front of the concert hall.

He left it in place there, and then dragged the police chief out, put him in the cage, and nailed more large pieces of wood across what was originally an opening.

Outside the cage he nailed another piece of wood so that the chief would not be able to dislodge it, and on to that piece Yuri stuck a sign that read, 'Here sits the most corrupt man in the City. He also beats his wife. You may feed him if you wish.'

Yuri had also left some food and drink and a pot to urinate in, before closing up the cage.

The police chief was livid. He screamed, uttering vile threats and curses about what he would do to Yuri when he was free, and making outrageous 'accusations' about Yuri's parentage, including accusing Yuri of being Jewish scum.

Yuri left him, and went back home for a short sleep.

Word spread quickly about the unusual sight in the city centre. The media came, tried to interview a furious man who just snarled venom at them but refused to offer any explanation as to who might have put him there and why he was accused of being corrupt.

His supporters were confused. Most were reluctant to show their faces. They didn't want to be dragged down with him. But what if he survived the humiliation? Would he not then favour those who had stood by him and condemn those who had turned a blind eye or had participated in rejecting him?

Gradually, some of the traders and business people who the chief had been taking money from started coming out. Those who came were less hesitant in expressing their opinions.

"About time someone dealt with that bastard."

"That's exactly where he belongs. I don't mind him staying there forever until he dies. We can feed him, give him a coat in the winter. But let him stay there as a warning to anyone else who thinks that because they are chief of police they can be the biggest crook in town."

"This cage was built for an animal, a pig I think, and it has one in there right now."

The police chief railed at these insults. "I'll see you in jail, everyone of you who insults me and who refuses to help me. I'm the chief of police and you are insulting a public official. It's the Gulag for the whole lot of you."

"Yes, and there will just be left in this city you and your three favourite ass-lickers. Is that it?"

The deputy chief pushed his way forward. He had an axe in his hand and lifted it to start chopping down the wooden pieces that blocked the opening.

"No. He hasn't been in there long enough."
"Let him stay."

These cries were quickly taken up by the crowd who surged forward towards the deputy, preventing him lifting the axe again.

"Step away, or I'll chop the arm or hand off anyone who interferes," the deputy threatened.

"Oh, really? So you are just like that corrupt pig? I don't think we are ready to have another one like him."
That had been spoken by Lothar Zemereck, a very tall, burly quarry worker who was considered to be one of the strongest men in the city.

The deputy chief lifted the axe again. "I'm warning you Lothar, step away. This is police business. It is illegal for you to interfere."

"I think we have had enough of his and your false legalities," and Lothar held back the deputy's arm holding the axe.

"Do it," screamed the police chief, "chop his arm and hand off if he resists."

The deputy turned to the chief. "So rather than you spend another hour or two here, you would prefer that I cripple this good man for the rest of his life? Even I won't go that far."

The building was an older but obviously very elegant building that had been looked after with care. He presumed that party officials and other prominent people must have been allotted the apartments. He waited a little until he saw that the doorman was distracted and then he slipped inside and made his way up the stairs to the fifth floor.

He knocked on the door. "Who is it?" he heard a woman calling.
"Mrs Garilova, I have a package for your husband."
"Why didn't you leave it with the doorman?"
"He wasn't there, and I was asked to deliver this personally."
"Who are you, and what is the package?"
"My name is Yuri. But I have been instructed to give the package to your husband alone. It is very important."
She opened the door a little, leaving it still on its chain. He smiled.

"I want to see the package."
"I am afraid I am not allowed to do that. It is just for your husband. I believe it is a confidential matter."

He was preparing himself to break the door open if necessary when she closed it, released the chain and opened it again.

"I suppose you had better come in, but I don't like this, especially not so late at night."

He entered the apartment. The woman was tall, slim, well-preserved in a long red evening robe.

He looked around. The furnishings were elaborate though to his taste old-fashioned. He saw a dining room with a large table and chairs around it. Another room off the entrance hall seemed to be a living room which was where she took him and pointed to a couch where he could sit. The couch was dark leather and matched a large armchair opposite it.

There was a credenza along one side of the wall, and a large samovar and a crystal vase were on top of the credenza.

An old man, with thinning grey hair, but upright, slim, carrying himself well, walked into the room.

"And who are you?"
"My name is Yuri. Do you recognize me?"
"No. Are you saying we have met before. Were we actually introduced?"
"Yes, we were introduced. I was introduced to Judge Garilov as accused 37648. You were introduced as presiding magistrate Garilov."
"So you are a person who came before me as an accused. I saw thousands of people in my years in court. I don't remember you. Should I?"
"It would have been eleven years ago. You might remember if I reminded you about a young man who didn't even know what he was charged with, and who questioned whether a lawyer who had never spoken to him could defend

him against charges he knew nothing about. When this young man protested and said that he would defend himself rather than have a lawyer he had not hired or briefed just agree with the prosecution's case and not seek to defend his client, you suggested that the lawyer had the right to do so, which actually was not true. I looked it up in the law books."

"I have no recollection of such an event, but assuming for a moment that it is true, what has that to do with you coming here?"

"Have you ever been to Vaygach?"

"No. Why do you ask?"

"Because you have sent many people there. If you send someone to a place, you really ought to have gone yourself to take a look at what you were sending people to."

"Why? They were all criminals and that was one of many places that we placed criminals in for a while so that they could ponder on the error of their ways and become rehabilitated."

"Excuse me. Are you a believer in reincarnation?"

"I'm sorry, I don't know what you are talking about."

"I'm asking you simply whether you believe that people come back from being dead and tell us about their experiences, perhaps the last few months or weeks or days."

"No. I don't believe that happens."

"Then in what life did you imagine those prisoners who had supposedly learned the error of their ways were going to return as better citizens?"

"Mr Yuri - I believe that is your name - you are clearly an accomplished debater. But I am too old to be debating at this time of the night such profound philosophical issues as whether people come back from the dead. I think it is time for you to go."

"Now you are being rude, Judge Garilov. My question to you regarding reincarnation was very simple because Vaygach is a death camp. You admit you have never been there. That is a pity. You should see how isolated it is. How cold it is in a very long winter. Under what miserable conditions the prisoners live. How they have to be up early in the morning to walk in the snow to work excavating rocks from a quarry, then walk back at night, to a pitifully small supper. They gradually starve. They become susceptible to infection and disease. And then they die. And for what crimes Judge Garilov?

For what serious crimes did you send young university students to die thousands of miles away from any family?"

"I was a servant of the state. I believe I performed my tasks with dignity and in an honest manner."

"You are a dignified liar. You are a dignified fool. You are a dignified murderer, former Judge Garilov. You sent people to these death camps without listening to their stories, without hearing their side of the case if ever there was a case. You were a disgrace to the concept of justice. If you tell me that you were no worse and maybe even better than some of your colleagues I would believe you and would conclude that they were even bigger fools, even more morally corrupt than you, even bigger murderers."

"I am getting more and more weary with your polemics, Mr Yuri. You evidently are very much alive. You survived what you tell me is a death camp. I think it is time for you to go."

"I didn't survive my sentence, former Judge Garilov. I am one of the very few who escaped and has remained free. I escaped because I saw my strength starting to fade, that I was weakening, and that if I didn't escape I would die as had so many before me. I am only a survivor in the sense of refusing to complete my sentence in a hole in the ground, dead."

"Okay, okay. Now please go," Garilov demanded irritably.

"Former Judge Garilov. You don't think I have come here after all these years just to admit to you that I escaped from the death that you sentenced me to, and that I am going to let you call the police the moment I leave to pick me up and put me back there, if they don't shoot me first.

Do you really still imagine that I am that stupid? You didn't think I was stupid eleven years ago when I challenged your behaviour, you claimed that you doubled the sentence you were originally going to give me because I spoke up."

"So what are you going to do with me now that I am an old man?"

"What does being an old man have to do with it? You took away my life. I was doing very well in university, you took away any career in that area. You sent me to a place to die. I escaped so I am now in a sense a nonperson, I can't go back to my previous life without risking betrayal and arrest. I have had to survive four years of brutal hard work and near-starvation in a death camp, and many years of hard work in an anonymous capacity instead of those years being years of productive intellectual academic or professional work. Years when I could have had a wife and a family and young children to bring up and enjoy and play with. And you think I am now going to let you enjoy many years of peaceful retirement with your wife and children and grandchildren. My, what an arrogant old fool you have become."

Garilov had been fighting to keep his composure. He had started to relax, thinking that this man Yuri had just come to him to debate and remonstrate. But now the initial sense of fear he had experienced started to return. He realized that Yuri had a more hurtful and vengeful purpose in mind.

"I am just going to cut the telephone wire so that you and your wife won't think of calling the police. I suggest you find a bag and put in it one sweater, one extra pair of pants, one change of underwear, and any toothpaste or shaving equipment and any medication that you need. We are going on a journey. You are going to be away for a while. And by the way, the same goes for your wife. She is coming with us."

Garilov was relieved to hear that. He would come to regret his sense of relief.

Yuri had easily found the code to open the security gate for the building's underground parking area. He took them in the elevator to the basement level, and then to his van, told them to go inside, and drove off.

He drove for nearly two hours. He was far away from the town now, just empty dark fields on both sides of the road.

He opened the doors of the van, and also took from behind the back seat two bags, one for each of them. He told them to open the bags. Inside they saw two big coats, two long white striped winter shirts, and rather thin pants. He told them to take their coats, jackets, and Garilov to take his shirt off, and to put on the replacement clothes. The substitutes were poorer quality garments, torn, threadbare, stained.

Yuri drove further for another hour and then stopped. He told the couple to get out of the van. They did.

"This is where we say goodbye. You have seen the route. You just follow this road all the way back until you come to the highway, and then you turn left and follow the highway all the way back to the city."

The old couple looked at each other and back at Yuri. "You are leaving us here? To walk back on our own, in the dark, in these torn, rags?"
"Yes."
"You can't, we won't survive, it's too far, it's too cold."
"I think it will give you a bit of an idea of what the thousands and thousands of people you sent to those camps experienced every single day. And they had no hope that at the end of the walk in the dark and bitter cold they might be picked up on the highway and taken in a warm car back to

their warm apartment and put back on nice comfortable warm clothes.

Do you know what they had at the end of their long walk? A long day of very hard work? No stopping to eat or drink. Not that they had much food to eat or drink anyway. They had to keep back a bit of bread or potato that they had saved to give them a little nourishment during the twelve hours that they worked. And then a very long walk back to their huts, tired, to receive a drink of water with a few shreds of a vegetable that somebody jokingly called soup, and a few potatoes.

Then most quickly fell asleep because they were so tired and had to be up at 4 a.m for the next day's work, and the same routine. I survived. Most didn't. What you are going to experience over the next few hours is the most minute fraction of that. You sent thousands to their deaths, in places so far away that their families will never visit. And for what, Judge Garilov? What terrible crimes do you imagine these people committed to deserve such an end to their lives? You were a monster, and you seem to have remained a monster because you show no remorse or regret."

"We are going to die, aren't we?" asked Mrs Garilova.

"I hope so," replied Yuri. "But I won't have killed you. You have just gone for a very long walk, not dressed very suitably, and you have got lost, which people of your age should really not have done. Goodbye Garilovs. May you rot in hell."

Yuri went back into his van and drove off. He would later leave various items of the clothing at different locations where poorer people lived, so that good use could be made of them.

It had taken Yuri a week to travel to Moscow and enter it quietly, and then find the Garilovs and research his plan for confronting them, and then devising the best method of making them suffer and die. He had no qualms, no feelings of guilt.

The unfair abruptness with which his previous life had been ended, all his hopes for academic and professional success shattered, the years of miserable experience in a labour death camp with starvation, brutality, extreme hard work, and the casual attitude towards death that had surrounded him had profoundly changed him.

He had thought of himself as a kind, caring, decent, tolerant person, who had no need or desire to hurt anyone. He still thought of himself as decent, kind, and caring, but he had much less tolerance now and none for those who would try to hurt him in any way, and he had become very accustomed to hurting back people who had hurt him or who would try to hurt him. He had no fear at all of police or of any other form of authority. The camp experience had erased that from his emotions.

He had been pleasantly surprised that he had been able to love. He thought that it might have something to do with the lovely women he had encountered. Yet they had told him that the men they had developed relationships with had even in circumstances of peace and comfort and relative freedom still not loved them or treated them well.

So he thought that perhaps his mind had achieved a strange balance. On the one hand a greater ability to love, and on the other hand an ability to act in a powerful and brutal manner towards anyone who would threaten him or try to hurt him. He thought that it was quite an acceptable outcome.

It took Yuri four more days to return.

A part of him was not surprised with what he found when he returned, yet he was also horrified, revolted.

Valentina's body was laid out on their bed, and the children had gone. She had been shot in the head and left.

Yuri had no doubt who was responsible. He went to the house of the former police chief. The man was not there. Yuri kept going back, and eventually after four attempts the man had returned. Yuri confronted him, broke almost every bone in his body, and then demanded to know who was the sponsor of this murderous attack.

Over the next few weeks Yuri killed the deputy police chief, the former mayor, and four thugs whom the police chief had hired to do the killing.

Yuri's killing of the chief was slow. He had not hurried. After paralyzing the man and leaving him to sit in his own urine and excreta for days, and repeatedly finding different bones to break, Yuri had finished him off.

He had found the police chief to be a strange man, one of those people who had the potential to be successful, with some personality strengths, but with a fundamental flaw of being highly self-destructive.

The chief had thrown away a good career because he had become greedy and power-obsessed, and he had thrown away a wonderful woman and family. Yuri's sadness arose from his disappointment that the chief had chosen to kill this lovely woman rather than let anyone else appreciate her.

It took Yuri a few more days to dispose of the bodies and then he left. He had found out that the children had been sent to Valentina's parents and that gave him some comfort. They had seemed to be good people from what she had told him.

He arranged for the business to be sold. It had been very profitable and a number of potential new owners made bids.

He did not choose to sell to the highest bidder in terms of money, but chose a young person who seemed dynamic and honest, who would want to succeed by providing good service.

He told many of the good people in the town that he had met, that it was time for him to move on. He told them that there were many good decent people in the town, and that they must not let the corruption that had caused so much rot in the town to return. That they had to choose fine people and make sure that power would not go to their heads. If a mayor or police chief was living too well it might be a sign that he had become corrupt and should be removed. He wished them well, and left with many tears being shed.

Yuri then left. He drove for some days until he came to another town that he thought might suit him. He settled there, made inquiries about bringing some of his money and buying a business and a home.

Three years later.

Yuri had been successful with his business again in the city he had moved to. He worked hard, the quality of his work was excellent and he made sure that the mechanics who worked for him kept the highest standards and he paid them well.

His repair garage developed a very good reputation quickly, and attracted many customers from districts far away from his location.

Yuri had kept a regular telephone contact with Igor and Miriam, and on a March day three years later Yuri received a telephone call that deeply troubled him.

Igor and Miriam told him that their now seventeen year old daughter seemed to have been kidnapped. It was suspected that she might be in Canada, working in the sex trade.

Yuri didn't hesitate. He spoke to his staff and took a plane to Toronto.

It didn't take him long to find out who in the Russian community was involved in the sex trade, and who the big bosses were.

He was given three names, and visited each of them. They all lived in large houses in the suburb of Woodbridge, which Yuri discovered had originally been a wealthy Italian section, but in recent years some successful Russians had moved in. Yuri had not been reticent to approach them and he brushed past their security guards.

The third person whose house he had come to was Felix Kaganovitch, but the person who came to speak to him was Yefim Alshtayn. Yefim appeared to be the front man, Yuri didn't know if he was the real boss or not. Yuri showed him pictures of Natasha. Yefim took them and asked him to wait.

About twenty minutes later Yefim came back with a bigger, heavy set but good looking man, probably in his early sixties, Yuri presumed this was Felix and the man confirmed that.

"You say this is your friend's daughter and she was kidnapped?"
"Yes."

"And you - they - are sure she is not here of her own free will, that she may have rebelled against her parents and wanted to get away to the west, have a new life?"

"Certain. She was a top student, doing well in high school, had a nice boyfriend, got on well with her family."

"And your interest? How do you come to be involved? To be able to travel here and come and look for her."

Yuri gave them a brief summary of his own history. He could see that their eyebrows were raised as he told them of his imprisonment, escape, and setting up in business.

"So you are one of those people who made the sacrifice so that we could come here more freely and have better lives?"

"I suppose you could say that," responded Yuri,.

"Yefim will make the inquiries and see if she is one of ours. She looks familiar but you will have to be prepared for a bit of a shock. By the time they come to us they have been treated in a not very nice way. It is to make them compliant and willing to do the work that we ask of them that I am sure you realize may not be what most of them expected when they were tempted or persuaded to come. They have usually been given drugs. If they have been in the clubs with men they make look older than they really are, they may have become dependent on the drugs. But I don't want to exploit someone like her that you say comes from a very good background, and you say she has a Jewish mother?"

"Yes. She does. A wonderful woman. Just find her. Then we'll see if she needs to be treated or rehabilitated."

It didn't take long. Later that evening Yuri was called and told to return to Felix's house.

The young woman he met there was indeed Natasha. She was heavily made up, she was still drowsy, he presumed that was from the drugs she had been given. She was dressed in a very provocative short dress, low-cut at the top, her young breasts almost popping out.

She remembered him - and started crying.

He put an arm around her, and told her he was taking her home.

But he didn't take her home. He took her back to the home of the people he was staying with, friends of Igor and Miriam who had moved to Canada some years earlier.

Yuri and Natasha called her parents, but Yuri had first spoken to his friend Jerry in California. It had been a long and emotional call, and when Yuri had called Igor and Miriam he had made a suggestion to them that they had accepted, and he now presented it to Natasha.

"I think that it might be better for you not to go back to Russia just now. I think that you would benefit a lot by going to my friend Jerry in California. You will be safer there, and you can go to school there. Your parents and brother will be able to visit."

Yuri spent some days with Natasha, walking with her in the parks and by the lake, taking her to eat. The family they were staying with were also very supportive, and being young and resilient Natasha recovered quickly.

Within a week she looked healthier, colour came back to her face, light to her eyes. She spoke more clearly, not with the almost slurred and fearful way in which she had communicated when he had first encountered her in Felix's house.

She understood the suggestion to go to California. It made sense. She accepted it. Yuri took her to the American Embassy. Jerry had already started the paperwork to sponsor her, and after waiting all day with hundreds of other would-be refugees or potential immigrants they obtained visas to enter the US.

Yuri took her to California. Jerry and his wife met them at Los Angeles airport and drove them to their home in Beverly Hills.

Yuri liked Jerry's wife immediately. She was a lively woman, very nice looking, friendly, obviously kept herself fit with regular exercise, and she seemed to be an aware and intelligent woman.

Yuri found out that she had been a school teacher before their children had been born, and then she had become a full-time mother until two years ago when she went back to teaching history at the local high-school partytime.

They had three children, a daughter also 17, a son of 14, and a younger daughter of 11.

His friend Jerry looked well. Jerry had become a successful lawyer specializing in real estate. He had put on some weight and told Yuri that he was aware of that and had embarked on an active exercise programme.

Yuri stayed with them for a few more days as Natasha settled in and they made arrangements for her to go to the local high school to learn more English and qualify for university entry in the US.

What surprised Yuri was what happened on Friday evening and Saturday. Jerry and his family had become traditional and practiced being Jewish. They went to shool on Friday evening and Saturday morning. Ellen, Jerry's wife, lit candles on Friday evening, made a traditional Shabbat meal, and Jerry made kiddush.

Yuri was impressed. In a quiet moment he had asked Jerry how it had happened.

"It was Ellen. She comes from a traditional home and she said this was important to her, so I tried it, and I liked it. Maybe because I liked her so much. But it grows on you, it's great for the children. You know so many families hardly ever eat together and so they don't talk much with each other. We eat together and talk every Friday night and Shabbat and all the festivals, we seem to get along much better than most of the others."

"You've done very well. Ellen is lovely, your children are a delight. You seem to be very well, successful, happy. I am very happy for you, and I think this will be a very good home for Natasha for a while. Thank you very much for agreeing to take her."

"You should come as well. What do you have to stay for there? Haven't they given you enough tsores in your life?" Jerry had used the Yiddish word for troubles. Yuri laughed. "You have certainly made me think about it."

But Yuri returned to Russia and to his work. He was on his own again. He met different women, had brief relationships with a few but nothing of any length or great meaning.

It was about fifteen months later that in their regular telephone calls Jerry had told him that Natasha was graduating from high school, that this was a big event and that Natasha was going to receive a special award. Jerry suggested that it would be very nice if he could come. Jerry had already told her parents and they were intending to come. Yuri agreed.

Igor and Miriam arrived earlier than Yuri and had an emotional reunion with Natasha. They didn't speak English and communicated with Ellen and others through using Jerry and Natasha as interpreters.

Yuri arrived, greeted Igor and Miriam with delight and they poured out their appreciation to him again - they had already spoken many times on the phone since he had rescued Natasha.

The award was announced after the graduating students had all been presented. The principal stood up to speak.

"Each year our teaching staff are asked if they can recommend a student for the Governor's Medal, which is given to a student who has accomplished something exceptional.

This year it is being given to a young woman who in the opinion of many of our teachers has indeed accomplished in an outstanding manner. This young lady came to us from another country, hardly speaking a word of English. I admit I was reluctant to accept her at first because she had had some very unpleasant experiences, but the family who were her guardians here were very persuasive, and as usual Ellen was right and I was wrong.

She has overcome a very difficult and traumatic background to become an exceptional student, and an outstanding contributor in many different ways to the atmosphere of the school. She has participated in a number of sports and cultural activities at a very high level, and she has been particularly sensitive and gone out of her way to make other students who have come from other countries feel comfortable and accepted here. And so on behalf of our teaching staff I am delighted to ask Natasha Revekzin to come up and accept the Governor's Medal."

As Natasha ascended the dais to receive her award, the principal asked her parents, and Jerry and Ellen to stand up, "and a very special man, Mr Yuri Goldberg, who has also come specially from Russia for this occasion and who helped Natasha change her life, to stand up so that people can see you." Natasha's classmates applauded, and congratulated her as she sat down again.

After the ceremony they all went out to eat and celebrate, and when they returned to Jerry and Ellen's house they were interested to see that the event had been filmed and was on TV on the late evening news, and would be circulated on the internet. They were featured briefly, and they received telephone calls asking if they would agree to be interviewed the next morning on TV.

They arrived at the television studio, were introduced to various people and were sent for some brief make-up to be applied to their faces.

They were seated in the chairs where they were going to be interviewed, when they saw a smartly dressed young woman in a coat walking into the set. Yuri looked, there was something familiar about her. The hostess of the show came on to the set and introduced herself. "I am Suzy Leston. Welcome and thank you for coming. I presume you are Yuri and Jerry. I don't know if you know this young lady, but she called us late last night and asked if she could be here this morning."

The young woman came forward, "Maybe you don't recognize me. I wonder if you remember him," and she pointed to an older man standing off to the side, wearing a cap on his head.

Yuri and Jerry looked at each other, "It's the captain, from the boat," and they looked at her.

"It's the captain, and you must be his daughter."

"Yes, and this is my father."

They both jumped up and she hugged them both and they brought her father to them.

The woman then explained to the hostess why she had wanted to come as soon as she had seen them on the evening news, and Suzy agreed that it would make a wonderful story to tell.

"My name is Elena Silver, and this is my father, Andrei Khovalov. I am a lawyer now in Baltimore. I have always felt very privileged that this wonderful country took me and my father in, enabled me to pursue a proper education, and eventually become a professional and a partner in a busy law practice.

But I owe my life and my success to these two men, who saved me from rape and death and enabled us to leave Russia and start a new life.

I was a teenager, I sometimes went out on the boat at night with my father. My mother had died five years earlier, and these men had escaped from the death camp, and my father was going to take them across to the mainland, which was very brave of him.

But my father had decided that I should have the chance to have a proper education, and he took this as an opportunity for us to also escape.

On the boat though, were some not very nice prisoners who had escaped together with these two, and those others tried to rape me, and they held my father at gunpoint as they were trying to rape me. I am sure that they would have killed both of us if these men had not stopped them.

What they did in stopping about twenty very dangerous and big men was incredibly brave. We never had the chance to thank them properly, and I knew when we saw them on television last night that we had to come here to meet them again, thank them and tell everyone the story."

After the show they all went out to eat and exchange their life stories since that time. They gave each other their addresses and telephone numbers and promised to keep in touch. Elena showed them pictures of her husband and her children, she was very proud of them. Her father lived in an apartment nearby and was a very involved grandfather, so they learned.

Yuri stayed for a few more days and was preparing to go back when he and Jerry and Ellen saw an item on the evening news that shocked them.

A young man, identified as the New York Consul for Russia, was announcing to the media that Mr Yuri Goldberg and Mr Jerry Sherman were escaped Russian prisoners, and that the Russian Ministry of the Interior was demanding that they be extradited back to Russia to serve the remainder of their sentence.

Jerry had become quite accustomed to American ways in the years he had lived there, and he knew that the best approach for dealing with such high-handed government mischief was to go public, via the media.

Jerry called a press conference for the next morning, and in front of many television cameras, radio microphones, and journalists, he told in a simple manner the story of the death camps, of unreasonable imprisonments for being Jewish and being a bright university student.

He said that they had not the slightest intention of allowing themselves to be sent back to a death camp to die, and that any official trying to co-operate with the Russians on this matter would by definition be identifying himself or herself as being corrupt and in the pay of the Russians.

Yuri had to restrain himself from laughing at Jerry's performance, it was so over the top, but he understood that this must be how they do things in this country and he hoped that it would work.

It did. But Yuri had taken note of the young Russian's name. He saw the continuing corruption of such young people as holding up the country from making progress.

Yuri travelled back by a round-about route. He did not want to risk being arrested again. He started to put his life baggage in order. He sold his business and transferred his funds out of the country, giving up the large discount that the smugglers demanded for their risk. He also sold his home, and took a place for temporary rent.

It had taken him eleven days to find her. He had gone first to the store where she had started working soon after he had left. They told him that she had stayed for three years and then had been offered a better position in a larger store.

He went to the larger store and was told that she had stayed there for five years and then had been offered a better position in a branch of the store in another town two hundred kilometers away.

He drove to that city and discovered that there were seven branches of the store in that city. He telephoned the central office, and after being passed from one secretary to another he was finally told which branch she had worked at - but was no longer there now.

But he went to that store and the manager told him that she had worked there also for three years, that she had been very competent and everybody liked her, and she had been offered a position in another company. The manager told him that he could look up the references to see which company she had actually gone to.

By the time the manager brought him the name and address of the other company it was after six o'clock. He thanked the manager and asked for a suggestion for a hotel to stay in for the night and a good place to eat at.

He set off the next morning for another two hundred and fifty kilometer drive, arriving in the city in the late morning. Each town or city had been bigger than the previous one, and each place had told him that she had moved to a better position. He was becoming increasingly impressed and pleased with her success.

He placed a call again to what seemed from the telephone book to be the main office of the company that she had moved to and was told that indeed she was with their company and that she was the senior manager on the women's dresses floor at their large branch on 1812 street. He asked for directions how to reach the store from where he was, and drove off.

He found a place to park on a side street near the store, and walked into the store.

It was a large superstore, clothing, furniture, household items, and seemed to cater to better-off people able to afford higher quality items.

He took the escalator to the women's clothes floor and walked around.

He did not know whether she would be there on the floor, or in an office, or she could even be out buying, or looking at other stores to compare their stocks and displays.

But then he saw her. She was in a corner talking to another woman. She had glasses perched on the end of her nose, but the crystal blue eyes were unmistakable.

He approached slowly, he didn't think she had seen him yet. She looked well. She was smartly dressed in what looked like a cream silk blouse and a pleated red skirt. There was the same outline to her figure, she was still voluptuous, but she seemed to have kept her weight under control, trimmed her figure.

He came closer, and she turned in his direction. A look of astonishment appeared on her face, and then a huge smile burst from her.

She turned to the person she had been speaking with and obviously excused herself and came over to him.

She looked at him; "it is who I think it is, isn't it?"
"I certainly hope so, Svetlana."
At the same moment they threw their arms around each other and hugged, and swayed and hugged for what seemed like minutes.

"My staff will think I've gone nuts, though I wouldn't mind continuing this for another hour or two." "How about all day?" She laughed.
"How did you find me?"
"With a lot of hard work."
She laughed again. "How long are you here for?"
"That depends on you. But first, let me tell you how wonderful you look, and second, how very impressed I am with your success in your career. I knew you had the potential to be very successful and I am so happy that it has come true."

"Thank you. You know that so much of my success is because of you. I have worked hard, very hard, but you got me started. You encouraged me to look beyond my small village, and to think that I could be more than what I was then. You are also looking well. Where are you living now?"

"That is a very long story. I would like to tell you about it and hear about your life since we last saw each other, but let me ask a delicate question first."

"I'll answer your question, at the least the one I think you are going to ask. No, I am not married and I am not in a relationship with any man. And you?"

"No, I'm not married. I have an almost-daughter from very good friends, and she is a part of the story that I can tell you if we can get together."

"The store is open until 6 and I usually stay a while after to make sure everything is put away properly for the next day. But I can finish a little earlier and you can come back with me for dinner."

"You invited me into your home to eat the very first time I met you. This time I would like to take you out to a nice place. I presume you know some nice places here. I only arrived in this city two hours ago."

"Thank you. I do like to eat out occasionally. But then you must let me go home first to change."

"You look lovely as you are. Ah, there is that beautiful blush I used to love. But of course. You tell me where to be and what time...."

"No, no, no. I want to show you where I live. We shall go together."

He wandered around the city, she had suggested a few interesting places to visit, and then he met her and accompanied her to her apartment in a more modern and less drab block than the usual housing in large cities.

She showed him around. It was a large three bedroom apartment. The furniture was neat, modern. The kitchen seemed well equipped.

"You have a beautiful home," he told her.

"Thank you. When my children were still living here it seemed busy and crowded at times. They would often have their friends visiting. Now that my daughter is away and my son is often away, there seems to be much more space."

"Where does your daughter live?"

"She is now in the United States."

His eyes lit up. "Really?"
"Yes. She has been living there now for two years."
"Have you visited her?"
"Not yet, but I was actually planning to go later this year. You have a look in your eyes. I remember that look."
"Let's talk about it at dinner. We have a lot to talk about."

She showered and changed and came out twenty minutes later in a burgundy knee-length dress with gold stitching on its lapels and a shiny black belt. He told her she looked absolutely gorgeous.

"So where do you live now?"
They were sitting in a quiet restaurant that she told him featured fish as its specialty.

"I have lived in three different cities for most of the years since you left, and I did the same thing in each city. I started working in a car repair workshop, saved some money, and eventually I opened my own businesses. For various reasons - actually for one main reason, the same reason each time - I left one city and moved to the next. As I mentioned, friends of mine had a daughter and something happened to her. She was kidnapped, and taken to Canada to become a prostitute. I was told about it, and with the help of some people there managed to rescue her and send her to my best friend, the man who had escaped with me from the prison camp, Jerry.

Jerry was living in the States and he and his family took her, saw that she received care and that she could return to school, and she did very well. She did so well after just a short time in the country and at the school, and so soon after being rescued from the horrible state she had been in - she had been heavily drugged to make her able to do the disgusting things they wanted her to do - that she was given a special award at her school. Jerry called me and told me, and that led to my going for the first time to the States to see her, and to see Jerry again and meet his family.

After I saw what life was like there, the freedom, the opportunities, and the lack of corruption compared to what we have, I decided that for the rest of my life I would rather live in that freer atmosphere than what we grew up with here.

I am pretty convinced that I can do well in the same type of work. Everyone drives a car there, even young people can earn enough in casual jobs to buy one. The distances are so big most people have to have a car, and cars always need to be repaired. So I have decided to live there."

"So you decided to come back here and close up things and say goodbye to people, even me."

"No. I have already closed up things over the past three months. I came back because I realized something very important was missing from my life, and that was a real companion, a woman whom I could love and trust and really feel at home with.

My friend Jerry has found that, and his home became such a wonderful place of recovery for this young woman Natasha. I want a home like that, a home of love and warmth, and I thought of the one woman in my life with whom I have felt that most, and I came to see if by any chance she was free and available."

"And have you found her, and is she free and available?" asked Svetlana.

"Oh yes, I have found her, though it took me quite a while to do so. I hear that she is free, I don't know yet if she is available. She does have a very good position here, and a very nice apartment. If she were to come with me it would mean learning a new language, although I am sure that her talents and skills would be quickly realized, and once she learned the language she could find a very good position. You know there are many former Russians in the US now."

"Have you asked her?"

"Not yet. But I think now is the time to ask her. Svetlana, will you please come with me to the States, live with me, marry me?" She looked at him.

"This is a bit sudden. And yet I feel as if my whole life has been moving towards this moment. Thank you for coming back for me Yuri. I'm thrilled that you should ask me to be your wife. I have managed well on my own for many years. But now that my children have grown up I had been thinking that I didn't want to grow older on my own, that I also wanted to share my life with someone, and there was always just one person who would come into my mind as the person I really wanted to be with, and that was you. I just thought it would never happen.

But before I say yes, there are a few questions that have been turning around and around in my head for years. I want you to answer them honestly, please, Yuri. Yuri, what did my husband actually do in the prison camp?"

"He was a guard. Most of the prisoners were like me, so-called political dissidents. Our regime at the time was convinced that there were always people ready to overthrow the country. Heaven forbid that there should be something like democracy, as if they had only had that in the west for a few hundred years. That there should be free votes, systems of justice, free markets for goods and services, freedom of movement, freedom of religion, freedom of expression. The guards were usually people who like your husband had been petty criminals and instead of being sent to jail for a long time were offered the "opportunity" - if you can call it that - to serve their time by being a guard in one of those death camps in the middle of nowhere. Most of them had no idea what they were getting into."

"Was my husband a nice, decent guard?"

"No, he wasn't. He was unhappy there, and he took out his unhappiness on the prisoners. He was mean and petty. There was a guard to a bunk of 28 prisoners, and two guards took us out to work and back. The guards had guns, and had the power to punish prisoners by sending them to solitary confinement for a day, or three days, or a week. In solitary you are on your own, in a tiny room with nothing, and even less food than usual is shoved into your cell each night - because you are not doing a day's work. Your husband wasn't liked by the prisoners, he hated them and they hated him, and so he sent a lot of people to solitary."

"The money you brought me wasn't really his money?"

"Well indirectly it was. You see when we escaped, he and the other guard were killed, and my friend Jerry and I took their wallets and used the money to bribe a ship captain to take us across the sea, and we used what little was left to buy our first food and simple clothes before looking for work. So after I earned some money, I decided that I owed it to his wife to at least tell her that he was dead, in case she didn't know, and give her some money."

"Did you give me a lot more than was in his wallet?"

"I don't know. We never counted what was in his or the other guard's wallets. I just gave you most of what I had earned."

"Why did you look so surprised when you first saw me? You just stared."

"I told you. I had never seen a woman with such beautiful eyes. You were - and are - in my eyes quite beautiful. And you were totally different from the picture. I even asked if it was you."

"And now the really difficult question, the one I've been struggling with for so long. Did you kill my husband?"

"As I've always said, you are a very smart woman. You asked me to tell you the truth, and I agree with you that a true committed marriage has to be based upon two people being truthful with each other, so I shall tell you the truth, even though I suppose it means the end of our relationship. Yes, I killed your husband."

"Can you tell me how and why?"

"He and the other guard were leading us out to work. We would go out at 4 a.m in the snow, about a two kilometer walk. Jerry and I had agreed the night before that this was the time to try to escape. We were getting weaker because of the lack of food and the constant hard work and we knew if we left it any longer we would be too weak. Also, your husband and I had an argument the night before and he was going to try to put me in solitary again, which as I said is a terrible experience that makes the person a lot weaker, and more likely to die soon after.

As we were walking we slipped behind the guards and broke their necks. It was quick and painless. We took their coats, their wallets, and their guns. We stopped a truck bringing in new guards and told them that our patrol needed the truck for an emergency and the camp was just around the bend, a short walk. It was actually over a kilometer and they weren't prepared for that cold and snow. The group got into the truck and we drove to the port and found a boat. So I suppose it is time now for me to say goodbye."

"Why. Where do you have to go?"

"I just told you that I am the person who killed your husband, the father of your children."

"You are also the nicest man whom I have ever met, the person who has treated me better than anyone else in my life, who helped make me the woman I am today. You have told me that my husband who was a petty thief was a nasty and mean man in prison. You have admitted to me that you have killed a person..."

"I've killed other people as well. When I lived in the different cities and had my car repair businesses, people tried to threaten me to take percentages of my business and they tried to kill me and people that I was close to. I did kill some of them."

"But everything I have seen of you has shown me what a nice and kind person you are," she commented.

"So to continue with the truth. Were you a good student, or just a trouble-maker?"

"The truth? The real truth? I was the only Jewish student admitted to the space research programme that took the top students from mathematics and physics. Of the top ten students we knew that seven, probably eight were Jewish. Five openly Jewish, with Jewish names and admitting it, three that looked Jewish and we thought were covering it up. I was the only one of them allowed into the advanced programme."

"And since leaving prison you have been a car repair mechanic."

"And a very good and successful one."

"Are you sad that you weren't in there, working in the space programme all these years?"

"And have given this miserable undeserving country the chance of being equal with or better than the United States? That we should be boasting like those totally corrupt East Germans, doping all their athletes and swimmers to win all the medals and then being shown up to be the biggest cheats, who shot people trying to leave their country? No, I'm so relieved that I haven't been there 'advancing' our country's great scientific progress."

She looked straight at him. She could see that he seemed uncomfortable, as if he was expecting bad news. But she wanted him to look into her eyes, the eyes that he said he liked so much.

"I am going to tell you a little story, that I sometimes told children when I was a teacher," she started.

"Once upon a time there was a wise king and queen, and they had a son who had been brought up in the palace, and so he was rather frivolous, not very mature, especially in his choice of women friends.

He was at an age when he should be married, and his parents were keen to have grandchildren to pass on their heritage, but none of the women their son had been introduced to had impressed them very much. Most of them were also from royalty from other countries, and often very arrogant, full of themselves, rather selfish and not very nice.

So they told their son that he had to go away from the palace and become more aware of the people of the country, of their needs, how difficult it was for poorer people and how it would be his duty and responsibility to be caring and look after them.

So he left the palace, dressed in poor clothes, and was taken far away, to an area of poorer villages, small farms where farmers struggled to make enough to feed themselves and their families.

The staff from the palace who had brought him, watched from a distance to see that no harm came to him, he still was the prince, the future king, but they didn't interfere as he went among the people.

As the prince wandered around, in his poor often-torn clothes, he sensed that the people were nice decent people, but seemed to be so occupied in their struggle to survive that no-one paid him much attention, or offered to help him in any way if he seemed lost or was looking for food or shelter.

By the fourth day of his wandering around, he was starting to become tired and hungry. He had mostly slept outside, in the open, and had managed on the occasional loaf of bread or piece of fruit that a stall owner had allowed him when he asked.

Towards evening, as he walked, tired, hungry, and it was starting to rain, a young woman called out to him.

"Excuse me sir, but you look very tired and you look as if you have not eaten much in the last few days. May I offer you some food, please."

He was very surprised, but very grateful and thanked her. She asked him to follow her. She walked with a strong stride and pace, and stopped at a modest hut.

"Please come in and sit down, I'll just be a few minutes warming up some soup."

The soup was delicious, certainly to a young man who had been wandering for days with little to eat.

As he started to feel better with the warm healthy soup, she brought out a plate of meat and vegetables and placed it in front of him.

"May I ask you how many days it has been since you last ate a good meal?"

He told her, and as he started talking he looked more closely at her. She was pleasant to look at, a bit chubby, but her nice smile, tuneful voice, and warm personality made her beautiful in his eyes.

She stepped outside for a moment, and then came back in.

"It has started to rain. Where were you planning to sleep?"

"I've been sleeping outside."

"Well, you can't now, you'll become ill. If you don't mind staying under the same roof as a woman you don't know, I would much prefer you stay here than become ill."

"I'm very grateful to you. Thank you very much. So since I don't know you, could you tell me about yourself," and she did.

Eventually it was obvious to her that he was very tired, and she showed him where he could sleep, and where the washroom and toilet were, and from where to bring the water.

He fell asleep quickly.

When he awoke the next morning, she had already left, but there was a note on the table where they had eaten, telling him where to find food for breakfast, and she wished him well. She had left him alone in her home, as if she completely trusted him not to steal from her. He also noticed that her handwriting was quite elegant.

He felt much better, having had a good night sleep and some proper food.

He found his watchers, and told them that they were to return after they had taken him home, and then to bring her to the palace.

She didn't understand what it was about when the watchers asked her to come with them to the royal palace, but the prince had instructed them not to tell her the reason or who he was, other than it was very important that she accompany them to the palace.

When she came to the palace, he went to greet her, brought her to meet his parents and said, "I've found her. This is the woman I want to marry. The nicest, most caring woman who offered me food and even shelter in her small home when no-one else paid attention to me."

The king and queen looked at their son, and they looked at the woman, dressed in simple clothes herself, not as slim from starving themselves as some of the princesses and wealthy young women their son had been introduced to over the past few years, but they knew almost instantly that their son had made the right choice.

"She has an inner beauty that radiates from her, and we feel it," said his mother.

"That is a beautiful story," Yuri said.

"So when do you want to go," she said.

"You just must give me a little time to prepare my company for my leaving, to give them the chance to appoint someone in my place and for me to help them for a week or two to adjust to the position. And then I am going to have to talk to my children. If we go to the US my daughter will be delighted, but I have to give my son the choice. Would you want him to live with us if he comes?"

"Of course. But are you saying 'yes'? Do you mean that you will still come with me to America and marry me even after what I've just told you?"

"You told me the truth, which is what I asked for. I think that I told you the truth about how I feel about you. You don't think that after all these years I am going to give up the chance to be with the man who has shown me the most love and acceptance that I have had in my life.

I promise you that I shall make a very good wife and that I shall give you all my love."

Yuri gave a big smile and leaned over and kissed her.

"So just to make sure that you won't change your mind, let us go tomorrow to buy a ticket for you, and then I shall go back to the US and apply for both of us to be admitted."

He asked her to be ready in two weeks, and said that he also had some matters to finish. He realized that it would take her a few days to talk to her son, to transfer her responsibilities at work, and then pack the most important items and be ready to leave with him.

He took a train to Novosibirsk, the city he had spent time in until he had been obligated to deal with the corruption. He was disappointed but not surprised to hear that the mayor and police chief still ran the town and continued the corruption.

He started with the police chief, quietly entering his house at one in the morning. He tied up the chief, ordered him to give the names and addresses of all the people who had been taking money from the hardworking citizens, and a list of all the people and businesses from which money had been taken.

He then shot the police chief

He went to the home of the mayor. He tied up the mayor and the mayor's wife. He went around their house putting all the computers and smartphones into a large bag.

As he had done with the police chief, he ordered the mayor to open his safe. The mayor responded in the same manner as the police chief, blustering, threatening, refusing, and Yuri did what he had done to the police chief, tortured him by chopping off his fingers one by one, alternating with his toes, while their wives even with gags in their mouths had made sounds indicating pleading with their husbands to give this man what he wanted.

Eventually both had, Yuri had taken all the money they had accumulated - which was a lot - but ignored other things such as jewellery and stock and bond certificates.

Yuri had not given either men or their wives any opportunity to call the others on their lists to warn them, and Yuri went around systemically to each of the houses and repeated the same action, until he came to the last person on his list.

"You were the accountant for this group, weren't you?" he addressed the man.

The man, Boris Andropov, looked very apologetic, "yes, to my shame I was."

"Why did you do it?"

"Like everybody else, I was greedy and I also thought it would protect my family. They would be safe from the assaults and beatings these people ordered to be done to those who wouldn't pay or whom they didn't like for any other reason."

"So what you are going to do now is prepare for me as exact a reckoning as you can of each of the people from whom money was taken, and estimate for how long money would have been taken and how much the eventual amount would have been for each of them. My guess is that you are a very careful accountant and you have computer records for all of them."

Boris Andropov's head seemed to descend even lower as he admitted that he did.

"And what about yourself? How much did you take for yourself?"

"I'm sure you won't believe me, but I only took what I reckoned to be my hourly rate for what I would have charged any citizen for doing their taxes."

"Why shouldn't I believe you?"

"Because I went along with the others. I didn't say no."

Yuri believed him. He asked Boris if he knew where the members of the ruling committee were now, and Yuri confirmed for himself that Boris didn't know what had happened to the others. He wasn't pretending to be contrite because he feared the same fate.

Yuri asked him where he kept his records, it was at his home, and Yuri told him he would wait until Boris had completed the work which they estimated would take many hours, and during that time Boris and his family would have no communication with anyone outside the house. Boris's wife would have to make food for them from what she had in the house.

That did not turn out to be a problem. Yuri found Boris's wife to be a pleasant woman and a good homemaker. They ate well over the next thirty six hours that Boris took to complete the work.

Boris asked Yuri a couple of times what had happened to the other members of the power group, Yuri had answered that he would tell him when Boris had finished the work.

When Boris eventually finished, Yuri opened up the sack containing all the cash he had taken from the homes of the police chief, mayor, and the other thugs that had terrorized the area for the past few years.

They counted the money, and then Boris made the calculations how much each person or family from whom the money had been taken could receive back.

Yuri then told Boris what he had done to the other members of the group.

Boris started crying, "so now you are going to kill me and my wife."

"No, I'm not," said Yuri. "What I am going to do is ask you and your wife to get dressed nicely, and to go with me to all these people on your list, and you are going to give them back their money with an apology that it shouldn't have been taken from them in the first place.

You are also going to tell them that it is their responsibility to make sure it doesn't happen again. They must not put into positions of power people that are corrupt bullies, and if by mistake such people do get into positions of power they must be stopped and removed as quickly as possible."

"And what about the money I took?"

"You told me you didn't take any extra money. So take out ten percent and put it in one envelope, and another ten per cent in another envelope. One envelope you will take personally to whichever organization here looks after orphaned or deprived children, and the other envelope goes to the organization that looks after women who have left their husbands because they have been abused and beaten. The rest you keep for yourself and your wife."

"You are not going to kill us, like you killed the others?"

"No. You are a decent person who was recruited by crooks and thugs. You and your wife are different. But you especially must speak up if you see anything like this happening again. Now go and have a better life."

When Yuri landed at Los Angeles airport, he was surprised that he was stopped at the Immigration desk and after a few minutes of the officer looking at his passport and then asking another officer to come and look at his computer screen and the two officers have a longer discussion, that he was then asked to go with them into another office.

A person who was obviously a more senior official then cautioned him in a very formal manner that he should answer all questions truthfully, and reviewed his identification details. His name, date of birth, place of birth, names of parents, and so on.

Apparently confirming that he was who he claimed to be as on the passport, he was then told that he was under arrest. Yuri asked why, and was told that an application had been made by the Soviet Consulate to have him returned to the Soviet Union as an escaped prisoner.

Yuri asked if he had the right to telephone a lawyer, which surprised the officials, and was reluctantly told that he could.

He immediately called Jerry. Jerry's daughter answered the phone and Yuri told her who he was, where he was, that it was an extremely urgent situation and that she should tell her father immediately, no matter what he was doing or wherever he was he would want to be interrupted and told about this.

He was then taken to a room that was empty apart from two chairs and a small table. He was told that the door would be locked, that he would be brought something to eat and drink, and that if he wished to use a toilet he should knock on the door and he would be escorted there and back.

Jerry again decided to play it from the beginning the 'American Way', as he had learned it. To appeal directly to the public. To arouse the public into thinking that the behaviour they were hearing about or seeing on their television was outrageous and totally unacceptable, and should be stopped immediately.

That's what Jerry did. He contacted every media source he could think of; television, news sources, the major radio stations, the major local and national newspapers, and told them that he would be giving a press conference about a matter related to Soviet interference with American justice.

Jerry was successful. He presented the story as a matter implying corruption at the Immigration services giving in to a Soviet request without exploring the matter properly. Most of the media were aroused to comment and some became quite indignant.

It took a few days, during which Yuri had to wait in a detention centre, and then reached national attention when at the weekly President's press conference the president was asked about it.

The administration had no choice but to back down. Too many people had heard the story and were disgusted with the behaviour of the Russians.

Yuri was released. Jerry had found an apartment for him to live in, and a place to start working until he could open his own garage.

Six months later Igor and Miriam arrived, and Yuri, Jerry, and Igor together bought a garage and Yuri and Igor started working there. Yuri had already acquired a growing reputation, and customers started coming.

Svetlana and her son came and they moved in with Yuri and married four months later at a ceremony attended by Jerry and family, Igor, Miriam and their children, and Elena from the boat and her father, Andrei, the captain.

Three Years Later:

"We have just received news of a story from Florida. A ten year old boy was left at a Child Service agency. The boy is believed to be of Russian origin, and there are reports indicating that the child had run away from home because he was being sexually and physically abused. The Agency is trying to identify the child and the child's parents and investigate the matter. In what may be a possibly related story, it is known that one week ago the Soviet Consul and his wife in New York had notified authorities and the media that their ten year old son was missing. We shall keep you updated."

AFTER THE BOMB

"Shlomi, it's Reuven. Like to go for a walk?"

Shlomi understood what Reuven was asking. "Sure, he replied. "See you outside in a couple of minutes."

"Reuven is going for a walk, I'm going to join him," Shlomi told Naomi, his wife.

"I'll call Netta." Netta was Naomi's closest friend and their husbands were good friends.

"Netta, Shlomi's going for a walk with Reuven."

"Yitzchak, Shlomi and Reuven are going outside for a walk," Netta called out to her husband.

"Did she tell you in which direction?"

"I'll call her back and ask."

By the time they reached the end of Chizkiyahu street they had become a group of fifteen men and six women. The women had older children who were able to look after their younger siblings for a while.

More people looked out of their windows and doors hearing the noise of people in the streets walking and talking together, and many joined them.

The white car with the large black letters UN painted on its side drew up to them and two soldiers climbed out, one tall and blond, the other much shorter and black.

"What are you doing. You know there is a curfew. Go back to your homes."

Reuven stepped forward. "This is our home, and this is our country. Not yours. We didn't ask you to be here. Now we suggest that you go back to your rooms. We are just going for a pleasant walk on a lovely evening."

The soldiers went back into their car. The Israelis could see that they were telephoning. Reuven and his friends continued walking.

A short while later, perhaps less than four minutes, a larger white van also with the large letters UN painted in black on both sides drove up and stopped in front of them. Another very tall blond soldier stepped out, followed by six soldiers with a variety of different physical characteristics. "What are you Jews doing out? You know there is a curfew. Go back to your homes."

Again Reuven stepped forward. "As we told your soldiers earlier, these are our homes and this is our country, and we are enjoying a pleasant evening's walk."

"In case you gave forgotten or maybe didn't even know," the tall blond soldier who seemed to be the leader, a sergeant or captain perhaps, responded in a sarcastic tone, "it was your own government that requested us to come to keep the peace. A part of keeping that peace is establishing a curfew."

Reuven kept calm, "I won't debate with you our internal political problems, or whether any unelected group has the right to invite foreign soldiers to come in to 'protect us' as you put it. But we see no need for a curfew and so we are out here enjoying a nice evening's walk."

The soldier took out a gun and shot Reuven in the chest. Reuven staggered back, fell, it became apparent that he was bleeding.

Shlomi went up to the soldier, pointed his gun at the soldier's head and fired. The other soldiers started lifting their rifles, but by the time they did so they were surrounded by about twenty men, many of whom had guns pointed at the soldiers.

"Has anyone called for an ambulance?"   "Yes," said Baruch, who was a doctor and was trying to see what he could do to help Reuven stay alive. The ambulance came within four minutes. "We're going to Tel Hashomer," announced one of the ambulance medics. "I guess he's going to need some major surgery if they're going to save him."

Both items of news spread rapidly over the country. The next evening a number of cities and small towns saw groups of men and women out walking. There was no UN presence.

In Raanana where it had started, by the third night there were at least a thousand people out walking, and in Rishon Letzion, a city often looked upon as emblematic of the modern secular but solidly patriotic Israel, estimates were that between five and ten thousand were walking. Stores had opened again in the evening, and even some amateur musicians had decided that this might be their big opportunity towards future stardom.

The meeting of officers was conducted in a very orderly manner. There were two hundred of them, the most senior officers from all the different units. They had been asked to nominate two speakers for each side, to support or not support the breaking of the UN temporary control.

The first three speakers had been quiet, clear in their presentations. The two speakers in favour of rejecting the UN involvement had said that while the effects of the bomb had been devastating and the losses huge, the damage had still been restricted to the Tel Aviv area. The armed forces especially in the many bases away from the main population centres were mostly intact, most officers had survived, and they were well equipped to defend the country against any further attack, and even launch one of their own.

The first speaker in opposition had said that at the moment the country was receiving much sympathy and support which would be withdrawn and they would be alienated again if they rejected this international help. The international support would benefit them in the recovery process until they were better able to retaliate.

It was the fourth speaker, the second opposition presenter who was most blunt.

He said that they had reaped what they had been sowing for years. That these expressions of sympathy were after the fact and were really empty and meaningless, because behind them lay much pleasure that we had got what we deserved. That the whole world was really delighted that the bomb had been dropped and it was because we had been arrogant, we had ignored the Palestinian suffering, we had been ignoring those among us who for years had been telling us that we had lost the moral battle, that our behaviour was unacceptable.

He had been provocative, and as listeners started to understand what he was saying, there were shouts of opposition, that became louder and noisier as he went on.

Avraham realized what this man was doing. He was deliberately stirring up what had been a very quiet and dignified meeting with the hope of causing sufficient disruption that they would be unable to take a vote.

Avraham asked to speak. Avraham was a senior rabbi in the armed forces and when he spoke people listened. He was a learned man full of common sense and was widely liked and respected.

"What we suffered was a cowardly attack. I have much more faith in our armed forces than I do in the United Nations or in the international community. Of course as a religious man I believe that the G-d of Israel won't let us down. But I don't think it helps us at all to blame ourselves for Iran doing what they had said they intended to do for many years.

"We had implored the rest of the world and especially the Americans to support us in stopping them. We held back as they kept reassuring us that sanctions were working, and that 'they had our back' and would never let Iran have nuclear weapons. Unwisely perhaps, we followed the pressures coming from those similar to the last speaker, who said that the most important thing was not to annoy and distance ourselves from our main allies, especially the Americans.

Their advice was wrong. We have paid for that misjudgement enormously. Now we have to do what we claimed we always would do, which is defend ourselves and not rely on anyone else. If the majority of our military here say that we have the capability to strike back in a very efficient and highly effective manner, then the sooner we do that the better."

There was applause from a number of people in the room, and then there was quiet. The Chief of Staff who was presiding took the opportunity to call for a vote. The opposition speakers asked for the vote to be a secret ballot, that was agreed.

It took only fifteen minutes to vote and for the votes to be counted. General Yirmiyahu announced the result.

"In favour of the proposition to reject the UN and international involvement and take action ourselves, one hundred and fifty seven. In opposition to the proposal and in favour of continuing the UN presence, forty three votes.

I think the result is clear, and as Chief of Staff I take the responsibility of asking the heads of all our branches to draw up plans for effective military action, and I am convening a meeting of our Executive for tomorrow at 6 p.m to discuss your proposals. Thank you all for participating in this meeting at a very difficult time in our history.

Our country will now be looking to us to restore our sense of confidence in ourselves and our ability to defend ourselves against those who wish to destroy us. I appreciate the contributions of those who made the case against our taking any action ourselves. I happen to believe that we came to the right and best decision this afternoon, but we must always keep our minds open to considering anything we might have overlooked, before we undertake what could be very dangerous steps that put many more lives at risk."

Zalman had prepared himself. He had taken his thinnest and sharpest knife and held it in his sleeve. When the armoured cars had noisily driven around his town at five in the morning, blaring the announcement that the Jews were to assemble on their streets at seven, he knew what was coming. He had heard about it from his grandparents who had come from Europe, and he had also read a lot about it. Their town had no rail line, there was no train service. There was only the other option.

Two soldiers approached his street, one appeared to be more senior than the other. They yelled at the Jews to form a line. The junior soldier asked for the name of the first of Zalman's neighbours, checked it on a sheet, and repeated the name to the senior officer who shot Moshe Azlagi in the head.

The two soldiers approached the next man, the junior asked for Yisachar Erez's name, checked it on his list, repeated the name to the senior officer, who then shot Yisachar.

Zalman looked at the gun. He recognized it. It carried eleven rounds. He didn't know whether the officer had used it before coming to their street. He was seventh in line, he saw.

The Arab soldiers continued along the line. As they approached Zalman he saw that after each shooting the senior officer would turn his head to his junior's list, as if he was checking the names that were already marked, and how many more were left.

They came to the man next to him, Mordechai Goldstein. The junior officer barked the request for Mordechai's name. Zalman leaned forward and with his left hand holding the knife plunged it straight into the senior officer's abdomen and sharply upwards, killing him instantly. With his right hand Zalman grabbed the dying officer's hand holding the gun and pointed it at the head of the junior officer and shot him.

Zalman took the weapons from both the dead Arabs, including the automatic rifle the junior officer had been carrying.

He called to Aharon and Shlomo who had been with him in the reserves and he knew were good shooters. He gave them each a gun from the dead Arabs, and they joined him. He kept the automatic. He told the other people who had been standing after him in the line to go back to their homes.

Zalman, Aharon and Shlomo made their way to the next street where they could see people gathered and see and hear that shooting was also going on there. They split up. Aharon and Shlomo approached from the main street, Zalman came to Bar Ilan street from a smaller side street.

As the two Arab soldiers who were doing the shooting on Bar Ilan turned to see Aharon and Shlomo approaching, Zalman came up behind them and shot them both.

The three Israelis asked the neighbours from Herzl Street who hadn't been shot which of them had recent army experience and were good shooters, and asked them to take the guns and other weapons from the dead Arabs, and to come with them to the next street.

They repeated the fight-back. The time delay had been longer, more Jews had been killed, but so had Arab soldiers, and weapons were being gathered.

They heard an armoured car driving near. They realized that it must be some of the leaders of this Arab unit driving around to see the progress of their murderous assault. The people who had the automatics ran to the street corners where they thought the car was approaching. They saw the car coming. It was an open top vehicle, four soldiers, presumably senior officers were in it. The Israelis quickly shot them all.

Zalman, Aharon, Shlomo, and Yisrael from HaKohen Street who had a reputation as one of the best snipers in the army, jumped in the armoured car and drove to other streets from wherever they could see Jews lined up or hear shooting.

Many Jews had already been killed, but it was not a large town, within an hour they had stopped the killing of Jews and had themselves killed every Arab officer and soldier who had taken part in the intended massacre.

As the Israelis became aware that they were safe for now, and that some of them had weapons again, a number had come together to Zalman and the leaders.

They started discussing what to do next. Meir who was on the town council said that those who had trucks should pick up the Jewish bodies first for proper burial, and then they would have to dispose of the Arab bodies.

There was some discussion what to do with the Arab bodies. Zalman finally said that they would take them to the school where the Arab unit had set up its headquarters, and they would ambush whoever came out to look at the bodies, and then they would invade the school and get rid of the remaining Arab soldiers.

They would then have to go to what had been their local weapon storage centre and take it back from the Arabs, and make sure that as many people as possible were armed and able to prevent any further attacks on their town.

Many of the women had been gathering in the synagogues during the day. Some were praying, others were supporting and trying to comfort each other. They had imagined at first that the older ones were going to be killed and the younger ones probably raped and kept for a while as sexual playthings for the Arabs, and there had been attempts by some of the women with army experience to strengthen the resolve of the older women to resist as best as they could, to be courageous, to not let their oppressors conquer them easily, without any negative consequences.

When the news came that the Arab soldiers carrying out the initial shootings had been stopped and killed, there was much relief, but for many there was agony as they discovered that their husbands or partners or fathers were among the dead. Nevertheless, they still came to whomever they could find to express their appreciation for fighting to save as many as they could, and for their victory, even if it might just be temporary.

In the north, it took a while for the news to reach there that there had been the takeover of a small town by the Arabs, but that there had then been this magnificent resistance, even though at a considerable cost.

Thirty three Israelis had been killed, but eighteen Arab soldiers and officers had been killed so far, and many weapons captured.

Zalman felt proud of what his fellow Jews had done. They organized the delivery of the Arab bodies to take place at 11 p.m. They knew that the rest of the Arab soldiers must be wondering what had happened to their colleagues. Surely it couldn't have taken so long to round up and shoot a few hundred Jews.

When the trucks pulled up and started dumping the bodies outside the school, some soldiers rushed out from the school and were easily picked off by the sharpshooters who had quietly walked along close to the school and positioned themselves.

The windows on the doors to the different school entrances were then shot out by the Israelis, and they could hear the panic inside as the Arab soldiers started arguing with each other what to do.

The Israelis waited. They had already recaptured the weapons storage building and Zalman had taken out some RPG launchers.

He handed one to Yisrael, who aimed at a window on the top floor. The rocket burst in and blew up the whole room. The Israelis heard screaming for a short while, then quiet, then screaming again as the soldiers in the rest of the building realized that the building was on fire, that the upper floor was collapsing above them, and their comrades had been killed.

Some ran out of the building again, and were easily picked off by the men Zalman had with him.

They made no move to enter the building. They decided to set up a watch to pick off any Arabs who might try to leave the building, and just wait for any still left inside to give themselves up because they were starving and frightened.

The next morning, two trucks were brought and all the Arab bodies were collected. Any identifications, especially of parents, wives, children, were removed, and then the bodies were loaded on to the trucks and driven to the Egyptian border.

The trucks were garbage trucks which had ejection load modes, and the bodies were ejected and left at the border. The Egyptians had been told through diplomatic channels that this would happen and they should accept the bodies for family disposal and not fire on the Israelis.

On Shabbat the week after Reuven came home from the hospital, Avraham went to the synagogue where Reuven would be attending. Reuven had made a good recovery after the surgery. A portion of his left lung where the bullet had entered and torn the tissue apart had been removed, and there had been no other major damage. Neither his heart, nor aorta, nor spinal column had been damaged. He had been in good physical condition before the shooting, and although there would be a period of rehabilitation he had wanted to be out of hospital as soon as possible.

He had asked to attend the synagogue to make the special blessing of thanks that survivors of illnesses and dangers traditionally make.

He went to the synagogue that his sister Rachel attended more regularly, and Avraham decided to visit that synagogue on this occasion.

When Reuven was called to the Torah to make his blessing, as he walked slowly to the reading platform, the whole congregation stood up in his honour.

Avraham also was called to the Torah, and after that part of the service was over, the rabbi of the synagogue invited him to speak to the congregation.

Avraham quoted from the portion of the Torah that had been read that morning, and compared the story of the large group of Jews who hadn't yet coalesced and identified themselves as a nation coming together to fight the marauding Amalekites who had attacked them as soon as they had escaped from Egypt. He reminded them of a passage from the special Haggada service that is read on the night of the Pesach festival, that tells that enemies that have similar behaviours and attitudes to that of Amalek arise in every generation and try to kill off Jews and Judaism.

He pointed out that for Jews it has always been a combination of their own physical strength and ingenuity and the invisible but guiding hand of the G-D we believe in that has enabled us to survive, and that both are necessary. It would be foolish to rely on physical ability alone, and it would be equally foolish to imagine that G-D is going to come to the rescue if you do nothing yourselves.

At the end of his talk people came up to him to congratulate him and express their appreciation, and he would ask each of them which unit they had served in and they would remind him of the visit he had paid to their unit. He was very well liked, a person whom people listened to.

He walked together with Reuven and Reuven's friends and neighbours, Reuven's sister Rachel had invited them for lunch.

Although Reuven was not religiously observant his sister had become observant during the period when her marriage was deteriorating, and when Avraham had heard that Reuven would be returning to the synagogue for the first time since his injury, he had indicated his wish to be present and the community had discussed the arrangements to be made. Rachel had suggested that she host the lunch.

As Avraham walked alongside Rachel and they started talking, she sensed a level of comfort between them. They seemed to communicate easily. She knew he was an outstanding communicator, that was his profession after all, and he certainly was a people person, she had seen that in the synagogue. But it felt more than that. She wondered.

Avraham had felt it too. He had been married when quite young, during his studying days, which was not unusual among the religious students. But his wife had been killed in a terrorist incident, and it had seemed to people who knew him that he had taken a long time to get over that hurt.

He was among those students who had taken the path of combining his Jewish religious studies with his army service, and he had been in an infantry unit, often in the far north of Israel, in the Golan area bordering Syria.

After completing that portion of his training and obtaining the Semicha or Rabbinical Ordination he had gone to university and taken a Master's Degree in Business and Economics. He had only become a practising rabbi after two of his former close friends and army buddies had been killed and he had sensed that the emotional support given to their families could have been much better, and he had decided that he would try to do that.

He had made it a priority to visit and comfort the families of those killed in action or from terrorist attacks, but he had also found that as an army rabbi he had a very large amount of responsibility, trying to meet the needs of both religious and non-religious young people doing their national duty.

Perhaps that had contributed to his not finding much time to meet the many women that family and friends had proposed to him. But with this woman he had felt those stirrings of real interest again.

She really liked him. She had been a bit concerned when the friends had suggested inviting the rabbi to be present at her brother's first shabbat after leaving hospital. She had imagined a long-bearded black-hatted older man, and Avraham was almost the complete opposite. Casually dressed in an open-necked, short-sleeved white shirt as most of the men in her congregation, and very down-to-earth in the way he spoke and related to people.

But he was clearly a highly intelligent and educated man with such a broad range of knowledge and experience, she wondered if he would think she wasn't smart enough to carry a conversation with him.

He didn't give her the chance to find out. He asked her about herself, about the teenage son and daughter that she had brought up almost on her own. She told him that she also worked in the army as a co-ordinator for the northern troops. She had graduated from Bar-Ilan University in Psychology and Social Sciences, but had been attracted back to the army by the prospect of teaching new immigrants about the features of a modern democratic society, and the responsibilities of individuals to find out about the privileges they had that might not have existed in countries they came from, and about what it meant to be able to vote freely, and how it was up to them to learn to distinguish between propaganda, rhetoric, and reality.

After a few years doing that she had been asked to work in the area of co-ordinating the resources and activities of different units in the north, and she became very knowledgeable about that area.

Avraham liked the way she talked, the way she expressed herself, that she was articulate, thoughtful, had a very pleasant voice and a very good use of language. He had the sense that he would like to really get to know her much better.

The lunch went well, there was no doubt that Rachel was a good cook. As they were coming to the end of the main course Rachel announced "Birshut Harav - with the rabbi's permission - my son and my daughter, Reuven's nephew and niece, would like to say a few words in honour of their uncle's recovery."

Rachel's son stood and spoke first, in a very modest and charming manner. He spoke about how his uncle had always been a source of inspiration to the family, how he had always been there for their mother, and how relieved they were to have him back healthy with them after his terrible ordeal.

Her daughter then spoke, linking the passages from the first prophets and kings of Israel that are read immediately after the weekly Shabbat Torah portion in the synagogue with her uncle's recovery, and their gratitude to G-D for him making such a quick and good recovery.

Rachel had asked the rabbi earlier on his own whether he would like to say a few words even though he had spoken in the synagogue and he had said of course he would.

"I am going to say something of perhaps a deeper level than some of you may be used to, but I see that I am among very highly educated and intelligent people," Avraham opened.

He then summarized for them a talmudic argument that was currently being debated in the pages of the talmud that people all over the world had been studying that week, and he showed how that argument had great significance for considering the response that the state should take after the devastation created by the bomb.

When Avraham explained the talmudic concepts, he made it seem easily understandable and able to be followed, and Rachel's son would have been the first to say that the language and expressions are far more complex, that it is the genius of great teachers like Avraham to make it appear simple and comprehensible.

"Your children are very impressive. You have done a wonderful job in bringing them up."

"Thank you. They are great kids, but my parents and my brother have been an enormous help. I do work and often have to travel up north and come home quite late and usually my mother or both my parents have come in when the children have come home from school and have made supper, sometimes even helped them with their homework."

Avraham hadn't really dated women for years. The women he had occasionally gone out with had been arranged by friends and family. But here he knew he had to take an initiative. And so as they were leaving and he was thanking Rachel and saying goodbye he quietly asked her if she would be agreeable to meeting again, just the two of them. She said she would be delighted to. They discussed how they would get in touch with each other. She was in the phone book, and she reminded him of her last name and the address.

The meeting had been called by Reuven with the help of his friends, and more than one hundred people crowded into Shlomi's living room.

"I think we all know what we are dealing with. We have a group of people who have decided that they are the ones to make the decisions, and to many of us it seems that they have decided to abandon the idea of the Jewish state. Calling in the United Nations was the first step, and no doubt it would have led to our neighbours coming in and taking bigger and bigger chunks for themselves, because the UN has never been able to stop any aggressive force.

We have to decide whether we are going to resist this, whether we are going to preserve our country as an independent country. If we agree on that then we shall have to mobilize public opinion so that we have a strong democratic mandate to continue as an independent country, and we shall need to take some very strong steps to see what we have left in terms of a military force to deter our enemies and those who might wish to take advantage of us after the tragedy.

So first let us see if we have a working majority who believe that we should remain the independent State of Israel, and therefore that those who are now strutting around claiming to be the leadership have to be removed. Can we do this by a show of hands, or do you want a sealed ballot?"

Almost unanimously those present agreed that a show of hands was sufficient.

Reuven then proposed the next point, removing those who now claimed to be the leadership.

There was a lot of argument, some of it was extreme. "They are traitors, they want to sell us out. They deserve the death penalty." "They already have sold us out. The question is how much more harm can they do every day unless we remove them quickly." "What we have to do - we have to do democratically. I am concerned whether we have enough time to organize an election campaign and find viable candidates before it becomes too late."

Reuven and Shlomi contacted the senior people in the army that they knew or had served with, and were quickly brought to the attention of the Chief of Staff.

They met with the Chief of Staff four days later.

"I really should have come to see you myself," started the Chief of Staff. "What you have done is amazing and you almost lost your life doing it. If we are to have a hope of preventing anything further in terms of a disaster, then your leadership will have been perhaps the most important contribution to turning the situation around."

Reuven and Shlomi then told him what had happened at their meeting and how they were confident that if such a proposition were put to many people all over the country they would receive much support.

The Chief of Staff said that he was completely in agreement, and then told them about the officers meeting and the overwhelming vote to take action and restore Israel's military strength and respond appropriately.

"Isn't your sister a major person in the co-ordination of our northern units?" asked the Chief of Staff.

"Yes, she is."

"Good. Because I'm going to ask her to report very quickly on the actual strength of our personnel and our equipment up there, as I'm also going to do for people co-ordinating the centre of the country and the south. I'm in full support of the political activity you are pursuing, I think it is very necessary. You are people of great leadership qualities and I am sure that I shall need to call on you to perform other tasks, and I hope you will make yourselves available."

"Of course," both Reuven and Shlomi responded.

Rachel reported back three days later, having visited a number of northern bases and spoken with the commanding officers of all the others. She had input the data of the number of soldiers available who had not been killed or severely injured by the bomb, and had asked the commanders about their state of readiness in terms of people and equipment.

At the same time similar inquiries were being made about the central area and the south.

The central area had been hit the hardest. The bomb had destroyed much of the centre of Tel Aviv and estimates of the numbers of dead and major casualties had settled at 1.3 million people. The numbers in the suburbs that might experience radiation sickness was still uncertain.

The south had been less affected, the cities were further away from Tel Aviv, but the southern commander had reported to the Chief of Staff something that he had found remarkable.

They had known that the city of Ashkelon close to the Egyptian border had been invaded and taken over by terrorists, but they only just found out that the local residents had recaptured it.

When the Chief of Staff contacted the commander of the largest base nearest to Ashkelon, he was told that they had been ordered by someone from the government to not resist and to stand down. The Chief of Staff inquired who from the government had given such an order and was informed that it had been a leading left-wing politician, Yaron Olin.

The Chief of Staff told the commander that Olin had no authority to give such an order, and then asked about the people who had recaptured the city.

The commander replied that such a group had indeed been successful and had widespread support and was led by a man named Zalman who had been an officer himself in the army, but that a battle was going on with the local police who were being influenced by the politician from Jerusalem.

General Yirmiyahu said he would be there within two hours. A helicopter flew him. He met with the base commander and asked to meet with the police chief and with Zalman.

When Zalman came in, General Yirmiyahu recognized him. "Shalom, you were with me in Lebanon, weren't you?" Zalman shook the General's hand, "Yes, I was. It was an honour to be in your unit. You were - you still are - a great leader and you taught us a lot."

"Thank you. Now let's get down to business here. Where is Olin now, and what does he want? You've taken back the city and stopped the killing. What does he want?"

The police chief spoke. "I think that he thinks that the Arabs will be back, and that we should then not resist."

"Is he nuts? I understand they were killing people until Zalman stopped them. What does he imagine is going to happen if you let them back. They will kill all of you."

"He thinks that if there is no resistance there will be no killing," said the police chief.

"Is he here in the city? Asked General Yirmiyahu.

The police chief acknowledged that he was at the police station.

Olin was a short, slim man with glasses, very full of himself.

"Ah, here come the trouble makers. Gentlemen, I don't think you understand the geopolitical factors that are significant here. We need to re-establish ourselves as a country that respects the rights of others, that doesn't oppress others, that doesn't discriminate against those who were here before us. We have been taught a very nasty lesson by the world because we were arrogant and thought we were better than our neighbours and didn't listen to the rest of the world. Well now, we are going to start listening."

General Yirmiyahu slowly turned and looked at the others. "Is this guy on the same planet as us? Which fantasy land does he think he is living in? Chief, lock him up please. He is a danger to the country."

"Ha, ha. Very funny, General. Who do you think you are. I'm a member of the cabinet, an elected member of our democratic parliament."

"Mr Olin. You are a traitor. There is no cabinet at the moment, and as the person most responsible for the security of this country at this difficult time, I am going to put you away for a while so that you cannot interfere with the work we are going to do to restore the independence and integrity and strength of this country. Lock him up please, and don't let him out.

He is to have no communication with anyone outside. He can watch TV himself, but take away his phone, his computer, anything he may be able to use to communicate."

Olin was led away, screaming and threatening that he was going to have the general dismissed and the others all put on trial. That he was an elected representative and they had no right to do this to him. They paid him no more attention.

Rachel reported on her findings from the military in the north. The reports were positive. More than 90% of the soldiers were alive and well, and at least 50% of the reservists appeared to have survived. Equipment and stocks had not been affected.

General Yirmiyahu called another meeting of the senior officers which included Avraham.

The general announced that the executive had made two recommendations which he now was putting to the larger group for their approval.

The first recommendation was that Israel retaliate in the strongest and most direct way by dropping equivalent bombs on Iran, and if this was approved then various officers would be asked to develop plans to accomplish this, which would also involve preventing any neighbouring countries interfering or trying to take advantage of what they might be perceiving as Israel's current post-bomb helplessness.

The second recommendation was that Avraham be their public spokesperson to the world in what would undoubtedly be a time of heated debate and furious public attack on Israel. He briefly outlined how suitable Avraham was for this role. Avraham was the son of parents who had brought him from England when he was just four years old and his younger sister two, two younger siblings were born in Israel, and he had grown up in an English-speaking home and spoke fluently without the usual heavy Israeli accent. Avraham was articulate, people found him easy to listen to and understand, and he carried a moral authority that people respected.

The recommendations were accepted unanimously.

General Yirmiyahu then discussed the status quo with them. The biggest direct threat at the moment came from the Syrians who were amassing many troops on the border, hoping of course to take back the Golan Heights. Jordan was also gathering troops.

Some officers expressed surprise that after their long and brutal civil war the Syrians would be in any position to engage Israel in battle, and the overall conclusion was that if any initial attack was repelled, the Syrians would have very little to fall back on.

A Jordanian attack was not taken very seriously, they were not believed to have a strong enough fighting force to challenge even a temporarily reduced Israeli army.

People wondered about the Egyptians. General Yirmiyahu said that for many years there had been good co-operation with Egyptian mainstream military, and that the invasion in Ashkelon had come from Hamas terrorists and that had been fought off. The General said that some people were already working on plans to redevelop the Gaza area and make it a peaceful modern residential and tourist centre.

That left the main threat of a follow-up Iranian attack, and that was a very large factor in the decision to retaliate immediately.

Two weeks later, the military went into action. First, night air raids focused on destroying the defensive capabilities of both Syria and Iran, especially their anti-aircraft batteries.

Then, within hours, before effective repairs could be done, six planes, each with a nuclear bomb on board, headed for Iran.

Each plane carried both nuclear and very powerful conventional bombs, so that each pilot would not know exactly whether his plane had carried a nuclear or a conventional bomb, and what sort of bomb that pilot had dropped on which city. The intention was in order to lessen the psychological burden of any one person thinking for the rest of their life that it was their plane that had dropped the bomb that killed hundreds of thousands or millions of people.

It was 3 a.m Israel time. An aide knocked on the door and waited to be admitted to Avraham's room.

"It's the President of the United States on the phone.

Avraham picked up the phone.

"Madam President?"

He heard screaming on the other end of the line.

"What the hell do you think you are doing. Turn your planes around immediately."

"Excuse me, Madam President. What is this about?"

"You know damn well what it's about. Don't fucking play games with me. Turn your planes around."

"I don't see the need for the abusive language. But please explain why we should turn our planes around?"

"Because I say so."

"Excuse me again. I don't think that is an explanation."

"You don't need an explanation from me. You do as I say."

"Madam President. Unless my aides just didn't wake me up to inform me, I don't believe that in the last few hours we became a state or territory of the United Sates."

"You don't understand. You have to turn your planes around and not attack Iran. That's an order."

"I must respectfully disagree, madam. We are a sovereign independent country. Your country may have been very generous to us over the years but you don't tell us what to do."

"In this case we do. Much more is at stake."

"Please enlighten me. What is more at stake than us defending ourselves?"

"We have an agreement with Iran."

"And that agreement that you have with Iran is what? That you will stop Israel attacking them?"

"Yes."

"You have an agreement with Iran that you will stop Israel attacking them. And what are they supposed to have given you in return? That Iran will not use its long-range missiles on the US?"

"Yes."

"You are being serious? You are not kidding me?"

"No. So now you understand, turn your planes around."

"Madam President. One of your predecessors claimed that he had made a deal that was best for everyone that would ensure that Iran would not be able to develop nuclear weapons. Clearly he was wrong. We were heavily pressured not to attack Iran years ago. We were told the US 'has our back'. Clearly that has not been the case. Clearly Iran has broken their agreement with you."

"We can make it up to you."

"Excuse me. You have discovered a method of bringing back to life the more than a million killed and perhaps hundreds of thousands more sentenced to die sooner or later from radiation sickness and cancer. Or perhaps you are going to forcibly evict a million to a million and a half Jews from the US and send them here to make up for the dead and dying?"

"Stop arguing with me and just do as I say."

Her voice was becoming more shrill by the second. Avraham thought that he was probably as angry as her but saw no point in giving in to the temptation to yell back.

"I am going to order our planes to shoot your plane's down if you won't stop."

"Our pilots are very capable. With respect I suggest that you don't try that path."

She started screaming again and Avraham told her that if she couldn't talk in a reasonable tone he would put the phone down and hope that next time they spoke would be calmer.

She swore at him, and he put the phone down.

He immediately called the Chief of Staff to tell him about the call and about the threat.

The escorts would be increased by another six fighters as soon as they could get there.

Avraham also called the ambassador in Washington to tell her to expect a call from the president, and how to handle it.

"Tell her that we are a sovereign nation. We have been viciously attacked. We have to fight back. We are not going to take the risk that doing nothing will lead to further nuclear bombs from Iran to destroy our other large cities and kill millions more people. Nor to the possibilities that some of our neighbours seeing our not taking action will be tempted to move in and carve out portions of our country for themselves, as happened a short while ago in the south. And please make it clear, that if US planes attempt to interfere with our action they will be shot down."

Two bombs were dropped on Teheran, the capital and main city. One bomb was dropped on Shiraz, one on Esfahan, and one on Tabriz. The sixth had been kept in case any of the other five had not seemed to detonate successfully.

The American Jets arrived at the same time as the Israeli support.

After the planes had returned safely and evidence of the destruction received, and it was known that it had been transmitted world wide, other planes were sent.

First, to bomb with regular - not nuclear - bombs the Syrian army contingents that had gathered on the border with Israel. Then, two days later, when the clouds from the nuclear bombs over Iran had settled, the approach roads to the main airports in Iran were bombed, and then the areas around each known Iranian bomb site were bombed. The purpose of this was to make it very difficult or impossible for the Iranians to launch any more nuclear bombs, or even to repair, supply, and service the facilities.

The Israelis had been deprived by the US many years earlier of having the equipment necessary to blast down to the deepest interiors where the Iranian bombs were being made. But destroying the surrounding infrastructure considerably reduced the Iranian's chances of being able to launch a second strike.

In the time period between the decision to take action and actually doing it, Avraham had called Rachel and they had gone to dinner together. It had been very enjoyable, they found each other easy to talk to. Both found the other person very interesting, and they both sensed that this could be a very meaningful relationship.

But with the retaliation bombing came the expected avalanche of criticism from the rest of the world. Led by the Americans, the British, and the French, there were the words they had heard so often in the past, "disproportion, indiscriminate, hospitals, schools, places of worship singled out, callous disregard for human life, etc."

As Avraham pointed out again and again, it was as if Israel had not been bombed first to start with, as if more than a million Israelis had not been killed 'disproportionately and indiscriminately'. There was that unspoken assumption that the Jews had it coming to them, that they deserved it, and had no right to hit back.

The platitudes of "we believe that Israel had every right to defend itself" were mouthed without any coherent guide as to what that could possibly mean other than "shut up and take what is coming to you."

Once again - led by the Americans - the message was being put out that Israel really was a nuisance, a thorn in the side of the rest of the world, and that there would be world peace, co-existence, and co-operation if Israel were to disappear. The New York Times lived up to the worst expectations the American Jewish community had of it, and strongly supported this notion.

"Time to drop our unconditional support of Israel" had been the headline in the Sunday edition and editorials, as if America's support had ever been unconditional.

But Israel's actions had been decisive. With the destruction of
Teheran and three other major cities, Iranians were in no mood for further blood loss and they retreated. Louder voices called for the resignations of the politicians and the removal of the religious fanatics.

At the United Nations many representatives called for Israel to be thrown out. Syria made a formal proposal which was supported by a number of Arab countries and countries with very large Muslim populations. The representative from Israel questioned why no such proposal had been made when Iran had unleashed a nuclear weapon destroying Tel Aviv and killing more than a million people, and as expected he was ignored. Many in Israel and in some western countries noted that this was yet again an example of the unacceptable biases of that organization and that leaving it would make very little difference to Israel. Israel had to look after itself, it needed a strong military and it needed to trade, and both those would require very strenuous efforts in coming years.

But the Israelis who had survived were pleased. They had come out of a very traumatic situation successfully, and at least for a time had silenced their enemies.

The United Nations did indeed throw out Israel from membership. Perhaps surprising to some people were the votes that showed that the United States and Canada had been among the leading countries favouring dismissal, heavily supported by most European countries.

But even more surprising was that some Arab countries supported Israel and voted against Israel being ejected. Saudi Arabia, Egypt, Abu Dhabi, the Emirates, being the leaders of this faction.

Avraham had asked Rachel to accompany him to the United Nations. Through the period of responding to Iran and the other potential attackers they had still found time to meet on a few occasions and developed a great mutual attraction and desire to be with each other.

When they returned to Israel Avraham asked Rachel to marry him. She had no hesitation accepting.

When the bombing finished and the Israeli military leaders were satisfied that any threats from their neighbours had been repelled or effectively discouraged, General Yirmiyahu had sat down with Avraham and suggested a plan. Avraham had taken the idea and formed a committee to find the best people to implement the purpose of the plan, and three weeks later they presented it to what had become the de facto cabinet.

"This is a plan for the redevelopment of Gaza. To turn what has been a hotbed of hostility and violence into a liveable paradise. We are going to build new housing after clearing away all remnants of the disaster that was. We are going to have schools and community centres and synagogues starting in each of three sectors, the north, middle, and south. After we establish the initial foundations it will be up to the people and individual enterprise to develop more. We are going to build a community initially for 60,000 people, and we are going to give first choice to the former residents of Gush Kativ who were pushed out of their homes in what had been an attempt to separate Israel from its palestinian enemies. The intention had been to give them a chance to show that they really can rule themselves and build a civil society. Hamas had demonstrated that to be an immature false hope.

Then two other groups of people are also going to be on the honorary list for first consideration; Ethopian and Egyptian Jews.

It did not take long for some of the western media to alert their staff to interview Israelis, pummeling them with just one comment, "Isn't this racist?"

Avraham had his answer ready; "It's not racist, it's not discriminating against anybody. It is putting certain deprived groups first. People who were forced out of the homes they had lived in for generations. That is all. I suggest you look at many of our neighbours who threw out all the Jews who lived in those countries for hundreds of years, and those neighbours who have made it clear that they will not accept any Jews at all. Those are racist. Not us. We have opened our borders to people of every religion, every ethnicity, every country of origin."

It took a year for the country to recover from the physical and psychological devastation of the bomb, the deaths and illnesses it had caused, before elections took place.

Reuven had fully recovered and he was asked to be a candidate for the party that was seen as the most likely to win a majority. The rules for the election had been changed to discourage small parties demanding coalition seats and holding up significant improvements and opportunities because small minorities had objections.

Zalman, who had led the revolt in the south, was asked to return to full-time army service as commander-in-chief of the Southern Command.

TRUE LOVE THAT REMAINS IN LATER LIFE

"How has she been today?" Tom asked.

"Her usual self. Quiet, reasonable, but not interested in getting up."

"Thank you," he said, and walked to her room.

"Poor man," Jennie thought. "He is so devoted to her, but I don't know if she even realizes who he is any more."

Jennie was the senior nurse on the third floor at Forest Wood Nursing Home, widely regarded as one of the better, private care facilities for older people who could no longer care for themselves, or whose partners could no longer care for them.

Tom went into his wife's room. As nurse Jennie had told him, Helen was sitting in bed. She smiled when he came in, but she didn't greet him as if she really knew who he was. She just gave him that warm friendly smile she had given to most people in the more than sixty years they had known each other.

He had brought her flowers, he gave them to her and kissed her. "You're looking particularly nice today, Helen."

"Thank you. Do I know you? There was a man here the other day, looked just like you. Do you have a twin brother?"

He tried to smile, it was difficult, this awareness that she no longer really knew who he was.

He visited nearly every day. He had retired, he had time. He would sit with her for an hour or two. He would chat, she rarely responded. He would tell her what local news he knew, and the national and international news that he had read on the internet last night or in the morning. Then he would take a break, go for his long morning walk and come back to help her eat lunch.

He would then leave, go home and do the activities that he was still involved with. He would go to his gym and exercise, sometimes get together with the few friends he still had left. He would return to the nursing home to feed her supper. Sometimes he would stay to watch a TV programme with her, and then return on his own to his home.

His mobile phone rang as he was walking home. He didn't recognize the number but answered.

"Hello Grandpa. It's Cindy, your granddaughter."

"Hi Cindy. How nice to hear from you. Are you alright?"

"Yes, Grandpa, I'm fine. Grandpa, it's been a while since I saw you and Grandma and I'd like to come and visit you."

"Of course. That would be lovely. My big house is almost empty now and there's plenty of room for you."

"Thank you Grandpa. Grandpa, I'd really like to bring a friend. It's my boyfriend. Would that be alright with you?"

"If he's a nice guy, of course it would, and I have no problem with you sharing a room. I know all you young people start your sex lives much earlier than we used to. When are you going to come?"

"We're driving, and so we'd like to reach your place on Thursday afternoon. Is it the same address?"

"It definitely is. You have my mobile number because you are calling me on it, so when you are near here please call so that I can be at home to let you in."

"Will grandma be there?"

"No, I'm afraid she won't. Maybe your mum and dad didn't tell you but I had to put grandma in a nursing home here, I just couldn't manage to care for her any more at home. But it is a nice place that she is in, and you can certainly come and visit her."

"I see. Well, we are still going to come and I'll call you when we are near."

Tom went home. He started clearing up the house and preparing a guest room for his granddaughter and her boyfriend. He then went out and did some shopping for basic necessities of milk, eggs, fish, vegetables, fruit, cereal. He hadn't asked Cindy what they ate, but he hoped that from these items she and her boyfriend would have enough to keep them fed for at least a few days.

Cindy was twenty six. She had a Master's degree in International Commerce and had started work at a large multinational bank. To her grandfather she was a beautiful, smart, lovely young woman. He liked her boy friend Derek. He seemed to be a very nice, decent young man who clearly adored Cindy. He had a Master's degree in economics and worked at a large brokerage.

After they arrived and Tom showed them around the house, he told them that he was going now to the nursing home to help Helen with supper.

"Don't they feed her there?"

"They provide food, and the food is quite good, but with someone like grandma you have to sit with her a long time to get her to eat it, and the staff often don't have the patience to do that, so you would see relatives like me helping their family members eat at lunch and supper.

"We'd like to come with you," announced Cindy.

"You've been driving a long way. I don't mind going by myself, I do it every day, and you two can rest and come tomorrow."

Cindy looked at Derek. "I think we'd like to come with you now. That is if you don't mind."

"No, of course I don't mind. I'll tell you a bit more about grandma as we walk. It's not a long walk, unless you want to take your car."

"No thanks. We could do with stretching our legs a bit after the drive."

As they walked Tom told them about the Dementia, how it had seemed to creep up slowly, but then reach a point where Helen couldn't remember where she had put things, couldn't remember whether she had switched off an oven, and would get lost walking even a few streets from where they lived.

She couldn't shop by herself, and it wasn't safe any more to let her cook by herself. Her personal care and hygiene that she had been so particular about when younger became lax, and when she became aware of that it upset her a lot.

Tom admitted that not only was there a lot of sadness within him that most of the time she didn't recognize him, but he was also concerned that she had become so immobile.

They arrived at the nursing home, and went in to see Helen.

"And who is this pretty young girl? Is this your wife? She's so young? Is she a new nurse here?"

Cindy sat on her grandmother's bed and told her grandmother who she was, and introduced her boy friend.

"I understand you haven't been getting up much grandma. Don't you think you would feel a lot better if you got up. It's so nice outside."

"Oh no, my dear," Helen replied, "I'm so tired. I think I'll just stay in bed and rest. Sometimes this nice doctor sits and reads me stories."

Cindy looked at her father. "Who is that doctor, he sounds very nice to sit and read stories to her."

"I'm the only person who reads stories to her. There are two doctors on staff, they only come twice a week to see all the patients, and they certainly don't have the time to sit and read stories to patients."

"Oh," said Cindy. "Oh." She looked at Derek and at her father. "I think we should try and get her up. Dad, would you like to make sure she's covered enough if we try and lift her."

Tom checked her robe and was satisfied. He then watched as Cindy and Derek together gently lifted Helen out of the bed and deposited her in a chair next to the bed.

"Well done. I think that's the first time four months that she has been out of bed."

"Tomorrow we're going to start getting her mobile again."

They walked back to Tom's house quietly. After they arrived, they sat down, Cindy went to the kitchen and started the kettle to make tea.

"It must be very upsetting for you to see your wife like this, after all these years," said Derek.

"It is, " said Tom. "You know, we used to say that we were sure that I would be the one to become demented first, and that she would have to look after me in that state. We never imagined it would be the other way round. But it shows you, you can't predict how life is going to turn out."

Cindy came into the living room with a tray on which were three cups of tea and pieces of a cake she had made and brought.

"It's sad to see Grandma like this. But she couldn't have a better and more loving carer than you, Grandpa," said Cindy.

"Thank you, my dear," said Tom, "and this cake is just delicious. I haven't been eating much cake myself recently. I brought your Grandma some cake for her birthday, and she nearly choked on it. The doctors and nurses said that a lot of older people in this state lose their gag reflex and it becomes easy for food to go down the wrong way. So I don't bring her cake anymore, which means I don't buy it for myself, and I try to make the food she eats as soft as possible."

"And what about you, Grandpa? Who's looking after you now?"

Tom laughed, "Oh, I can take care of myself, thank you."

"I'm sure you can," said Cindy, "and very well too. But what if something happens and you can't. And what would happen to Grandma if you couldn't be there for her?"

"Cindy, my dear, those are great questions, and the truth is that I haven't wanted to look at them yet. But I think that the two of you have had a long day, and it was so nice of you to come with me to the nursing home, but I should really let you go to bed now. I've left some cereal and milk and other things I hope that you might like for breakfast. I'll see you tomorrow morning. Have a good night."

Cindy came over and gave Tom a big hug, and Derek thanked Tom for letting them stay in his house.

Cindy and Derek went to their room, undressed, showered, and went to bed.

"What do you think, Derek?"

Derek knew Cindy. They had lived together for a year and were very close. They had known from early in the relationship that this was special, that they had a strong closeness and sensitivity to each other.

"I think you are asking me how I would feel about us moving here to help look after your grandfather and support him in his care for your grandma."

Cindy hugged Derek. "Yes, you really know me, don't you? That is what I would like. I know I can make the move in terms of work, but what about you?"

"I would do it. I would do it because he is such a great guy and I would like to think that I could be like that for our parents and my grandma if they were in a similar situation, and that if we start having kids that they would be able to see such a demonstration of what real love and decency and caring is."

Over the next two days, Cindy and Derek took Tom to the nursing home most of the time, and then took Tom shopping and took him out to eat, which he had not done himself for a very long time.

They also started taking Tom out for long walks during the day when Helen was asleep. Tom had been a very active runner and football player until the past couple of years, and he had lost a bit of his previous physical vitality, and the walking stimulated him. He felt more lively, invigorated.

Cindy and Derek were able to lift Helen into a wheelchair now, and took her for walks that she had not had for at least a year.

She seemed to appreciate it and thanked them.

It was on the fourth evening that Cindy and Derek approached her grandfather and suggested that they move in.

"Thank you, my dear, but I really can take care of myself."

"We know that you can grandpa. You are amazing. But we also think that you are lonely, coming home to an empty house every night, and even though you talk to grandma it is one-way, there is very little that she understands or can say to you.

We don't want to get in your way at all. We just think that having us around and having us join you sometimes in visiting grandma can help ease the burden a little."

They knew that it might take a long time to persuade him, and that might not be accomplished on this visit. But Cindy hoped that they had implanted the idea in his mind and that his mind might work on the possibility and give it serious thought.

"Have you gone out of your mind, Thomas? You take in that young couple into your house and the next thing you'll know will be that they'll ship you off to the same place Helen is in."

"Why would you say that, Mrs Jenkins?" Tom asked his neighbour from across the street who had dropped in after Cindy and Derek had left to do some shopping.

"Because that is always what happens when young people make what seems like a generous offer. The young people move into a relative's house and quickly they take it over, dump the owner in a nursing home, and they have a lovely house to themselves, and it didn't cost them a penny. Or maybe a few pennies to feed you until you were ready to be sent to the nursing home."

"I don't think that my granddaughter is like that, and so far I've been very impressed with her partner Derek, he seems like a very nice man."

Mrs Jenkins left, but her views stayed in Tom's mind. He didn't see either Cindy or her husband as not being genuine, but Mrs Jenkins' comments had made him uncomfortable.

When they arrived back at the house with bags full of groceries, fruit, vegetables, healthy foods, Tom told them that he still needed time to think over their proposals.

Cindy wondered what had changed, because the previous evening Tom had seemed very positive to the idea of them moving in to be with him and help him.

Nothing more was said overtly, but Cindy had a sense that Tom was looking at her differently. She couldn't have articulated clearly what concerned her. It was just a sense that something was different.

They had succeeded in persuading Tom to come out walking with them after supper each evening, and had gradually increased their pace and the distance they walked.

The kitchen and refrigerator were also well stocked with healthy food now, cereal and fruit and vegetables and eggs, and a lot of fish which they were pleased to see Tom really liked.

It was about three weeks later when Derek was in the supermarket and overheard a conversation coming from the next aisle.

"I told him. I told him that those young people would move in and within a few months would ship him off to the nursing home and say that he can't be managed any more at home. And they would have a beautiful home, tax free, for nothing. Silly old fool. They never learn, these smart men."

Derek was shocked - and yet he was not surprised. He had suspected there was more to the story but had not been able to find any real evidence.

And now he understood.

He came back to the house and told Cindy. She was upset to hear it. They talked together trying to decide what to say to her grandfather.

Cindy decided she wanted to be straightforward with him. He seemed to be quite capable mentally and she was going to tell him and leave to him to decide.

About a week later Cindy approached her grandfather after they had come back from the nursing home visiting Helen.

"Grandpa. I know that one of your neighbours has talked with you and made you doubt our intentions. If you really believe that we have come here with a plot to throw you out and put you in a nursing home, that is very upsetting. We are only here to help you and do whatever we can for grandma, but if you don't believe us and trust us then we can pack up our things and leave. We don't want you to worry any more than you already do about Helen."

Derek added, "I've known Cindy now for a while and we've been living together, and I can tell you that she is the most honest, decent, caring person I've ever come across. She really loves you and your wife.

Look at your refrigerator and your kitchen cupboards now, aren't they filled with really good food? And the walks we've been taking. Don't you feel a lot more energetic since we've been doing that together? Does it really sound as if all the good stuff is to prepare you for a nursing home?

Don't you realize that it really is to help you stay healthy for a very long time? We know that we haven't been as much in your life as your neighbour has all these years, but I know I would trust Cindy more than any neighbour. She is such a great person."

"I know. She really is," agreed Tom. "And I am so grateful for everything that you have done these last few weeks. I really do feel a lot more alive than I had been feeling for the past couple of years, and I realize it has a lot to do with the two of you. It's not only Cindy, you're pretty good too Derek."

"Thank you. It's very nice of you to say that. But I get my good stuff from Cindy. She's my inspiration."

Cindy was in tears. "Thank you Derek, and thank you grandpa. You mean a lot to us, and I have good memories from the time when grandma was better. I wish we had been able to spend more time with her, but when we were younger and in high school and university we wanted to be with our friends and explore the world, and spending a lot of time with grandparents didn't seem like such an important priority.

Now when you're older, and grandma can't really communicate with us anymore, it seems sad that we missed a lot of good opportunities. I hope that when we have kids we'll teach them to take more interest in their grandparents while their grandparents are still young enough to have meaningful relationships with them."

"So. You are intending to have children?" asked Tom.

"Absolutely," insisted Cindy. That was another of our reasons for moving here. The possibility of starting a family here. It is such a nice environment for kids to grow up in."

"Well, I'm delighted to hear that," said Tom. "It really would be very nice to live to become a great-grandparent. Then I'd better let you two get off to bed to start making babies."

Derek and Cindy both laughed, "we're not quite as methodical as that, grandpa. We still try to make our love-making fun."

Tom decided that he had to call his son and daughter-in-law, Cindy's parents, and hear what they had to say.

Michael and Georgina had moved to Canada when Cindy was eight and her brother Leslie was six. Michael was a doctor and he had thought that opportunities in Canada were better for doctors at the time he had moved. Michael had told his father that was no longer the case. A combination of fee controls and cutbacks and huge increases in petty bureaucratic regulations had made the practice of medicine in Canada much less desirable, and not surprisingly neither of their children had chosen to enter medicine.

Georgina was a high school teacher of economics, which probably had been the inspiration for Cindy's choice of career, and Cindy's attraction to a man with a degree in economics.

"Hi, Michael. You know we have your daughter and her man friend with us at the moment. Tell me, from a totally objective neutral viewpoint about my granddaughter."

Michael laughed. "Of course I can be totally objective. But Georgina can be even more neutral and objective than me." It was Tom's turn to laugh.

"But seriously," said Michael, "I don't know what you are looking for or why you are asking, but Cindy is just an amazing young woman. She's bright, smart, beautiful, and the most honest, upright, decent and loving person."

"Thanks Michael. I knew I could get a totally objective opinion from you."

"Now Dad, tell me why you were asking."

"Cindy and her young man told me that they would like to move in to help me cope better and make it easier for me to visit your mother. But then, one of my gossipy neighbours, raised a concern that according to her many young people want to move into their parents' or grandparents' home, take it over, push the grandparent or parents into a nursing home, and then they have themselves a very nice house, totally free to them.''

Michael listened, then said "Dad, I'm sorry to say this but I suspect that your neighbourhood has had problems for some years, and some not-so-nice people have moved in. I wouldn't believe that neighbour if she imagines that's what Cindy is like."

They carried on chatting for a while, how Georgina was doing and their son Leslie, whether Michael was thinking of retiring. No, he said, he was too young and still enjoyed what he did.

Tom continued thinking, and watching, and what he saw pleased him.

He told Cindy and Derek that he had given their idea a lot of thought, and he would be very honoured if they would move in.

Cindy cried, "thank you so much Grandpa," and Derek shook Tom's hand and expressed his appreciation.

The next morning, Tom was aware that he felt different, that he felt more energetic. That he now looked forward to the day with joy, and not with those depressing thoughts or feelings that bother so many people. He knew who was responsible for making him feel that happiness again.

BAD FROM THE START

He was tall, handsome, strongly built. He wasn't too bright at his studies but he was captain of the junior football team. Many of the girls wanted to go out with him, even some from high school although he was still only in middle school.

Most of the girls in her grade would have agreed that Jennifer was very pretty. She was also one of the best students in most subjects, and she was a good all-round athlete, runner, swimmer, basketball player. But Jennifer was shy. She was not very out-going. No-one had a bad word to say about her but she was definitely not one of the party girls.

Carlos had taken a liking to her. He told his admirers that he thought she was really 'hot' and that he was going to go out with her and have her.

When he approached her in the corridor at school one afternoon she tried to politely say no to him. She didn't find him very likeable or very smart. She knew he was football captain, and she thought that he believed that every girl was just dying to go out with him. She wasn't. She thought he was just a show-off. None of the girls he had been out with had come back from dates saying they had a fantastic time with him.

But he persisted, and some of the other girls made comments about how all the girls wanted to go out with him and she was very lucky that he had asked her, and she should go out with him.

Reluctantly, she said yes.

He told her he would pick her up from her house on Friday evening.

Her mother, Diana, was concerned. Jennifer was going out on a date without much enthusiasm. Jennifer didn't seem to take her usual time and care in getting ready for the date.

Diana Hartwell was a trim, usually cheerful woman in her early forties. She was a math teacher in another high school. She loved her three children and spent a lot of time with them. Jennifer was the oldest at 15, Barry was 13 and Sylvia was 11.

"I get the impression you're not thrilled about this date."

"I'm not. I'm not sure if I really want to go, but it's too late for that."

"You can change your mind, you know. It's a woman's privilege."

Diana laughed, but Jennifer said, "I'm going to go. I said I would. I just hope it works out o'k and that it's not a disaster."

They heard the noisy horn of a car outside their door. They both looked out and saw a car outside their door. They looked at each other, each knew what the other was thinking, that it was not very mature of the young man to just sound the horn noisily expecting her to come out, and not come to the front door and introduce himself to her parents.

Carlos continued to lean on the horn of his car, obviously impatient.

Jennifer kissed her mother goodbye and left.

"What took you so long?" No 'hi, you really look lovely', thought Jennifer.

"Guys that I have been out with before usually come to the door and introduce themselves to my parents before we go out."

"Well, I'm not other guys. I'm me," Carlos announced rather arrogantly.

They drove to a movie theatre. Carlos mentioned a new horror movie that Jennifer had no interest in seeing. She looked at the different movies playing at the cinema and suggested two others. Carlos wasn't interested.

Carlos didn't initiate much in the way of conversation before the movie started so Jennifer tried to engage him in some discussion. She asked him which courses he was taking, what interested him, did he think of going to college.

"To play football," he told her. He wanted to get a good football scholarship to a leading football school, and from there be drafted by a NFL team. He could earn much more money that way and live well, rather than studying boring stuff for years to be a doctor or a lawyer.

Her father was a hard-working lawyer, his comment did not go down very well with her.

Mercifully, the movie started. But perhaps she had hoped for relief too early. Because as soon as the movie started Carlos started groping her. He put his arm around her and started grabbing her breasts. At first she gently lifted him off in the way that she had done before with guys, and the guys who really liked her had taken it well and smiled, as if they knew she might later but were just testing her. Carlos didn't smile. He pouted.

A few minutes later he tried to put his hand between her thighs and caress her genital area. Again she gently lifted his hand off with a smile.

He grumbled something and she said to him that this was a first date and they hardly knew each other and he should be patient. She didn't tell him he should also be respectful, because she already realized he had no concept of what that might require.

He directed his attention to the movie, responding noisily to the more horrific aspects. She found it funny at times, sickening at other times, but mostly boring.

He didn't suggest going for a coffee or ice cream afterward, but said "let's go for a drive."

She didn't see herself as being given much of a choice, which didn't please her, and she was hardly surprised when he took her to the popular park 'romantic-spot'.

He unzipped his pants, took out his penis and said to her, "suck my dick".

She couldn't help it. She laughed.

He growled at her." I'm not joking, I said suck my dick."

"No. I don't do that with guys anyway, and certainly not on a first date.

I like to get to know a guy first and see that he really likes me before I even kiss him. I'm certainly not going to take a guy's thing in my mouth when all the guy does is just take it out of his pants and says 'suck it'. Guys go to massage parlours if they want that."

She didn't know where it came from, but suddenly her head was spinning and her nose was bleeding.

He had backhanded her very hard in her face. "I said suck it, bitch."

"No."

He hit her again and tried to force her head down on to his penis, she resisted.

He leaned over and punched her full in the face, yelling at her, screaming at her.

She was crying now, her face hurt, her nose was bleeding. She pushed open the door of the car and ran out. He still had his penis out of his penis and hurried to put it in and zip himself up before charging out of the car after her.

But she had a good start, she was fast, and she was very afraid. She ran to the main street and ran along near the cars, screaming 'help, help'. Most of the cars ignored her. Maybe they thought she was a prostitute thrown out by her pimp.

But one car screeched to a halt, not too far ahead. She ran to it and climbed in, Carlos not too far behind.

"Someone beat you up?"
"Yes, I think he's running after me."
"Jump in."
The driver was a woman, looked to be in her early fifties.

"Your face is bleeding. Let's go to the hospital."
"No. Please take me home first, and I'll get my parents to take me. I really appreciate you stopping to pick me up. That guy was horrible. Can you believe it was a first date?"
"Are you sure, you are bleeding pretty badly. Here, take a tissue and hold it over your nose."
Jennifer directed the driver to her house. "Could you please sound the horn loudly a few times, I'm sure someone will come out."
Jennifer didn't want the woman to drive away without her parents thanking her, and Jennifer - being a lawyer's daughter - was already thinking that her dad might want to know who the person was who might be a witness.

They arrived at her home, and the woman driver did as Jennifer asked. Her mother came out after a few minutes. She looked towards the car, gradually came closer, and Jennifer opened the car door.
"Oh my - what happened to you Jenny?"
"That pig, my date, started hitting me in his car, I jumped out and ran, and this kind lady picked me up and brought me home. Could you please thank her for me, and ask her name.

I think I should go to a hospital and be checked out. He hit me in the face and head pretty badly, I want to make sure nothing is broken."

"Dad's inside. We'll take you in just a moment."
Jennifer ran into the house, looked at her face in the mirror, and called for her father.

He was shocked when he saw her, and even though her sweater was covered in blood he gave her a big hug. She told him briefly what happened and that she wanted to go to a hospital.

He said "of course," and asked her if he could take a quick photo of her face before they left. She agreed, and also told him about the woman who had picked her up and driven her home and might still be outside.

They arrived at the hospital. It was a quiet evening, not too busy, and they did not have to wait too long to be seen. An emergency room doctor examined her and sent her for x-rays. He had told her he didn't think her nose was broken, and although she had been dazed by Carlos's first backhand across her face the doctor didn't think she had suffered a concussion or any head injury.

They waited another hour until the doctors checked the x-rays. Her nose had stopped bleeding, and she was reassured that no bones had been broken and she was sent home.

Her father called the police when they returned home and reported the assault. Two police officers, a man and a woman came to the house to interview Jennifer and her parents. She identified Carlos, her father showed them his photographs of Jennifer's face when she had come home. The officers left.

The next morning, Jennifer's parents wanted her to stay at home but she insisted on going out. They went together as a family. On Saturday they walked in the park, and went to a movie they all wanted to see. On Sunday they went for brunch together.

On Monday morning, Jennifer insisted on going to school. The bruising on her face had become quite obvious and there was a lot of swelling. She refused to put on any make-up. "I hope the other girls ask me what happened to me."

Her father drove her to school and after dropping her off he parked his car and made his way to the principal's office. He introduced himself and asked to speak with the principal.

He told the principal what had happened. The principal told him that he had received a message that Carlos had been arrested by the police, his parents had taken him home, and he was due to appear in court that morning.

Jennifer went to her first class. Most of the kids who were in the room gasped when they saw her, the boys as much as the girls.

"What the hell happened to you, Jenny?"

She told them. Slowly, clearly, articulately, exactly what had happened.

Pamela Bartek snorted, "If Tom asked me to suck his dick I would have."

But Lisa Goldstein went to Jennifer and put an arm around her. "It must have been horrible. What a lousy date. Are you o'k? Did you have to go to hospital?"

One of the boys asked, "What's happening with Carlos? Was he arrested?"

Jennifer said, "I think so."

A couple of the boys then asked, "What's this going to mean for the football team?"

Some of the girls groaned. "You've got to be kidding," said Samantha Armstrong. "Jenny's had her face bashed in by a real pig and all you're concerned about is the football team." "Thanks, Sam," said Jennifer.

The principal walked into the class. "I suppose you've all seen Jennifer's face and you probably all know that Carlos was arrested and is going to have to go to court. It must have been a terrible experience for Jennifer and I hope you will be supportive of her.

For those of you on the football team, I'm sorry, but this is such unacceptable behaviour that even if Carlos is not put in jail or sent to a youth reform centre he's not going to be captain or play for our football team any more.

That may be a disappointment for those of you who thought we had a chance of winning some championships this year, but we are not going to have people coming to games and making comments asking if that is the rapist there? Is that the guy who beat up the young woman on a first date?"

By the time of Carlos's trial, four other young women had come forward and told police that Carlos had assaulted them. With that record, even though it was the first time he had been charged, he was jailed for six months and ordered to do two hundred hours of community services under tight supervision in a women's shelter.

Carlos learned well in jail. Not the usual school subjects that he had not paid attention to in class because he thought they didn't matter - he was going to become the great NFL star - but many more 'informal' classes from experts in such occupations as lock picking, breaking and entering, money laundering, casino organization, prostitution management.

It didn't take Carlos long to be recruited into three different criminal gangs. Denny Landstone's drug pushers saw Carlos as a great potential asset for school campuses, Livio Saltrini's group looked at Carlos's size, strength, and good looks and saw him as an ideal front man for the prostitutes they were bringing in from Eastern Europe and who needed to be broken in to accept what was the real work they were going to be doing in this country, and Jimmy Hart's cohort of fast tough drivers who couriered drug supplies and drug dealers all over town quickly got to hear about the tough ex-con who before he went to jail had loved fast hard driving.

Carlos also had his own agenda, and high on his list was getting even with that Hartwell bitch.

Carlos progressed. He was young, attractive to many girls and seen as a big tough guy by many boys. He boasted about his achievements as football quarterback, and he became very popular as a drug pusher. He soon realized that even though he had a flair for it and was very successful, even better money was to be made being higher up the supply ladder.

The women trafficked in from Eastern Europe easily fell for him. He seduced them, and then had his way with them sexually in a very aggressive manner. He charmed them into bed - he had learned from his bad experience with Jennifer Hartwell - but once in bed he was brutal. He jumped on them and thrust himself inside them when they were hardly ready and lubricated. He pumped furiously until he ejaculated.

He gave them and himself a few moments, and then turned them over and forced himself inside them anally. Occasionally he did use some lubricant to start doing it that way, but after ejaculating again inside them, he would again lubricate them slightly and push himself inside them - not necessarily to have another release, although he could achieve that often - but more to get them used to having anal sex, which was very much in demand and a big seller in the work they would be doing.

He enjoyed the sense of power he had with them. He wasn't particularly aroused when some of them became aware of what was happening and turned angry and resentful and bitchy. But he really liked those who understood and who concluded that submission was the safest and most practical path for them.

The madams taught him about the sex toys - he hadn't known what sex toys were when he was still in school - and then after the madams had trained the women in becoming experts using the various toys they would turn the women back to him to practice on.

But what rivalled for him even the enjoyment of the women, was being an enforcer for Jimmy Hart's group, beating up some of the people who were slow in paying. He relished that, it gave him enormous satisfaction. He would tell some of the victims when he was beating them up that it was even better than good sex.

Another lesson Carlos had learned in jail was how to play off one group against another. He had made himself very useful to three different organizations. They weren't in direct competition with each other but an asset like Carlos was not easily found, and when one such became available a smart leader would not want to lose the person.

So Carlos was rewarded very well. He bought himself a nice condominium, a very expensive sports car, and fashionable clothes.

He hadn't found the need to have a relationship with any one woman. He didn't trust women and he could get all the sex he wanted, in as much variety and experimenting in as many different ways as he desired, and certainly far more than any one woman could ever offer on her own.

But sometimes Carlos's tendency to act rashly, to behave in an arrogant manner thinking that he was so desirable that no-one would refuse his demands, still led him into trouble.

Natalyia had attracted him because she had combined lustrous dark hair and dark eyes with a slim upper body and voluptuous hips.

He had taken her for a quick drink and then back to his apartment, and after taking her clothes off had wasted no time in turning her face down and attempting anal sex with her.

She had screamed, and had jerked her body upward and thrown him off. He had not bothered to find out more about her and didn't know that she had been through some unpleasant war-time experiences and had developed fighting survival skills.

He had tried to slap her around as he did with most women who put up some protest and who usually quickly gave in when he asserted his masculine authority.

Natalyia didn't give in. She fought him bitterly until he started punching her in the face and body seriously. He broke her nose, broke a number of ribs, and bloodied and bruised her face and upper body severely. At one point she seemed to lose consciousness, and he took her down to his car, drove off, and dumped her by the side of the road in one of the seedier parts of town. He drove back to his apartment and tried to wipe away all trace of her having been there.

He had thought she might have been dead, or that if she was still alive that she wouldn't remember much of what had happened, and anyway after the beating would be too frightened to do anything about it.

He was wrong on all counts. She wasn't dead. She recovered consciousness and was able to find someone to take her to a hospital.

At the hospital she was treated and the police were called and she told them the full story, even admitting that she was an illegal resident.

Carlos was charged, and to his surprise yet again was sentenced, this time to five years in jail.

Carlos had learned from his experience in jail, and he was out after three years. He had behaved himself, had gone to classes, had focused even more on developing his powerful body, and his reputation as an enforcer and member of some of the leading criminal organizations gave him a privileged and protected position. No-one bothered him, and he received all the comforts that a prisoner could receive.

When he came out, the gangs were happy to have him back, although old man Saltrini gave him a long lecture about respecting limits in 'disciplining' - as he called it - the young women.

Jennifer Hartwell survived her last few months at school. Her grades were not as high as she might have liked but her parents and teachers were sympathetic, they told her she had done very well considering the upsetness she had experienced.

She went to a few parties - there weren't many in the last few months anyway as students strove to increase their marks before going off to college. Some of her classmates invited her, others still seemed uncomfortable or clearly resented her and rejected her.

She was invited to the prom by one of the nicest guys in the class Davis Carter. She hadn't known Davis was attracted to her, and she was pleasantly surprised by the mature graciousness with which he treated her. It was well-known that after the prom was the occasion for many students to have their first sexual experiences, and for those already well-acquainted with the intimacies of the opposite sex the opportunity to spend a full night in a nice hotel with a partner was a new pleasure to be enjoyed.

Davis had not pressured Jennifer but had been very gentle with her, so much so that she had made the first move to kiss him, and then asked him if he really liked her. He had told her that he did very much, but that he had not wanted to make her feel threatened in any way.

They didn't have full sex, but had some very intense deep necking that led to both of them reaching very satisfying orgasms. They had both dozed off for a short while, and then he had taken her home.

They dated a few times until they went to different colleges. They never did have a complete love-making experience, but she remembered him very fondly. He was the nicest man she had gone out with, and she had hoped that they might eventually get together for a full relationship. But he was killed in a freak car accident in Thailand in his second year of college. She was devastated.

She applied for Law School, her LSAT marks were excellent, she had recaptured her good studying abilities.

In her third year at college she had two brief affairs - one with a professor - that helped her overcome her fears of sexual assault, and at Law School had three more relationships, each lasting for six to nine months with nice people, with each of them recognizing that they were not ready for a permanent relationship and still wanted to experience other people. Parting in each case was amicable.

Jennifer graduated comfortably. She had studied hard, her professors had liked her - sometimes even loved her - and she received three good offers to article.

She chose a medium-size firm in midtown Phoenix, an office that offered a broad range of areas of specialty. She had interviewed three of the senior partners and three junior associates and received a positive impression of the attitudes and relationships between partners and juniors. They left her in no doubt that juniors were expected to work long and hard hours, yet there was a sense that the hard work was consistently appreciated.

Jennifer worked hard, she did good work, and she had realized the benefits of regular exercise. She ran four times a week, and worked out with machines at a gym that the firm paid for.

She met some men at the gym, went out with a few but none seemed quite right for her.

She had not found it very easy to make women friends. She knew that she was vulnerable to become easily hurt and disappointed if she thought that someone she liked didn't really like her very much. She still kept in touch with some of the nicer women from her schooldays, but most of the others she could hardly remember.

If Jennifer had been asked at that time in her life whether she thought much about Carlos she would have answered 'not at all'. But as is true of so many women - even very smart women - she was very astute about others but not very self-aware.

Jennifer perhaps didn't even realize it herself but feelings and fears about her experience with Carlos were only just beneath the surface of her consciousness, and made a significant contribution to her difficulties with long-term relationships.

She was thirty two, a junior partner, recognized as hard-working, very capable, a very nice and decent woman who kept herself physically fit, ran ten kilometer charity runs in good times, and gave up one evening a week and a weekend day every two weeks to work with deprived children, and she was still single.

She usually enjoyed the conference that this year was being held in Las Vegas. It was one of the largest legal conferences, often there were many interesting sessions and she usually came away having learned something new, and having met new and interesting colleagues from all over the country and other countries.

But she was pleasantly surprised this time to have met a really nice man, just two years older than her, who came from the same town. She had thought she knew most of her colleagues in Phoenix, especially those of her own age group, but obviously she hadn't.

Steven was a little taller than her, he also kept himself fit by running regularly, and he worked in a mid-sized firm, his own area of practice being Child Protection. That surprised her even more because her volunteer work often brought her close to situations that might become legal issues, and she was surprised that she had not met or heard of Steven before the convention.

They really hit it off. They found themselves talking easily with each other, knowing and understanding what the other person was talking about, and finding a real pleasure in their initial meetings.

Jennifer had been disappointed in the past thinking that meeting and becoming romantically or sexually involved with exciting men at such conferences might lead to a permanent relationship.

She had then tried the 'this is only for good recreational sex' route and had not been very happy with how she felt about herself after those encounters.

And so this time - especially knowing Steven was from the same city - she held back on any more romantic and physical expressions of her attraction to him. He seemed to either accept that from her, or have his own personal reasons for acting in a similar manner. He made clear his pleasure in spending some time with her, and when the conference finished and they were both going to leave he indicated his interest in meeting her again in Phoenix, but he also refrained from demonstrating excessive affectionate or sexual desires.

After they returned to Phoenix he called her within three days. She was delighted to hear from him. They agreed to go out to dinner. It went very well, they enjoyed each other's company, they arranged another date for the weekend, and after the second date both had no doubt that they wanted to be in a relationship with each other.

They met again for dinner during the week, went to a movie together on Friday evening, and spent Saturday together driving out of town for a long walk, and starting to tell each other their life stories.

Jennifer found that Steven had also been hurt in two previous relationships. Seven years earlier a woman he had been living with for three years had become involved with a man who had been a boyfriend in her school days and had made her pregnant. She had always had regrets about the abortion, and the ex-boy friend had come back tormenting her with accusations of being a 'child-killer' who had only considered herself and the effects on her and not considered his wishes at all. Her obsession with this man had destroyed the relationship between her and Steven.

Then two years ago a relationship with a woman he had lived with for two years had broken up, because - according to Steven - she had become so depressed not knowing what to do with her life, having no sense of direction after trying two different master's programmes, that she became very difficult to live with, and he admitted that he could no longer cope with her.

He had a lot of guilt feelings thinking he had abandoned her, but said that he had felt dragged down, that he knew he wasn't focusing on his work, was always worrying what was she thinking, what might she do, how was she going to be when he arrived home? Miserable, crying, angry, complaining, questioning, demanding? Life had ceased to be enjoyable around her, and he had thought that he was still too young to be dragged down by someone so unhappy with herself.

Jennifer had been impressed. He had told her these things in a straightforward manner, he seemed able to acknowledge that he might have failed in some ways, he didn't accuse the women of being 'bad' people.

Jennifer told him a bit about Carlos. She realized that it was the first time for many years that she had talked about that experience with any man, and then she said that it might have contributed to her not being able to make a permanent relationship up to this time in her life.

That surprised her, she had never openly expressed that thought. 'It must be something to do with my age,' she thought.

Steven was very supportive. He empathized, and after she had told him of her other longer but ultimately not-permanent relationships he said to her that it was very fortunate for him that she had remained single, otherwise he wouldn't have been able to have the opportunity to develop a relationship with such a lovely woman.

That pretty much did it for Jennifer. Her sense that this was the right man for her, the man that she could spend many more years together with, marry, and have a family with, grew stronger each day. She eventually told him that, he agreed, and they started making plans to marry and announce their engagement.

And they did so one week after Carlos was released from his latest incarceration.

Carlos heard about it very soon after, because some people had heard him talk about 'that Hartwell bitch' and told him about her becoming engaged. Carlos quickly discovered who she had become engaged to, where they both worked, and where they both lived. He was going to extract his revenge, and he was going to make sure it would be excruciatingly painful.

Carlos had returned to his previous colleagues. He had not betrayed them when he had been arrested even though offers had been made for a reduced sentence if he co-operated and gave details of the criminal activities of the people he worked with, and that loyalty had paid off. He had been welcomed back, even though his older bosses told him that it was time he grew up and controlled his temper better and used his rage to punish those who deserved it rather than innocent and ignorant young women.

So Carlos had more junior people working for him, and he started some of them off following Jennifer and Steven and making careful notes of their regular daily activities, the times they left and came home, when they went out or went shopping, where and how they exercised.

As professional people, even though Jennifer and Steven were very active young people they still both led quite disciplined lives. After a few weeks Carlos had a clear picture of their most frequent activities and their usual time schedules.

Steven was the first target. Early one evening, out running, he was attacked by three hooded young men.

Although he was taken by surprise, Steven surprised them back. Two had tried to hold him so that the third could administer a severe beating to his face and body, but Steven had started to recover. He stepped hard on the insteps of each of the thugs holding him. That caused them to yell and temporarily loosen their grip on Steven. He pivoted and slipped out of their grasp and quickly brought their heads together and clashed those one against the other.

And then he ran, and there was no stopping him or catching him. He ran to his home, and as soon as he was inside the door he called Jennifer. He told her that he had been attacked and warned her to be aware of the possibility that she might also be attacked.

Steven and Jennifer were resourceful, and they soon found out that Carlos had been released from prison just a few weeks earlier. Steven didn't really know Carlos, but Jennifer convinced him that there was a strong possibility that Carlos was responsible for the assault.

Through their colleagues they were able to have a meeting with a senior police officer involved in organized crime who filled them in on some of Carlos's activities in the past few years, and they met with some other officers who specialized in protecting celebrities and others who had been threatened.

Steven and Jennifer learned about varying their daily routines, about being able to notice when they were being followed, becoming alert to seeing what at first was a strange face in two or more locations near them.

They no longer ran separately but ran together after taking a drive and making sure that they were not being followed, and carrying phones programmed to call police with just one touch.

It helped. Eventually Carlos himself followed them. Brash as ever in a loud sports car, as if he didn't mind being noticed – or perhaps had not learned a vital lesson from his years of incarceration.

They hadn't noticed him coming because he had guessed where they were going, and had driven there by a different route.

They had just started their run when he drove up to them, and came out his car swinging a baseball bat. They both pressed the call button on their telephones and gave their location.

"Won't matter," yelled Carlos. "You'll be pulp by the time any cops get here, and I'll be out of here."

Steven and Jennifer had no doubt that Carlos meant to keep his threat, but unlike Carlos they had learned some valuable lessons preparing for this possibility.

As Carlos approached them swinging his baseball bat, Steven lunged forward grabbing Carlos's wrist with one hand and punching Carlos hard in his armpit with his other hand, temporarily paralyzing that arm.

Jennifer also grabbed the arm holding the baseball bat and held it upright while launching a hard kick at Carlos's groin. Carlos doubled-over in pain and shock.

Carlos had become very strong pumping weights in jail, but he had little opportunity to develop any speed. He had slowed, and Steven and Jennifer were much faster in their actions.

They forced the baseball bat out of Carlos's hand, and aimed a few more hard kicks in his testicular area, and each took a powerful swing at Carlos's nose. As she saw Carlos's nose bleeding Jennifer felt a great sense of satisfaction.

A police car came along. Steven explained the situation and Carlos was taken away.

A psychiatrist testified at the trial that there really was no hope of rehabilitation. Carlos was a vengeful person whose obsession with 'getting even' or getting the better of Jennifer was incurable in her opinion. The severity of the past attacks, the multiple history of assaults, and the planning and mobilization of others to try to hurt Jennifer and now the man she loved had mounted too much to be ignored.

Carlos was sentenced to twenty five years in jail with no possibility of parole for the first twenty years.

He never served the full sentence. Russian inmates who had been friends of some of the women he had abused killed him in a staged 'prison fight'.

Four months after hearing that news Jennifer became pregnant. She was 37, she had thought that she and Steven might not be able to have children of their own and were starting to explore the possibilities of adoption.

It had taken twenty years for her emotional burden to be lifted. But her joy made up for every hurt moment.

EVOLUTION

"Come here you bitch."

He was drunk again and in one of his angry moods. He was almost always angry. Well, it wasn't a surprise. He couldn't keep a job, and he and mum were always fighting. Mum was as angry as dad was, and she got drunk nearly as often.

But she knew that tone of his. She knew what he had in mind. There didn't have to be a reason for him to beat her. He just did it because life had treated him rottenly - so he believed - so he had to take out his frustration on someone else. And that someone else was usually her.

"You come down here or it'll be even worse for you."

She wouldn't go. She had had enough of his beatings, his insults, his rage. He had never been a real father to her.
The door of her bedroom burst open. He came in, red faced, livid. Her mother followed him in, panting from rushing up the stairs behind him.

She remained sitting on her bed. He slugged her, full force in the face, staggering her, and then he pushed her down on the bed and turned her over on her front.

Her mother sat on top of her, on her back. She was a heavy woman. Isabel was pinned down. Her father pulled her shoes off so that she could not kick out effectively, and then he reached into the front of her jeans, unzipped them and pulled down her jeans and knickers.

"Now you're going to get it. Now you'll do what I tell you, you'll jump when I say so, you lousy little cunt," he yelled.

Isabel responded, "Who are you? You are certainly not my father. No father could be such a pig to his daughter."

"You'll be the one who will be screaming like a pig soon."

She knew what he was doing now, lifting that strap of thick leather cut from a belt. He had nailed it to a piece of wood and made that into a handle. And then he started lashing away at her.

She buried her face in her sheets. She wasn't going to give him the satisfaction of screaming, of crying, of begging him to stop.

But the pain was too much. She had steeled herself to take more and more each time without crying, but he seemed to hit her harder than ever before and she knew it was going on longer.

As the strap hit parts that had already been hit and bruised the pain became too great. She started sobbing, as quietly as she could, into the sheet.

She could feel him tiring. He was drunk. The lashes became less strong and slower, and he stopped. Her mother got up off her back, and they walked out of the room, leaving her on the bed, in tears, with an extremely bruised bottom.

After a while she got up and did what she had learned to do after a beating. She went to the bathroom, took a towel and made it wet with cold water. She went back to her room, lay on the bed and pressed the towel against her bottom. That would reduce the bruising.

The towel started to become too cold. She stopped pressing with it, and put it aside.

But she couldn't go to sleep. She was in pain, and she was full of rage. It felt like a torrent, building inside her. She cursed and swore silently, all the obscene names that she could think of.

She switched off the light in the room and dropped off to an uneasy sleep for a few hours.

When she woke she saw on her clock that it was a quarter to one in the morning. She sat up, her back rested against a propped up pillow. She thought for a long time. A powerful feeling of hate was building inside her.

She put on another pair of knickers, a pair of shorts and a t-shirt, and quietly stood up. The house was quiet, she could hear both parents snoring away.

She went down the stairs quietly, to the kitchen. She knew where the longest and sharpest knives that her mother used for carving meat were kept, and as quietly as she could she chose two. She felt their edges. Yes, they were very sharp indeed.

She went up the stairs, again making as little sound as she could. The door to her parent's bedroom was closed but she knew it wouldn't be locked. She listened, to make sure that the snoring was continuing, and then she opened the door.

They were still asleep. She plunged one knife and then the other into her father's neck, again and again.

He woke briefly, choking with the pain, blood filling his throat. He clutched his throat, and she pulled back the sheet covering him and plunged the knives into his abdomen, repeatedly.

Her mother woke up, and screamed. But he was dead already.

Isabel went downstairs. She felt quite calm, at peace. She picked up the telephone and called the police.

"My name is Isabel Taylor. I've just killed my abusive father. This is my address. 48 Langham Crescent. You can send around police officers to investigate."

"Shall we send an ambulance?"

"He's dead."

"Well, we usually send fire and ambulance anyway, so we'll do that.

They should all be at your place within the next ten minutes."

She sat in an armchair downstairs, holding on to the knives.

She sat quietly and calmly in the armchair until she heard the sirens of the fire engine or ambulance or both approaching, and then she heard knocking on the door.

She opened it and let the fire rescue and ambulance men in. She told them that her father's body was upstairs.

They were quickly followed by two police officers. She held up her hands to show she had no weapons and invited them in.

She sat back on the armchair. She pointed to the knives beside her. "These are the knives I stabbed him with, they have my fingerprints and his blood. You will probably want to take them away."

The police officers looked at each other. They were surprised by her calmness. They wondered if she was mentally disturbed, in some sort of state where she had mentally dissociated herself from the reality.

"I think that we should caution you that you have the right to not say anything to us, but that if you do say anything it might be written down and could be used against you."

"Thank you."

One of the officers spoke into his mobile. "It's Officer Walters. Officer Hughes and I are here at the house. We think we ought to have a senior female here. We are dealing with a young teenage woman and we think a female officer might be more suitable to talk to this young lady."

Sergeant Walters turned to Isabel, "You heard that. I've asked for a senior woman officer to come. Are you going to be o'k waiting like this for a little while, or do we have to handcuff you?"
"No, I'll be fine. My work is over."
"What or who is that screaming upstairs?"
"That's my mother. She was asleep when I stabbed him and she woke up. They were both sodding drunk, totally out of it, when he beat me. She held me down so he could beat me. I had just had enough of it."

"May I ask, how old are you?"
"I'm 16."
"You're 16 and your dad was still beating you?"
"Yes, pants and knickers off, the whole thing. Unbelievable, isn't it? But that's what being drunk all the time gets you, lousy perverts. Both of them."
The police officers were quiet. About fifteen minutes later there was a knock on the door. One of the police officers went to open the door and a woman walked in.

She was a little taller than medium height. She had light brown hair, what looked to be a sturdy but feminine figure. She wore a dark grey business suit, a jacket and knee length skirt.

She introduced herself, "I'm Detective Diane Chartwell. I'm with the homicide division," and she looked at Isabel.
Isabel looked back. She has nice eyes, thought Isabel. There was something about this woman that gave Isabel a sense of confidence.

Diane looked at Isabel, at the way she had been seated. She did not seem to be anxious or particularly upset. Diane took in the knives, she saw that Isabel had not attempted to wash the blood off her hands or clothes.

There was something appealing about this young woman, thought Diane. She is not a monster, she's not a psychopath, not even an uncivilized thug.

"And I presume you are the young woman who called the police and told us that you killed your father."
"Yes. I'm Isabel Taylor."

Diane looked at the two officers, "yes, we've cautioned her," offered Officer Hughes.

"Would you like to tell me what happened, or do you want to have a lawyer present?"

"No, I'm o'k telling you. There's really not that much to it. My father has been beating me for years, especially when he is bloody drunk. Which he was again tonight when he came home. He was in a foul mood - as he usually is these days - and yelled for me, which I knew was going to be a beating. I stayed in my room. He came up followed by my mum. He pushed me over on the bed and mum sat on me. He pulled down my pants and knickers and beat me with that strap of his. He's done it many times before, doesn't care that I'm now 16, and she encourages and helps him. I think this was the hardest, longest beating he'd ever given me. I just decided I'd had enough of these beatings. I took a wet towel to lessen the bruising for a while, then I slept for a bit. Then I woke up, and I just sat for about an hour, just sitting and thinking. Then I went downstairs, took out those two knives, and went upstairs and stabbed him. That's the story. I suppose I'm going to jail for a few years, but I won't have them beating me and yelling at me for the rest of my life."

"You say that it was the worst beating you've had. Can I have a look?" Isabel glanced at the male officers.

"Of course. Officers, could you please turn around. If she attacks me I'll yell." Diane had the sense that this young woman was not going to attack anyone else.

Isabel pulled down her jeans and knickers and showed Diane the bruising.

Diane expressed a sharp breath. "That looks really bad. How do you feel? Does it still hurt?"

"It hurts. But I'll get over it. Knowing it's never going to happen again makes it easier."

Diane took out a small camera. "Do you mind if I take a few pictures? The more evidence we have the better chance you will have of explaining why you did what you say you did."

Diane asked the officers, "do you know if the crime scene photographer is here?"

Officer Hughes answered, "I don't think they've arrived yet. Only fire and ambulance are up there. If he's dead they'll have to call the coroner as well as the crime scene unit."

"Can you find out if they have declared him dead, or are they going to take him to hospital?"

Diane took some photographs from different angles. "Thank you very much. You can get dressed again. Sergeant Hughes, can you see what the situation is please?"

Diane looked at Isabel. "Why don't we sit down for a few minutes, if you can do that comfortably."

They started talking. Diane asked Isabel about her school situation, which class she was in, which subjects she was taking, whether she liked school, what else other than school did she like to do.

Isabel found Diane easy to talk to. She responded to Diane's questions and elaborated. Her parents had been quite uninterested for a long time in what she did, either at school or outside school. Here was someone who was listening, even if it was a police detective building a case.

The sergeants came down the stairs. "They're declaring him dead, and asking for the coroner and the crime scene unit. We called. They should be here soon."

"Good."

Diane turned to Isabel. "Would you mind very much if I made us a cup of tea in your kitchen. I presume there is nothing there that would interfere with our investigation, no blood, or no struggle there with your mother?'

"No. Everything was upstairs. Look, I can make you a tea - oh, I suppose you would want to fingerprint me and have me photographed with the blood on my hands."

"Yes, I'm afraid so. So let me make the tea. You can come and tell me where things are in the kitchen."

Diane was impressed with Isabel's self-awareness, her willingness to let herself be labelled as the killer without any trace of doubt. As if she wanted to accept that role and not have anyone take it from her. That she needed it to justify to herself what she had done.

They went into the kitchen. Isabel pointed to where the cups and saucers were, Diane could see the kettle, and Isabel told Diane where she might find a few biscuits.

As the water was boiling in the kettle Diane asked Isabel more about herself and about her parents and grandparents. While they were talking there were more knocks on the door.

Sergeant Hughes opened the door. "It's the crime scene unit. I'll take them upstairs."

Diane called out. "Could you ask the photographer to come in here first for just a few minutes."

The photographer came in. It was a middle-aged man. Diane turned to Isabel. "I hope you don't mind. Mr Peters has seen just about everything in the years he's worked with us."

"It's o'k," said Isabel.

"I'm also going to ask you to come to the hospital with me for a doctor - a female doctor - to examine you."

"I wasn't raped."

"No. But we'll need a proper medical examination and description of the bruises."

Isabel understood, and then turned around, pulled down her jeans and knickers again and let the photographer take some pictures.

"We're going to have to take you to the station now to process you, take fingerprints, and then we shall charge you. The charge may not be what you will eventually go to court about, that will be for the lawyers to decide. I'm afraid you are going to have to stay overnight in jail, and then you'll appear before a judge tomorrow morning. I don't know if your family has a lawyer, if not we'll provide a lawyer for you and you will be able to discuss the question of bail. Because of your age, and because you don't seem to be a danger to anyone else, and I'm assuming you don't have a criminal record - "

"No, I don't."

"Then you might have a chance to be released, if there was somewhere for you to go where we knew you would be safe, no danger to anyone else especially your mother, and that you would be absolutely reliable to appear in court for the trial when it takes place."

"I'm not running anywhere, and even if I don't think that fat pig has been a real mother I have no intention of killing her."

The trial did not go well. It was a woman judge, a hard woman, very formal, unsmiling, who seemed to have little compassion.

Her summing up focused on what she referred to as the 'facts' in the case, but the facts were focused on the killing and the evidence from the weapons, the fingerprints, and Isabel's mother's testimony, that she saw Isabel stab her father repeatedly.

Any 'facts' about the brutal beatings, Isabel's father's repeated assaults, and her mother's encouragement and assistance in the beatings were put aside by the judge as secondary factors, not to be considered in the jury deciding whether Isabel had killed her father.

Isabel had absolutely refused to consider a plea of being 'insane' or psychologically disturbed when she killed her father. She had insisted on telling the jury that she had indeed killed her father because he had repeatedly abused her and she had decided to finally put an end to that, even if it meant going to jail for many years.

The prosecutor had said that there were many other alternative approaches that a young woman being abused by her parents could have taken, other than killing the abuser.

She could have gone to the police herself. She could have contacted children's social services and asked to go to a foster home, she could have run away. She could have gone to friends to stay, and alerted a friend's parents that she was in a very disturbed home situation. Why didn't she choose any of the other alternatives instead of killing her father?

She was sentenced to eight years in jail. Her youth and the history of the beatings had been taken as mitigating factors for the sentencing, the judge told her. The jail time could have been much longer.

She was sent to a medium-security centre. Diane had come to speak with her before the prisoners were taken to the jails. Diane told her what would happen when she arrived at the jail and was processed, and had given her some advice about how to handle some of the challenges Isabel would face.

Isabel settled into the jail routine. She spoke little to the other women, she was one of the youngest at the prison. She had brought some books with her, and when offered the opportunity to use the prison library she had taken it.

She had already been at the prison for four weeks when she was approached by a guard and told that she had a visitor.

She was surprised. It was not a normal visiting time. She wondered if it was a lawyer coming to discuss her appeal.

She made her way to the visiting area, was searched, and took a seat.

Her eyes widened in surprise as she saw that her visitor was the police woman, Diane.

"Hello, Isabel. How are you doing so far?"
"I'm alright, thank you."
"Anyone giving you a hard time, any trouble?"
"No."
"Now that you've settled yourself in, I wonder if you are ready to consider taking some courses at the university. It's not very far from here."
"I'm only 17 now. I wouldn't get in, would I?" asked Isabel.
"I've seen your marks. You did very well. I think we could try and get you in. The term starts in four weeks."
"How would I get there and back?"
"We could see if the warden can make arrangements to have staff members take you and bring you back."

"I don't know what courses to take."

"You can start with some general courses that don't commit you to any particular final degree path, and then you can choose in terms of what you have found that you really like."

The arrangement was that she would be taken by a guard three evenings a week to the university. It was a forty minute drive each way. The guard would wait for her until 9.15 p.m, classes were supposed to finish by 9 but sometimes ran a little over if students asked questions.

Isabel was going to take three 100 level courses, and the warden of the prison had decided that going in the evening would lessen the risk of Isabel escaping, or developing inappropriate relationships with the very much larger number of students during the day, who also tended to be younger, while the evening students were often more mature adults seeking to upgrade their qualifications.

Isabel hadn't objected, she had felt thrilled to be offered the opportunity, both to go to university as well as being able to get out of the prison for a few hours.

She chose a philosophy course, a biology course, and an Italian course. She had looked through the university calendar with Diane who had come to be a regular visitor, Isabel's only visitor. They had agreed on philosophy as an introduction to the fundamentals of western democratic society, biology as a possible entry for any future career in the field of health care, and Italian as a further development of foreign language skills that both agreed were increasingly necessary in the world of high-speed travel and communication.

Isabel loved the courses. She found she was able to keep up with the classes easily. Many of the other students had not done very well in high school which was why they were returning now to improve their CVs. She also knew she had the advantage that she had most of the day free to study while most of the other students worked during the day or were full-time mothers of small children.

She finished her first year with 'A's in each of her courses. She continued taking courses in the summer programme - she did not have a vacation on a sunny Mediterranean beach on her calendar - and took two more courses in Anthropology and Economics.

The economics course had been a surprise to her. She had not thought she could understand economics or would have an interest in it, and had been surprised when Diane had suggested it. But she had come to implicitly trust Diane's judgment, and once again Diane had done something that was so good for her.

After just three weeks of the course Isabel had started to realize why so much of what happened in the world was dependent upon economics. How some nations thrived while others lagged. Why her own country had experienced its difficulties, as well as its periods of great success. By six weeks she was reading the financial section of the newspaper immediately after the fashion section, and even before the help and advice columns that she had in the past turned to.

Two more 'A's were her reward for her summer studies. Isabel and Diane now looked at 200 level courses, and she was going to ask to take five.

The warden was skeptical, she was impressed that Isabel had done so well in her first year, but she thought that five trips would be too much of a drain on the staff time, and would be an extra cost for the prison in terms of the overtime pay that the staff members taking Isabel required.

Diane stepped in. "I'll take her and bring her back one evening. I presume you can trust a police officer."

"Of course, Detective Chartwell."

Isabel was thrilled when she heard that Diane would be taking her one of the nights. Very few things in her life so far had ever thrilled Isabel. The chance of going to university, the courses, obtaining 'A's, and now Diane taking her and bringing her back, spending forty minutes each way alone with Diane - Isabel had a strange sense of feeling privileged, something she had never felt before. She had tended to see herself as being deprived, cheated out of a normal childhood with normal loving parents that she knew most other girls and boys in her classes did have in their homes.

But sometimes life is too good to be true.

One of the guards taking Isabel in the autumn term of her third year was a guard with whom Isabel did not have a good relationship. Isabel thought there was something sour about that woman, Kate. Isabel could understand that some or most of the guards were just doing the trip for the extra money, but most had been quite nice to her, one or two had even sat in on some of the courses and said how much they enjoyed the experience and would discuss a class on the way back, or the reading they had both done before the class the next week. At least two had actually enrolled themselves to take courses.

Kate was different. Kate was older, an unhappy divorcee with grown children who had little to do with her. The rumours were that Kate went on vacations to places that were notorious because older English women looked to be picked up for brief highly sexual flings by very young local boys. Kate herself encouraged the rumours, maybe she thought it made her more glamorous in the eyes of her co-workers. She would show them many photographs of the young handsome men on the beach, slyly implying that this one or that one had been her ecstatic lover. Isabel understood that Kate had probably volunteered to take Isabel just to boost her income for her vacations, but Kate still seemed to emit an attitude of resentment towards Isabel for going to university and doing so well.

Kate did not come in to the Tuesday night class Isabel was taking, and would wait for Isabel in the corridor outside the lecture hall, making sure that Isabel had no opportunity to socialize with other students after class, and also that other students could see that Isabel was in the company of a prison guard, as Kate insisted on wearing her uniform - which none of the other guards saw the need for.

One evening in November, Isabel came out of her class at 9.10, but Kate wasn't there. Kate had never told Isabel what she did while Isabel was in the class, but on a couple of occasions Isabel had seen Kate rushing to be at the meeting point by 9.15, and a man looking at Kate as if they had spent time together and just parted.

Isabel waited. Kate eventually came, it was about 9.45. Isabel said nothing, Kate did not apologize, nor offer any explanation.

But the next morning Isabel was summoned to the warden's office.

"I understand you came back late last night from your course, Ms Taylor."

Isabel saw that Kate was also in the warden's office.

"Yes ma'am."

"Why were you late?"

"I was at the usual meeting point at 9.10. Officer Wimsett was delayed."

"That's not what happened according to Officer Wimsett. She says that you didn't arrive at the meeting point until 9.45, and that she had the impression that you had been drinking and smoking cigarettes."

Isabel realized the situation was hopeless. Kate was lying, but Isabel wasn't going to stand for any more bullying in her life.

"That's not true, ma'am. I don't drink, I don't smoke, and I was there at the meeting point at 9.10."

Isabel could see that Kate was smirking. Kate knew what would come next.

"Ms Taylor. In a situation where a prisoner and an officer are in disagreement, I have to give more credit to what the officer says, unless the prisoner can give me proof that what they are saying is true, and what the officer says is incorrect. If you do not have any proof of what you are claiming, then I am going to have to suspend your taking courses at the university until I can be sure that you will keep to the rules we established. You were given a very special privilege, that you may have abused, and even though I know you have done very well in your courses so far, I wouldn't want to think that we have been too liberal in granting you this privilege, and that you have taken advantage of the privilege and misused it."

Isabel was shocked. She felt very hurt, and very angry.

"That is so unfair. I know I'm very lucky to be able to go to the university, but I've always been extremely reliable. I don't have any opportunity to spend time afterwards with the other students and go out with them in a normal way as all the others do, and go for a drink, or a coffee, or to chat, or go to a movie. I accept all that. But I've never abused the privilege, and now you're telling me I have to stop because one officer was late, doesn't tell the truth, and accuses me."

But it was useless, and Isabel knew it. As she left the warden's office she saw on Kate's look a mixture of triumph that Isabel had lost her privilege, and rage that Isabel had dared to challenge her in front of the warden.

But Isabel was used to standing up to bullies, and fighting back hard, if necessary.

When the late afternoon time came that prisoners were allowed to make telephone calls, Isabel waited in line and then called Diane.

"Diane, it's Isabel. Something terrible has happened. Is there any way you can come here? I don't want to talk over the phone."

"I'll be there as soon as I can."

Diane arrived and asked to meet Isabel in the library. Isabel told her the story.

"So you say you were there at the meeting point at 9.10, and she wasn't. Exactly where was this meeting point?"

Isabel told her. Isabel added her own impression that Kate had conveyed a negative attitude towards her from the beginning, that Kate had seemed to want the job, but not to enjoy it at all.

"Let me see what I can do, Isabel. You've been doing so well, and I know you wouldn't have wanted to mess it up. Let me try and find out what happened.'

"I told you what happened. The problem is that a guard has lied. The warden believes her, and I'm screwed with my courses."

"Let me see what I can do. In the meantime, please don't do anything stupid to get your own back on her."

Diane went straight to the university, and to the location Isabel had described as the meeting point after Tuesday's class.

Diane looked around, and found what she was looking for. She then went to the campus security office.

She introduced herself, and told the manager in charge exactly what she wanted.

Ten minutes later the Closed Circuit Tape for Tuesday evening for that location was brought to her, and she was shown the viewing area.

It did not take long for Diane to fast forward through the tape until she came to 9 p.m, and then she watched slowly and carefully.

As Isabel had said, Isabel had arrived at the meeting point chatting with two other students. The time on the tape read 9.09. Diane could see Isabel looking around for a few moments, and then continuing to chat with the friends.

This behaviour continued for a while longer, every few minutes Isabel would look up and around, as if she was looking for someone.

It wasn't until 9.41 on the tape that another woman came into view and approached Isabel directly, gesturing to Isabel in an abrupt manner as if saying, "we have to go now."

The other woman was older, she had thick curly hair, she was dressed in a prison guard uniform, she seemed angry, unpleasant. Diane could feel how embarrassed Isabel must have felt being met each week by this dumpy unhappy woman.

Diane asked the security manager for a copy of the tape. That took a few minutes to make, and then Diane drove back to the jail and went straight to the warden's office.

The warden knew her. The warden was not particularly fond of Diane but knew her to be a very competent detective, and a woman of great integrity. The warden wondered whether Diane had come to ask for leniency for Isabel.

Diane strode into the room. "I understand that Isabel Taylor was late back from her class yesterday, and that you have punished her by stopping her continuing her courses. I won't even discuss whether that was an overreaction, considering how well she has done up till now. But what if she is innocent and your guard was lying?"

"Detective Chartwell. I know that Ms Taylor has been doing very well in her courses, and I also know that in spite of the crime for which she has been incarcerated she seems to be a young woman who in most areas of life has very good values, and indeed, there is a reasonable possibility that she is telling the truth. But I am sure you are also aware from your own work culture which is not that far removed from ours, that the only way we can maintain disciplined and well-functioning units with a high sense of morale is by showing solid support for our staff until we receive very solid evidence that they have done something wrong."

Diane put the tape on the warden's desk. "Here is your evidence, Ms Simpson. Shall we view it together?"

The warden knew she had little choice, and she started her own video machine and inserted the tape.

The warden saw Isabel arriving at the meeting point at 9.09.

Diane then said, "I won't waste your time waiting for the next thirty two minutes to pass, unless you insist. Otherwise, I'd like to jump to 9.39, and let's watch briefly."

They did. After a few minutes the warden stopped the tape and said to Diane. "I guess I'm not surprised. You're going to have the union very upset with me over this."

"You can move her out quickly so she doesn't have a chance to tell others, and also you can tell her that if she blabs too much she won't be able to get any good employment elsewhere."

Isabel was able to resume her courses. Diane offered to take her on the Tuesday in addition to the usual Thursday that she was already taking Isabel.

They enjoyed their time together, Isabel would talk about the courses and Diane often had interesting questions or comments to make. Isabel felt thrilled that here was someone who seemed genuinely interested in what Isabel was doing, in what Isabel thought.

Isabel also found that Diane was obviously very intelligent and she seemed to understand a lot of the material that was new for Isabel. Isabel asked Diane about her education, she was very impressed to hear that Diane had a Master's degree. Isabel hadn't thought that many police officers had higher education.

Isabel also had a sense that Diane was treating her as an adult, younger perhaps - but not as a child, and that made Isabel feel very warm inside.

One evening, taking Isabel back, Diane's car broke down. She called immediately for assistance, but realizing that it would take time coming, and repair might not be immediate, the car might even have to be towed to a garage, Diane called the prison. She identified herself and explained the situation, and told them that Isabel might be very late returning, or that if it was extremely late Diane might take Isabel home with her and bring her to the prison early the next morning.

It took an hour until roadside assistance arrived. The mechanic confirmed what Diane had suspected, which was that the fuel injection was not working properly, and would require replacement and that might take two hours the next morning. The car was towed, and from the garage Diane had arranged for a cab to take them to Diane's home.

Isabel was very impressed with Diane's home. It was a small house. It seemed to Isabel to be very pretty, a nice small garden in the front, it looked well-kept, and inside it seemed very warm and comfortable.

There was a large combined living and dining room, a compact small kitchen that still had room for a table and two chairs. The kitchen cabinets were white and looked new.

Diane showed Isabel the bedrooms and bathrooms, and then invited Isabel to join her in the kitchen for a tea and light snack.

They chatted together, Isabel complimented Diane on the beauty of her home and thanked her for taking her to the classes and now bringing her to her home and already calling the prison.

"You do so much for me. Nobody has ever done anything like what you have done. I appreciate it so much. You've been so good to me," and Isabel grabbed Diane's hand and kissed it. "Thank you, thank you, thank you."

Diane smiled. "You're in a bad place that you don't really deserve to be in. I saw from the first moment that you were really a very decent young woman in a very difficult and unfortunate situation, but you had a judge who didn't see it and wouldn't understand it.

I just thought you deserve a much better deal, and I've felt very good spending this time with you and seeing you thrive in your school work, and grow as a woman, and I think you'll be able to put the bad stuff behind you and have a good life. I certainly want to do whatever I can to help you achieve that. I've dealt with enough really bad people, really nasty evil people, to be able to help someone who really is a very good person, and who has great potential."

They talked more, and then Diane showed Isabel the alternative bedrooms and where the bathroom was, and brought Isabel a robe, some pyjamas, and a change of underwear for the morning. "You can give those back to me next week."

They said goodnight, and Diane gave Isabel a big hug, holding Isabel for a few long seconds.

Isabel looked up at Diane, looked into Diane's eyes, and said to her, "Will you be very offended if I kiss you?"

Diane looked back at Isabel, she could see the yearning in Isabel's eyes, the desire to feel loved that a person who had never felt loved in her life was expressing.

"I would feel very honoured if you would kiss me," Diane said gently and softly.

The kiss was mutual. It was light at first, then it was repeated, a little longer and with more passion.

"I've never kissed a woman before. Some guys kissed me in school, but that was just kids experimenting, they didn't really know what they were doing and I didn't know much more."

"I've also not kissed a woman before, it's a first time for me, but it's actually very nice kissing you."

"Thank you. I know I don't have anything much to compare it with in terms of experience, but it does seem very very nice indeed. I can't imagine it can get much better than this."

Diane laughed. "I think it's a bit early to jump to that conclusion, but I hope you'll have many nice kisses in your life."

"You say the nicest things. Where did you learn all this?"

"It comes with life experience, and allowing yourself to experience whatever life has to offer, not running away from good opportunities. You actually did something very brave and you didn't run away from an opportunity, and even though it got you into trouble it also liberated you in a very important way. It got you away from continuing to be beaten up and abused by your parents.

I know that the prosecutor said you could have chosen less lethal alternatives - but we both know that was very unlikely. You had the courage to choose the one option that would free you in the long run - even though you had to pay a big cost in the short run.

But you are still going to be very young when you get out, and you may by then have a university degree, and you can really make something of your life. I think it was very brave of you, and I think you would have been much worse off if you had continued to be abused for another few years.

And Diane leaned forward and kissed Isabel again. "Now let's get some sleep."

But neither of them could get to sleep, and about an hour later Isabel knocked on the door of Diane's room and asked if she could come in.

"Of course."
Neither said anything more. Diane lifted up the cover of the bed inviting Isabel in. They kissed, held each other, and took off each other's pyjamas.

Diane took the initiative in kissing and caressing Isabel. Diane knew she was older, much more experienced, and that Isabel needed most of all to feel loved, desired, to have the sense that someone else saw her as beautiful, and Diane gave those feelings to Isabel.

Isabel responded. Isabel admired Diane's beautiful body and told her so, and Isabel caressed and kissed Diane's breasts, and Diane's shoulders, and Diane's abdomen, and Diane's back, and Diane's thighs and Diane's bottom, and Diane reciprocated enthusiastically.

And then Diane took Isabel gently and laid Isabel on her back and parted her thighs and kissed the hair around her genitals, and then Isabel's vagina itself, and gradually opened Isabel up and Diane put her mouth and tongue inside Isabel, seeking out her clitoris and then caressing it with her tongue.

Isabel was enjoying everything, and finding herself being swept along by a feeling she couldn't quite understand, but it seemed to take her over, and she heard herself moaning softly, at first not even realizing it was herself who was moaning, and then realizing that the moans were not moans of pain but of great pleasure.

And the wave she was feeling became stronger and stronger, and it engulfed her and she felt her thighs and her bottom tighten and then she felt a sudden surge, as if something had been released inside her.

"Was that an orgasm?"
"It certainly looked and sounded like one to me," said Diane.
"Wow. It felt great. I don't think I've ever had that before."
"Now that makes me feel really good. To be the first person to bring you to what I hope will be many such experiences of great pleasure."
Isabel turned on her side and looked into Diane's eyes. "Thank you. It was really lovely. But what about you?"
"My turn will come eventually, I'm sure. I think this should be very special for you, something for you to remember for a long time, and it makes me feel very good having helped you have this pleasure."

They both slept well. Diane brought Isabel back to the prison the next day, and went straight to the warden to explain the circumstances. This time there were no problems about Isabel's lateness or staying away the night.

"She's probably due for a try at parole anyway. I don't know if there is anybody she would be staying with. Would it be you, if she started some weekends on parole?"

"I would be very happy to have her stay with me. I would have to make it clear that I can be called out on emergency situations, and she would be unsupervised if that happened. But I believe she is quite trustworthy and responsible."

"I agree. I'm willing to give her the opportunity. I hope she doesn't abuse it. I agree with you that it is unlikely. But one never knows. I don't think there is a person in a similar situation of responsibility who has not been burned a few times by people they thought they could totally trust."

Isabel came at first for a weekend once a month, from Friday evening until Sunday evening. Diane took her out on Friday evening to restaurants and eventually to clubs. She insisted that Isabel not smoke or drink alcohol. If a guy offered to buy her a drink it would be a juice or a diet soft drink, but Diane encouraged her to dance with men. Although Isabel was mature for her age in so many ways, she was also quite inexperienced with men. When they went to Diane's home afterwards Isabel would ask Diane about dating, about going out with men, what men expected, how to handle them.

Diane didn't talk very much about herself. She had told Isabel that her father was an accountant and her mother a nurse, and that she had two younger sisters who were both at university.

Isabel asked Diane what made her become a police officer. Diane told her that a very good school friend of hers had been attacked when they were 15, and Diane had seen how insensitive male policemen had not treated her friend well, and one woman officer who had tried to be kind and supportive had been openly ridiculed by a boorish male officer. Diane had thought then that she might become a police officer herself and treat women, especially young girls, with a lot more sensitivity, and not be bullied by crude male officers.

"And how has it worked out?" asked Isabel.

"Times are different now from even a few years ago. The men know that they can get into big trouble if they are rude to women officers or bully them and they are much more careful, and there are some really good women - only a few now but it will grow - who don't take any nonsense from men. I think I have quite good relationships with most of the men I've worked with," replied Diane.

Diane admitted to Isabel that she had not had great success in relationships with men. She had wondered if some men were intimidated by her being a homicide detective. She had been out with a few policemen but felt more comfortable with men who weren't in the police but were in another field.

They talked about their sexual feelings together, but only twice more did they repeat the love-making. Diane told Isabel that she hoped that when Isabel was released she would be able to date men and she didn't want Isabel to think that she could only have love-making with a woman, and Diane herself wanted eventually to marry and have a family.

The years went by. Isabel continued her courses. Diane received two promotions.

Isabel met with a committee of the Parole Board to discuss early parole. She received strong support from Diane, from the warden, and - she was surprised to hear - from some teachers at the university, though she wasn't told their names. Isabel was a bit surprised, but she thought that when that guard Kate had been meeting her dressed in prison guard uniform and very openly treated Isabel as if indeed she was a major criminal being allowed a very brief supervised pass to take a course or two, that some people must have noticed and perhaps done a little research and found out who she was and what she had done.

The Parole Board also received an objection - a foul-mouthed tirade - from her mother. Diane had stepped in and countered that, explaining how the mother had assisted father in brutally beating Isabel, and that Isabel wanted to have nothing to do with a mother who had never loved her.

Early parole was granted. Isabel would live with Diane until she found a place of her own, and strict probation requirements had to be followed. Her date of release was to be the morning after her graduation from university.

Diane took Isabel to rent the gown and hat she was to wear for the graduation ceremony. Isabel had applied for a ticket for Diane to attend, and the arrangements were made for Diane to pick Isabel up from the prison to take her to the ceremony.

Isabel wondered what was happening. Everyone else seemed to have been called and received their degrees. Now the President of the university was at the microphone again. Was she not being allowed to receive her degree in public because of her still being in jail? Had they just decided to let her sit with her graduating class but they wouldn't call out her name in public in case anyone recognized it and protested?

She became aware that the president was speaking.

"Ladies and gentlemen. Each year the teachers of the university make an award to a student whom they consider to have been a special student. The criteria for this award are fairly wide, but in recent years the award has usually been given to students who have overcome unusually difficult circumstances or handicaps or disabilities and have come to our university and have been outstanding students, and by their presence here have made a distinct contribution to the university.

Our professors put forward their recommendations, and either by what they say or by the number of teachers putting forward one particular person, we make the choice.

This year, I am delighted to announce that our teachers have nominated a young lady, who has overcome some especially difficult circumstances to become an outstanding student obtaining 'A's in every course she took. Will Isabel Taylor please come to accept the Teacher's Award for..

She didn't take it in at first. The professors on the podium were standing and applauding. All around her the other students were looking at her, wondering why she didn't stand up and walk to the platform to receive the award. One or two then started talking to her and telling her what was happening.

"Me? He called my name?"
"Yes. You. Now go. "

She stood and walked along her row past her fellow students and up to the platform. As she did so the other students stood and applauded her. She held her head in her hand for a while, she knew there were some tears.

She mounted the steps and shook the president's hand and accepted the award. She thanked him, and she turned to the faculty gathered on the podium and thanked them.

"Do you mind if I say a very brief thank you, please?"
The president was gracious. "Of course."
She moved closer to the microphone. "I am deeply, deeply touched by this award. I never expected anything like this. Thank you all so much. I would like to say that I have

enjoyed so much being here at the university. Every teacher I have had has been wonderful. But there are some special people that I would like to thank publicly.

First and most important is the person who first encouraged me to be here, to think that I could do this when I never imagined I could be at university let alone do well, and she has been with me all the way, always encouraging and helping me. Her name is Diane Chartwell. I know she is here, and I'd like her to stand up so you can all see a wonderful human being who took an interest in a very lost soul and nurtured that soul to be what you see today.

I would like to publicly thank a person who probably isn't here, but who took a chance in supporting my being here. She could easily have refused, and then I wouldn't be here. But she did, and I am grateful, her name is Julie Simpson.."

A voice rang out, "and she most definitely is here, I wouldn't have missed this for anything, congratulations Isabel, you really deserve this."

Isabel looked up, "Thank you Ms Simpson. And the third person I would like to thank - as I said all the teachers have been so interesting and helpful, and I think I've learned so much from all of you whom I've had the privilege of being in your classes.

But if I could just mention Professor Gordon. You always made special time for me. You inspired me. You listened to me and helped me understand in such thoughtful ways some ideas and topics that were quite difficult for me at first, and you always treated me with such kindness.

Because of my background I had never been to London, or to places like the British Museum or the National Gallery, and to be taken by you and your wonderful family was such a very special privilege that I shall always treasure deeply. Thank you Mr President."

Diane hugged her as she came down from the podium. "Thank you. That was really beautiful, what you did and said."

"You deserved it, and a lot more."

They walked outside after the ceremony. Most graduates had family members, parents, grandparents, brothers, sisters, some had wives, husbands, girl friends and boy friends, all busy posing for and taking photographs.

Isabel brought Diane to meet Professor Gordon and his family. He and his wife gave Isabel a big hug, and she met again their son Dan, a tall, handsome young man of 19, and his younger sister Heather who was 16.

"Handsome young man, isn't he?" Diane said to Isabel.

"He is, but he's a bit younger than me, and he's a professor's son, and he's going to university himself already, and they are a very healthy loving family, and they've been very nice to me, but they certainly don't need someone with my background complicating things for their son."

Diane looked at Isabel and spoke firmly, "You've just graduated with all 'A's, you're being released tomorrow. You have to look on this as a fresh beginning to your life. You are so much more a person now, and you are free now from that horror of a life you had as a kid. You can see that people really like you and love you and think that you are very smart and very nice. You have to put that abused child behind you, and see the great adult woman that you are becoming," and gave her a big hug.

Another very handsome young man came over to congratulate Isabel. Isabel introduced him to Diane.

"This is Professor Johnson. I took a class in Theoretical Physics with him. About the most difficult class I think out of all my classes, but he certainly tried to help me understand it, even though I'm still not sure whether I do."

He laughed, "Well, Ms Taylor, you did very well and it was a pleasure teaching you. I much prefer students who ask questions because they don't understand the material at first than those who keep quiet and remain not understanding it as demonstrated later by their test performances. You are the sort of student that real teachers really like to have in a class, because you say aloud what the others want to say but are too embarrassed to ask. But also, I was very interested to meet this woman that you expressed so much appreciation for, I presume this is her."

"Indeed it is."

At that moment some fellow-students came over to Isabel to congratulate her and wish her well, and that left Alan Johnson and Diane the opportunity to talk a bit on their own.

Alan put Diane at ease, "Most of us on the staff do know Ms Taylor's background and your role in her life, so I don't have to ask you what sort of work you do, though I wouldn't be surprised if what you are doing now is a little different from what you were doing when you first met and became involved with Ms Taylor."

Diane was fascinated. She had never really had a personal relationship with an academic, and certainly not one as young, handsome, and apparently quite sensitive, tactful, and charming as this man.

Six months later:

This was her first full 10k run. It had been difficult but she had enjoyed the challenge. Having so many people around helped, and the charity - Children's Cancer Support - was one of the most important she had heard about.

At last she was approaching the finish. She could see the big clock ahead, it was at 42.30 now so she hoped she would finish somewhere around 43 minutes, which was much faster than she had expected for her first competitive 10k run.

As she came into the chute at the end she heard a name being called and looked around. She was very surprised to see that it was Dan Gordon, and he was in running gear.

"Isabel. Hi. I didn't know you were running in this."

She waved to him. "Hi, Dan. Can you wait a couple of minutes until I'm through?"

"Of course."

After she completed her finishing registration and was told where she could find the drinks and post-race food, she met Dan who gave her a big hug.

"You did very well, 43.10. That's a great time. Have you been running long?"

"No. I don't know if you knew that I came here to train at the police academy and one of the instructors suggested I run to keep up my level of fitness. So I've been doing it and this was my first 10k."

"Well then, your time is fantastic."

"What about you?"

Just then a reporter with a camera crew came over. "Mr Gordon, could we do a brief interview?"

"Sure. Could you excuse me for a few moments Isabel?"
"Of course."

The reporter started, "So you're one of our great hopes for the Olympic 800 metres, Dan. Why did you do this longer run? Is it a part of your preparation? Isn't the 800 now just a long sprint?"

Dan laughed. "Yes, there's a lot of truth in that. But to be able to keep up that long sprint you've got to have the stamina to survive it, and something like doing fast 10k's may help."

"You finished 8th, didn't you? Against a top-class long-distance field. That's pretty good."

"I'm pleased. I'd like to do two or three more to convince myself that I can really keep up the pace for nearly half an hour. But then I'll probably focus more on speed. But I'll say it again. I'm really thinking more in terms of the Olympics four years away then this time around."

"I'm sure that if you go this time it will be a great experience for you. Thank you, and all the best Dan."

"Thank you."

"You finished 8th? What was your time?" asked Isabel.

"29.16" replied Dan.

"Wow. I didn't know people could run that fast."

He laughed. "So how are you doing here?"

"Before I talk about that, how long are you staying here? How are you getting back? Where are you going to have lunch? Have you made any arrangements?"

"So many questions. I have already had a brief snack and brought something with me for the journey back. I just came for the race, and I'm going back by train, there's one about every hour."

"Then you can come back to my place for some lunch and you can shower and change, and I can take you to the station."

"That's very nice. But I don't want to put you to any trouble."

"You and your parents did an enormous amount for me. This is just the least I could do. I see you have your bag already. Let me pick mine up and then we can take the shuttle back to the start where my car is."

As they walked and then went on the bus, she told him about being admitted to the police college with Diane's help and her experience training there, and her first couple of months working and earning money. When they were near to her home she stopped at a large supermarket and said she needed to buy a few items. He accompanied her into the store and then she suggested he take a cart and choose some fruit and vegetables and she would look for eggs and tuna.

Four months later:

Isabel picked up the telephone. "Hi, it's Diane. Is everything o'k with you?" "Sure."
"Good. Because I am going to make a request that you absolutely cannot say no. You have to say yes, and then I'll tell you more about what is involved."
"I'm listening."
"I want you to be my maid of honour at my wedding." "You are getting married?" screamed Isabel.
"Yes."
"Who to? I mean to whom?"
"You know to whom, you introduced us."
"I did?"
"Yes, at your graduation."
"Professor Johnston?"
"Yes."
"Oh, that's wonderful, that's really great news. When?"
"We would like the first week of June, we've just put money down on a hall and a caterer and we know which church we like. Let me tell you about being a maid of honour."
Diane did. That Isabel had to look after Diane. Traditionally, that was to protect the bride against any rivals snatching her, and to protect her virginity until she could give it to who had been chosen for her. In modern times, it had become looking after the bride and making sure she turned up at the right time in the right places, having accomplished all

those things that a bride needs to do in the days before the wedding and during the wedding.

"We are arranging for you to say with the Gordons, they've already said that they would love to see you again and have you stay with them, and I think that their delicious son Dan who raved about how nicely you had treated him in London, is coming from Oxford for the weekend to be at the wedding."

A shiver ran through Isabel's body, a sensation she hadn't quite experienced before. She hoped that Dan hadn't shared too many details of that wonderful afternoon.

"That's very nice of them. What sort of gift do you think I should bring them? I know when people stay at people's houses on such occasions you're supposed to bring a gift."

"That's true, I won't pretend it isn't. But it doesn't have to be anything expensive. From you something that is modest and has something of a personal touch I'm sure would be perfect."

They continued talking for a while, Isabel telling Diane about the work she was doing, Diane asking whether Isabel had run into any difficulties with work colleagues who probably knew about her background.

"Most have been very good, very helpful and supportive. I've heard once or twice that there were some people who thought it was inappropriate for the police to take me, but it seems that others said that I was a very good choice, that I could bring a very different and unusual perspective to working with some of the more difficult people they had to deal with."

Dan picked her up from the station on the Thursday before the wedding. She felt an inner thrill seeing him again. He looked even better than when she had seen him in London.

He gave her a huge hug when they met, and brought her to his car.

"I'm really pleased to see you again so soon. I hadn't expected to, with my studying and training and your new work. Have you been very busy?"

"It's been unbelievably hectic. But I've enjoyed it, and I think I'm learning something new every day. I've been out on some really difficult situations, and we have to go into some unpleasant neighbourhoods. I've seen stuff that has reminded me of what I went through as a child, which has made me realize even if I knew it already, that lots of other children go through as bad or even worse stuff. What about you?"

"Nothing bad for me, other than sometimes boring lecturers and some really hard training sessions. But I think both are growth situations where I feel my limits are being pushed and expanded."

They arrived at his parent's home. His mother greeted them, her husband was still at the university.

Isabel wondered what Mrs Gordon really thought about her. She had always been warm, friendly, gracious, but she must have become aware of the attraction between her son and Isabel. Would she really welcome a real love relationship between them?

But there was work to be done. Isabel telephoned Diane after she had put her bag in the room they had prepared for her and had a quick shower, and Diane outlined a very busy schedule that would start as soon as Isabel could come to Diane's home, to prepare for the wedding rehearsal.

The next two and a half days seemed to just fly. From church to hall to caterer to discuss final menus to flower arranger, photographer, musicians to decide on the music for the church, band for the music at the dinner and dance. It seemed one more thing every few minutes.

But it was fun. Diane maintained her usual calm, she didn't panic or become very upset if something didn't seem to be right, the two of them just worked to straighten it out.

The wedding itself was beautiful. Isabel had never been to a wedding before, and she felt deeply touched by it. Diane of course looked lovely in her gown and Alan Johnston was the handsome groom that any young woman might desire. Isabel herself had chosen a navy-blue short dress with gold trimming above the waist. It had been quite expensive for her, but she thought that Diane had done so much for her that it was important that as maid-of-honour she also look smart.

Dan told her she looked stunning. They sat together, and danced together. Diane told her they danced as if they were glued to each other, and their athleticism was obvious.

As maid-of-honour Isabel made a short speech toasting the bride, though she had some nice words to say about her former professor. She told the guests that Diane had been the person who had given her a life, that to her she was the most wonderful woman in the world, and now that she had found such a great partner for herself she hoped that together they would always make each other as happy as Diane had made her.

Diane thanked her, and said that it was Isabel who had actually introduced them, and for that she owed Isabel as much gratitude as Isabel believed she owed Diane.

One of Alan Johnston's rugby team-mates who had been his best man, they had been friends since high school, talked about the deceptive appearance of the quiet soft-spoken theoretical physics professor who was a terror on the rugby field, but who also was a man of great loyalty and integrity.

At some weddings it was traditional for the bride to throw a bouquet towards the single women, and often the other women would let the maid-of-honour catch it, that she should be next in line to be married. When Diane told Isabel about this tradition, Isabel politely declined.

Diane wondered why?

"Because I think I know who I want to marry. But it's going to take a while. He's a bit younger than me and not quite ready yet. But I can wait. I've been used to waiting a long time for really good things to happen, and I can wait for him."

Diane knew who she was talking about. "Does he know about this?"

"Not consciously. But I hope it will eventually come to him."

Diane questioned, "He's at university where he meets thousands of attractive very bright young women. He's a leading athlete and gets to meet tons of very athletic and attractive and smart women from all over the world. Aren't you afraid someone else might snatch him away before he realizes you want him?"

"It can happen. But I think I would rather he met many of these other women first and then settled on me, rather than marry too young and after a while wish that he hadn't because there are so many more attractive and smarter women than me available."

Diane gave her a hug. "He'll never find anyone better."

When Dan found her after that short private chat, Dan saw a glow on Isabel's face.

"I wish I could produce such a glow on your face."

"There is a glow you produce. It's inside, in me. You always make me feel happy and special around you."

They couldn't continue the love-making that had begun so pleasurably in London while they were in his parent's house, but they made arrangements for him to come to London, and she would go to Oxford for one weekend.

That contact - repeated every few months - would have to do for now. She knew he needed time to spread his wings, fly, and then eventually come back to her. Life had been so good to her these last few years. She had very fulfilling work. She could wait for her love.

DOCTOR CHARM

"Good morning Ms Stevenson, my name is Janet Deluca and I am the prosecutor in this case. I am going to be asking you some questions about your relationship with Dr Simon."

Rosemary Stevenson was a tall, slim, very attractive blonde woman, dressed in a light green jacket and straight skirt. She seemed poised, and when she responded her voice was clear and she expressed herself succinctly.

"Good morning Ms Deluca, and members of the panel," she replied.

Janet Deluca then asked Rosemary Stevenson to take her through the development of her relationship with Dr Simon.

"We met at a party, about ten years ago. I had recently graduated and my first position was with a chemical company. We put on an evening for doctors to tell them about the research we were doing and how it might one day be applied to their work.

Barry, Dr Simon, was one of the doctors present. I tried to chat briefly with as many as possible and Barry was one of them. He asked me some things about some new experimental products, and I found him articulate, intelligent, and charming, and I suggested getting together for lunch during the week and talking more. We did, and that led to dates and a very pleasant relationship for four months."

"Why did it stop after four months?"
"I was head-hunted and I received an offer from a company in Seattle that at that time in my life was just ideal. I took it, and with a lot of sadness left."

"So when did you become his patient?"

"After I returned from Seattle. I was looking for a family doctor. I had married and we had one child, and we needed a family doctor."

"Oh. So you became his patient after you married and after your personal relationship with him?"

"Yes."

"And how has he been as your family doctor?"

"Wonderful. He's very patient, always seems to have time to listen. He's knowledgeable and very thorough. We're very happy with him as our doctor."

"Thank you, Ms Stevenson. You may ask questions of the witness if you wish, Dr Simon."

"Thank you. Good morning Ms Stevenson. Thank you very much for coming and clarifying the history and nature of our relationship. You were a delightful partner during our personal relationship and I feel honoured that you and your husband chose me to be your family doctor when you came back here. Essentially the accusations against me are that I have had sexual relations with patients of mine during the time they were patients. Just to clarify for certain, you are saying that has not been the case since you returned, married, became my patient, became a mother."

"Yes, that's quite true."

"Thank you very much."

The next witness was also tall, dark-haired and tanned, sturdier than Rosemary Stevenson, dressed in a white blouse and black pants.

"You are Jennifer Grayson, I believe?"

"Yes."

"Can you tell us a bit about yourself, Ms Grayson."

She did. Jennifer Grayson was an accountant with a well-known large accounting firm. She was a junior partner.

She was married with two children, and she played indoor and outdoor soccer with women's teams and with co-ed teams.

"And when did you become a patient of Dr Simon?"
"After I married and had my first child. My husband and I had moved before the baby was born, into our first house in a different neighbourhood, and I remembered that Barry worked in a practice in the area, so I asked if we could become his patients?"

"But you had had an affair with him before that, hadn't you?"
"Oh yes. We met when I was at university and playing on the soccer team and I played against him. We chatted and he asked me out and we dated for a few months."
"And he was also your doctor then?"
"Good heavens no. He was still in medical school. We were young. We liked each other. We had a nice time together. And then he went off to Italy for a few months, I think it was some sort of student exchange programme for medical students, and by the time he came back I think both of us were ready to explore other possibilities."

"I see. So are you sure that there was never a time when you might have been his patient and having an affair with him?"
"No. Both of us were single. But since we became his patients we couldn't have that sort of intimate relationship, could we? And I wouldn't call what we had as an affair, because I think of an affair as being between two people who are married to other partners, and we were both single at the time."

"I see. Thank you Ms Grayson.
Dr Simon, you may question Ms Grayson."

"Thank you. Thank you very much for coming Ms Grayson. Just to make things clear, did I ask you to come here today to be a witness?"
"No. I received a call from a person who described herself as an Investigative Officer for the Disciplinary Society.

She asked me if I had had an intimate relationship with you because inquiries were being made about your behaviour, and I said yes, we did have an intimate relationship, and that was that. She didn't ask anything further about when it was, whether it was mutual or whether you had assaulted me or anything like that."

"So she didn't ask you whether it had occurred before I became your doctor, or since I became your doctor?"

"No."

"Thank you very much."

The third witness was a light-brown-haired woman, visibly pregnant, and wearing a colourful maternity dress.

Janet DeLuca introduced herself and confirmed that this witness was Laura Jamal. Ms Jamal told the prosecutor and everyone else in the room that she herself was an attorney, working in civil litigation with a prominent law firm.

She testified that she had met Barry Simon at a course on Marital Difficulties and the legal consequences. She had been interested from the law perspective, while he had come as a doctor interested in the dynamics of relationships that break up.

He had asked for her telephone number and they had dated for about six months. It had been a good relationship, but she had been ready then to marry and have a family and he wanted to continue his pleasurable single life. While she was very disappointed, they had parted on quite amicable terms.

She was married now with one child. Her husband was of Moroccan origin and they had lived there while he finished his studies and then returned here. When she became pregnant she had realized the need for a family doctor and after trying out three others had become very happy with Dr Simon.

Once again, it seemed that the sex relationship had taken place long before the women had become patients of Dr Simon.

One of the panellists turned to Janet, the prosecutor.

"I am wondering Ms DeLuca, do you really have any strong evidence of wrongdoing on the part of Dr Simon, because we haven't heard any so far?"

Janet asked for a break, and after the lunch break she asked the judge if she could postpone the case until the following morning. The judge agreed.

The next morning Janet opened the trial by telling everyone that she had given much thought to what had been presented to the court over the past few days. That given the uniformity of the witnesses all saying that they had become patients of Dr Simon after their personal relationship with him, that there was no case to continue. She was withdrawing the charges. She apologized to Barry and told him that he was free to leave and there would be no negative findings placed on his record.

Barry left, accompanied by two of his witnesses who had stayed and who had immediately hugged him and congratulated him. They went to a coffee shop and chatted for a while. He thanked them, gave them both a big hug, and he went to his office and they to their activities.

Later that week, sitting in his office, his secretary told him he had a call. He asked who it was? "Wouldn't leave a name," he was told.

He picked up the phone, and was surprised to hear Janet De Luca introduce herself, and ask to meet him, for lunch if he was free.

He was intrigued, he wondered why she wanted to meet him on a personal level. He even wondered whether she was trying to trap him by meeting in this way.

He met her at a busy restaurant. She was dressed informal-smart, in a dark grey sweater and a pleated wool skirt. He thought she looked quite attractive, more than she had seemed at the trial.

"I called you because now that the trial is over I wanted to get to know you a bit better, because I found you a very interesting man, and a number of very smart women seem to have had similar thoughts. So just in case you are wondering, I am not out to trap you, or anything like that. I just want to know you a little bit better."

She then introduced herself more fully in terms of her background, her family, where she went to school, and then inevitably her athleticism.

He reciprocated, told her more about his family background, his education, his development as a doctor, and his choice of speciality. They continued talking and as they did so Barry found himself becoming more relaxed, less wary, she was easy to listen to and easy to talk to.

She had known she was attracted to him. It had shocked her at first during the trial, and she had reminded herself that the whole point was that many women found him very attractive. The only issue had been had he crossed that boundary of not developing a sexual relationship with a patient.

But she had wanted to find out for herself in the quite different setting of a social meeting, not quite a date but perhaps a preliminary exploratory meeting towards a date. And she was finding it very pleasant. He really was a charmer, bright, intelligent, articulate, and he seemed genuinely nice. It was not an act or a façade.

So who was going to make the first move towards turning this or another meeting into a date?

Janet realized she had to. He might still be suspicious that she was playing him to see if he really had been guilty.

They had been talking for more than two hours. "This has been the longest lunch meeting I've ever had, but it's also been the nicest," said Janet. "But I have to move on. I'd like to get together again with you, if that's o'k with you?"

Barry looked straight at her. "Getting together can mean a business conference, or a date. Just to make sure, is it a date? Because I've very much enjoyed your company and I would like to get together with you again, for a date."

She felt relieved. When he had said "business conference" she sensed that he was still concerned, and then when he understood 'date' and added that he had 'very much enjoyed' being with her, she almost audibly breathed a sigh of relief.

"Date. Definitely a date."

"Then telephone numbers, e-mails, please."

"I see we are both practitioners of efficiency."

Their dates went well, very well. They found each other intellectually stimulating. They compared their work and their experiences with different situations. They went to movies together, went for walks and started running together. He was delighted that she could keep up a good pace for the three or four miles they ran together a couple of evenings a week, and the five or six miles they ran together on either Saturday or Sunday.

They drove down to the lake and ran along the shore, and then out of town to hilly areas, challenging themselves, and usually finished up going to one or other home, showering and eating together.

It became a warm close mutually appreciative and respectful relationship.

They started a sexual relationship. That took a little more patience on his part, as she admitted it had not been an easy area for her. She had always felt self-conscious about her body, she had not had very good early experiences. Her first partners in high school and at university had been immature, rushed, and not really aware of her as a person or paid much attention to pleasing her, just needing to satisfy themselves and confirm their masculinity. That had led her to withdrawing from love-making for some years, he was her first partner for a long time.

He was very considerate with her, very attentive, above all very loving. They started with showering together, a new experience for her but one that she found she really enjoyed. He had a very nice body, and he raved about hers. Told her she was gorgeous, beautiful, very pleasing to him and he showed it in his touches and caresses and kisses and expression of pleasure and delight.

It all made her feel truly appreciated, even loved and desired, and she told him so, that she had never really felt that before in her life. He felt deeply touched. He also became aware that it provoked within him a deep sense of responsibility. That this woman who had come across as a tough lawyer was in fact a very sensitive and vulnerable human being.

Their closeness increased. They spent more and more time with each other. She became very comfortable with his presence, with their intimacy. She felt loved, he felt very appreciated and cared for.

So what happened next came as a total shock.

It was seven months later, Barry received a call from Rosemary. Rosemary told him that she had received a call from a woman who had said she was from the Disciplinary Board and they were looking into the allegations again. There was a new prosecutor who wanted to interview her. Did Barry know about this?

No, Barry had not heard anything. He said he would look into it. He called the other women who had been witnesses, and two of the others said they had also received calls and were going to call him but he had called them first.

He asked them to call the person who had called them and ask why, on what grounds was a new prosecutor wanting to bring up something that had been decided in open trial.

He also asked Janet to do the same, and he called the other two women witnesses whom he had not yet contacted, and they confirmed that they had been called. He asked them to do what he was asking the others to do. Over the next two days he heard back from all of them. No details were being given, just that new information had come up that the new prosecutor wanted to explore.

Barry was very straight forward. He suggested to them that they had been put through an unnecessary ordeal already once, and without much more detailed information there was no obligation on them to be interviewed again. The only person that might be under any obligation to respond was himself. They should just simply refuse. They all agreed.

The call eventually came to him. That a new prosecutor was re-opening the case. Barry decided that this now required legal help and he called a good friend who was a very competent lawyer, Jeffrey Feldkorn.

He met with Jeffrey, outlined the situation, and asked Jeffrey to find out on what basis was the new prosecutor seeking to open the case. Jeffrey called the prosecutor, who told him little more than that the Disciplinary Board had received an "anonymous tip" alleging that he and his witnesses had all lied at the trial. Jeffrey had asked the prosecutor for the identity of the person who had contacted them, and the prosecutor repeated that the caller was "anonymous".

Jeffrey said he had expressed astonishment that a prosecutor would seek to re-open a case after an open trial, in which five witnesses had clearly stated there was nothing to the allegations, and the previous prosecutor had acknowledged that, and at the end had withdrawn the allegations. To do this on the basis of an "anonymous tip"?

Jeffrey said he had told the prosecutor that anyone could call in who had a grudge against a person and make an anonymous allegation, and some people could even make such calls just for the sake of mischief.

The prosecutor had not accepted Jeffrey's rejection of the basis for further pursuit of Barry.

Jeffrey advised Barry to make it clear that he would not agree to be interviewed again by the new prosecutor or another staff member, and Jeffrey said that he was advising Barry's witnesses to refuse to participate. That they had already given their testimony, it was all on the record, and they had no reason to want to revisit the matter.

The prosecutor tried to influence Jeffrey to believe that a negative impression would be created for his client by these refusals, but Jeffrey hinted to the new prosecutor that starting a new case and trial on the basis of an 'anonymous tip' would be a disaster for the image of the Disciplinary Board.

But the Board went ahead and a date was set. Jeffrey and Barry turned up. None of Barry's witnesses came. Jeffrey told Barry that he had received no indication that the prosecutor was bringing new witnesses, which would be an appropriate courtesy to the opposite side in a proper trial.

As the prosecutor stood to open the trial Jeffrey also stood and spoke. He introduced himself and then announced that he had called representatives of the media to come.

"I am now going to tell the media present that all allegations against my client were found to be completely unwarranted over a year ago. The Disciplinary Board is now seeking to revisit the matter on the basis of what they call an 'anonymous tip'.

We are demanding that they disclose exactly who is the person that gave them such a tip. Have they examined the reliability and veracity of the person. They certainly have not given us any opportunity to explore whether such a person exists in reality, and whether such a person would be in any position to refute the testimonies of all the witnesses who testified at the previous trial, as well as my client's own evidence.

If the prosecutor cannot produce such a person and the evidence upon which the person's claim is based, then we are leaving. This is not a totalitarian state where you can manufacture false non-existent evidence because you don't like someone.

So in simple, admittedly blunt, English, either put up or shut up."

Harvey Trayoner was the prosecutor. He stood. "May we proceed now?"

Jeffrey stood again, "are you giving us the name of the person who is making the allegations?"

Trayoner responded, "please stop interrupting Mr Feldkorn, you've made your points. We'll now proceed with the hearing."

Jeffrey stood again. "You used the word 'hearing', evidently you seem to be hard of hearing. I've made it very clear, you either give us the name of the new accuser or we leave."

"I'm under no obligation to do that, Mr Feldkorn, but your client is under obligation to remain here, and should he choose to leave then he will be liable to further disciplinary action which could include losing his license to practice."

"Thank you, Mr Trayoner. You have indeed confirmed that this Disciplinary Board considers itself far above the considerations that are a part of normal legal court practice, perhaps more like the behaviours of totalitarian state regimes. We have no respect for such attitude and behaviour. Good morning."

Jeffrey and Barry left, reporters already rushing to interview them as they made their way out.

Jeffrey felt very satisfied with how the brief hearing had developed and the obvious enthusiasm of the media for the story, and he didn't realize that Barry didn't quite share his joy.

That was not because Barry was disappointed with what had happened. He was actually quite pleased.

But there was something else that was bothering him. He had not heard from Janet for more than a month, and his calls to her had not been returned.

Two weeks later, Barry decided to call Janet's parents. He had developed a good relationship with Janet's mother, and he asked if he could come and speak with her.

When he met Mrs De Luca, he told her that he had not heard from Janet for six weeks. He had not been aware of any big argument, that he had done anything particular to upset her. Was Janet unwell? What had happened?

Janet's mother explained, "Janet was very upset and she has gone away for a while. She asked me not to tell you at first, that she wanted a bit of time away. I know that she had become extremely fond of you, and I'm not exactly sure what upset her. I have respected her wishes until now, but I think that after this period of time maybe she should tell you herself. So I'll tell you where she went and you can decide for yourself if you want to try to see her."

Mrs De Luca told Barry that Janet had gone to a place along the ocean. She had rented a beach house and was staying there. She gave Barry the address. Barry realized it was about a three hour drive.

He drove on Friday of that week, after finishing his practice hours. It was bright, sunny, but with quite a nip in the air. It took him three hours as he had expected, and he parked his car on the street running parallel with the beach.

He emerged from the car, stretched his legs, and started walking down to the beach, and then along the beach.

He didn't know who saw whom first, but as they drew nearer to each other he saw her look closely, as if she couldn't quite believe what or whom she was seeing.

She stopped in front of him, "well, this is quite a surprise." He gently put his arms around her and gave her a warm and not overly pressured hug. "I'm pleased to see you. You're looking well."

"Thank you. My mum told you where to find me?"

"She did. I went to talk to her and she explained to me that you had wanted some time away. You chose a very nice location."

She smiled, "yes, it has been very pleasant here. You know I resigned from that job at the Disciplinary Board."

"No, I didn't know. I thought maybe it was a leave of absence."

"That's what it was going to be at first. But when they launched that case against you again I decided I didn't want to be associated with such an organization any more."

"So what will you do?"

She took his arm and turned them around. "To start off, go for a nice walk with you along this lovely beach. I presume you've been driving for at least three hours and you need to stretch your legs and get some fresh air."

He thought that was such a sensible and thoughtful approach. "Great idea," he said.

As they walked she told him how she managed with the house she was renting and with shopping, and what activities she was doing to keep herself busy. He was reminded how much he enjoyed listening to her, what a nice pleasant voice she had.

Eventually they turned back and then reached the house she was renting and she took him inside.

He took her in his arms and gently kissed her. She kissed him back. "I really missed that most of all," she said. "Can we repeat that, I'm sure I can do with some more.'

He did, and then she showed him around the house.

He saw that she had made it comfortable, although the property itself seemed a bit old as was the furniture. But he told her she seemed to have made the best of it.

"How long more do you have it?"

"At least until the summer, but it wasn't my intention to stay that long. I was thinking of three months. I should be seriously looking for new work now."

"What have you been thinking of doing?"

"That's one of my problems, I'm not quite sure. I certainly don't want to go back to the Disciplinary Board."

"What about setting yourself up as a specialist in defending doctors like me who have been charged by the disciplinary board. You certainly have an insider's understanding of how they work and the weak points in allegations and charges that are made."

She looked at him. "What a fantastic idea. I think I want to marry you right now," and she blushed deeply and put her hand over her mouth. "Oh, I'm sorry. That wasn't very appropriate."

He took her in his arms again. "I don't think I've ever been proposed to like that before, but it wasn't inappropriate at all. It was totally charming.

I think the idea of us marrying is a wonderful idea. I know you have a very good heart, you are a totally decent woman who can recognize when something is very wrong and stop it, even if it costs you in some way, like eventually giving up a very nice job.

That you also are in my eyes a really very beautiful woman, with a voice that I love listening to, you're athletic, you are smart, together we would have great children.

Yes, I'd really like to marry you."

"You would..," she started. And then she started crying.

"I'm sorry. It's the sea, the air, being away from civilization for so long, and then seeing you and being so happy to see you. It's made me a little nuts, I think."

He asked her, "So that wasn't a genuine proposal?"

"Can we sit down?" she said. As they sat, she took his hands in hers and started talking.

"Being away here, not working, not being with people, walking up and down this lovely beach, trying different dishes - and I'm going to try one or two new things on you before you leave, you have been warned - I thought a lot about you and about us, and I see you much as those very nice things you said about me, and how much I've grown to like you and to fantasize what it might be like to be married to you and have children with you.

So though you may have thought of me as a lawyer very careful with my words, sometimes things come out spontaneously that surprise even me.

Yes, I've been thinking a lot about marrying you, and I'm sorry that it wasn't the most romantic proposal. But now that I've said it and you responded so positively - which just reminds me again what a fantastic guy you are - I have to admit that I'm terrified.

I'm terrified that I'm clueless about being a wife and being a mother. You've made going out easy, because you are so bright and smart and such good company, and you know what you've done for me in terms of lovemaking. Something that was very uncomfortable for me and that I shied away from for years has become with you an absolute delight. Yes, the fantasy of being married to you thrills me, but the reality frightens me.

I also wonder why you would want to marry me. I saw those beautiful, very accomplished women, that you went out with before me, so why me?

I think I might be scared that you would become bored with me and look for someone else."

"So let me tell you why I want to marry you. I was pleasantly surprised and it bothered me a little that when I first saw you as the prosecutor that I thought you were very attractive. I had to remind myself that you were out to destroy my career.

But as the trial went on and I could see you treating those other women with respect and with great fairness, and as I sensed you becoming convinced that they were telling the truth, that I had done nothing wrong but was a good guy, appreciated by these women as both a person and a good doctor, I saw you losing enthusiasm for the prosecution and although I was mostly relieved when you stopped it, I was also impressed with your decency and dignity.

Then, when you asked me out for lunch I was wary again. What is she up to? Does she want to trick me in some way into revealing that I really am a scheming predator, and of course you came across totally differently. As a very lovely, intelligent, decent woman that I felt very comfortable with. And for both of us it just took off from there.

To me, you are beautiful. But not just physically. Your character, the way you talk, the way you treat people is so full of kindness and warmth. I think the role of prosecutor didn't really suit you best. You would probably make a much better defender.

But with me, it feels so natural, so open, so comfortable. Somebody that I want to be there for, and someone whom I sense would be there for me.

Your concerns sound perfectly normal to me. So I take it that my initial acceptance is now being confirmed by you. Oh, I'm getting to sound like a lawyer, I wonder where I get that from?"

She laughed, as she wiped her tears away. "Shower and bed first, or supper first?"

"From what you said earlier, I think that shower and bed for us is a pretty sure thing, whereas supper is still experimental. So let's go for the sure thing first."

GOOD MORNING

"Good morning, I'm Lenny Pressburg. I'm here as a doctor for the next three months."

"Welcome Dr Pressburg. I'm Elizabeth Hendrickson, I'm the secretary to this unit. People call me Liz."

She was a full-figured woman with a cheerful face, lovely eyes he thought, a nice smile and a pleasant voice.

"She actually runs the unit and everything around here. She knows everybody and everything and if you need or want anything done she's the person to do it."

The speaker was a tall, very slim woman with dark - probably dyed he thought - hair.

"And I'm Sue Kintrell. I'm one of the nurse therapists here. Nice to meet you. We have been desperate to have another psychiatrist here, we've been just overwhelmed with work the last few months."

"Well, Ms Hendrickson - "Liz, please," she told him. "If you are the person who knows everything here, perhaps you could show me around."

"With pleasure, Dr."

"Larry, please."

The two women looked at each other.

He asked, "did I say something odd?"

Liz responded first, "let's just say that the chief here would never let anyone call him by his first name."

Liz stood up and suggested that he walk with her. He saw that she wore low heels and he estimated her height at about five feet and four inches. She wore a light blue sweater - matches her eyes he thought - and a knee-length pleated navy skirt.

She took him around the hospital, showing him the different units and offices of various staff members. He noticed she didn't say anything about the chief of the department, he didn't comment on that.

She brought him to the staff lounge and made the introductions. There were two other psychiatrists on staff, two psychologists, six social workers and twelve nurse therapists, although all were not there.

He went around to each of them, introduced himself with a smile, and repeated their names to try to start memorizing them.

Liz told him that each morning there was a staff meeting that was a combination of an intake meeting and patient review meeting in which the staff could discuss the progress of patients, and hear views on handling difficulties or lack of progress with particular patients.

He enjoyed listening to her. She had a nice voice, spoke clearly, smiled often.

She suggested that before the staff meeting began he might like to have a cup of coffee with the staff, which he readily agreed to.

He would only find out later that this was an important assessment factor for Liz and some of the others. How willing was he to be a part of a team, or did he set himself apart as superior because of his qualifications and experience.

"Hi, I'm Danny Goldman. I've read some of your work which I really found very helpful and I'm looking forward to learning from you while you are with us."

"Thank you, Dr Goldman. Can you tell me a bit about your own background?"

Danny did, and Lenny found out that Danny was a relatively newly certified psychiatrist, who was eager to obtain as much general experience as he could before settling on any one or two areas to focus on.

As they were chatting one of the psychologists suggested that it was almost ten o'clock, when the staff meeting would start, and they all started to walk towards the meeting room.

A rather primly dressed man, in his mid-fifties thought Lenny, medium height, chubby, wearing a dark suit, tightly knotted tie, polished shoes, walked in.

"That's Doctor Morgan, chief of the department," said Liz. Before she could say more, Lenny had walked over to Doctor Morgan and introduced himself, putting his hand out to shake Dr Morgan's hand.

Dr Morgan looked at Lenny's hand as if it was an organ of contamination and turned away. He sat down and said to Lenny, "as you are new here it would be best if you just listened and see how we do things here."

Dr Morgan then turned to the rest of the staff and said, "All right, let's get started."

One of the nurse therapists then introduced a new patient that had been admitted two nights earlier and reviewed by the nurse.

The nurse held a fairly large file in her hands, and indicated it was the patient's file from previous admissions to other hospitals in the area that had been sent to them electronically and printed out.

"And so what is the diagnosis?" asked Dr Morgan.

"According to the file she has been given a diagnosis of Bipolar Disorder."

"And so you know what to do in terms of treatment?"

"Yes, Dr Morgan."

"Then next case," said Dr Morgan.

"Now hold on just a moment," said Lenny. "You say that she is a 38 year old professional woman who hasn't worked for the past two years, and has cuts along her forearms though none deep enough to require stitches.
That she has had a series of broken relationships with men and that she is a regular marihuana smoker. Now putting aside for a moment what any other unit thought about her, are there any other diagnoses that you might consider for this woman?"

"Excuse me, doctor. We know the diagnosis. Let's move on," Dr Morgan announced in a brusque manner.

"No. Actually we don't know the diagnosis. So far we've only been told what another unit has said. I'd like Ms Crandon or anyone else for that matter, to think what else might explain this picture. Perhaps, Ms Crandon, if I ask you how you would characterize these cuts or slashes on her forearms?"

"They are suicide gestures, doctor. That's enough. Move on," interjected Dr Morgan.

"I don't think anyone seriously believes they can commit suicide by making superficial slashes along their forearms. Certainly not an educated professional woman in her late thirties. So what other types of gestures might these be? And let me give you a clue, two words, one begins with an 'A' the other with an 'S'."

"Attention-seeking," called out a few other staff members together.

"Yes, attention-seeking. And if that is the case, would any of you now like to offer our diagnosis, not another unit's perhaps inaccurate suggestion?"

"Is it all right if we psychiatrists offer our suggestions, or do you just want the non-medical staff to come to the right conclusion?"

"I don't want to embarrass anybody, so please go ahead."

"Thank you. When we take a fresh look at the material as Dr Pressburg has suggested, I think it becomes much clearer that this woman has a Borderline Personality Disorder."

"Excellent, Dr Akwame."

"Majar, please."

"Thank you, Majar. And if indeed Borderline Personality Disorder is a much more accurate diagnosis, then what might be the implications for treatment?"

Danny Goldman spoke up. "Although these can be very difficult patients to treat, and she sounds as if she has been in and out a number of times suggesting that no-one has really tried to deal adequately with her the person, then it is generally accepted now that the first line of treatment is psychotherapy, not medication. That in fact medication has very little to offer except for a brief time if people are admitted in a brief psychotic state."

"Exactly. Thank you, Dr Goldman, Danny. There is a very important lesson to be learnt here. Just because a patient has been given a certain diagnosis elsewhere, does not necessarily mean that diagnosis is correct. And in fact if you just accept another diagnosis without really examining for yourself whether you agree with it or not, you might then just add to the confusion, and that ultimately fails the patient, because it reinforces that 'x' is the diagnosis when it isn't, and you may continue giving the wrong treatment which has been the treatment offered for a long time."

"O'K. That's enough. Doctor, I want to see you in my office. Now."

The other staff members exchanged glances, Lenny just smiled. He had dealt with people like Dr Morgan before.

He followed Dr Morgan to his room. Dr Morgan went behind his desk and sat down.

Lenny looked around the room, he did not see another chair. He went out of the room and heard Dr Morgan shout, "Where the hell do you think you are going?"

Lenny ignored him, found a chair and brought it into Dr Morgan's office and sat down, smiling benignly at Dr Morgan.

Dr Morgan looked as if he was going to burst a blood vessel. "What are you doing with that chair? I didn't say you could bring it in here."

"No, you didn't. But you said you wanted to talk with me, so if we are going to talk sitting down, then I need a chair also."

"No you don't. When I talk with people in my office they remain standing."

"Then I suggest you stop that policy immediately. From what I can see you have good staff here who are adults, not six year old children. It is extremely disrespectful to them to not provide a chair for them to sit. I won't accept it, and I shall make sure that none of them accept it in the future. Now, what did you want to talk about?"

"As I told you before the meeting started, you are new here. Your role is to be quiet and learn and see how we do things here."

"As far as I am aware, this is a hospital that is intended to help troubled people. That means we put the welfare of the patients first, which especially means finding the best diagnosis and offering the most appropriate treatment.

What you intended to do in not questioning the diagnosis or treatment of that patient was negligent, incompetent, and ignorant. You may have intimidated others into not questioning you but that won't work with me. It is a pity that we are starting off on the wrong foot here, the rest of your staff seem to be very nice, friendly, and competent people. If you have nothing constructive to say I'll leave and see where I can be of help."

With that Lenny stood and started walking out of the room. Dr Morgan yelled "Get back in here," Lenny ignored him.

Dr Morgan rushed out from behind his desk and picked up the chair to throw at Lenny, but Lenny had ducked out of the room and closed the door as the chair crashed into it and broke.

Lenny went back to the meeting room where the intake and discussion had taken place.

One of the psychologists spoke up, "Well, you seem to have made an enemy on your first day. What does a psychiatrist have to say to that?"

"You all have been here longer than me. I suspect you all have your own views of Dr Morgan. My concern is that we do the best for our patients and that younger staff be given the opportunity to obtain the maximum learning we can offer them."

"Well said," commented Majar Akwame, "but Dr Morgan can be a nasty enemy."

Lenny busied himself visiting as many wards as possible and talking with the staff, trying to obtain a feel of them and of the work they were doing.

Before the hospital day finished he approached Elizabeth Hendrickson, "Since you know everything, can you recommend a few nice restaurants to me," he asked her.

She mentioned a few, wrote some on a piece of paper, and made a suggestion which one or two he might try first.

"Since it is my first time here, unless you have other commitments perhaps you'd like to join me."

She looked at him, "That's very nice of you. Thank you. Yes. If you don't mind I'd like to go home and change first. Perhaps we could meet at the restaurant, say at 7 o'clock."

It was a cool evening so she came in a coat which she took off when they met inside. She was wearing a dark blue sweater and a short pleated skirt. He thought she looked very nice and said so. She gave him a big smile and thanked him.

Talking was easy. They told each other about their backgrounds, where they had grown up and what they had done with their lives.

She had married quite young, had two grown children. The marriage had not worked and she and her husband had divorced. She had remained single, her son and daughter were both married and she had three grandchildren.

He had been married, but lost his wife to cancer five years earlier. He also had two adult children, both married and one child each.

After her divorce she had worked and also taken night courses at university and had finished a degree. He was impressed. She told him that though people might have thought that with a degree she could pursue something more challenging than receptionist-secretarial work, she had actually found that the reality often was that she became the administrator of a company or institution and that gave her a sense of satisfaction without feeling overwhelmed.

The time passed. He told her he enjoyed the food and enjoyed even more her company.

She had come with her own car and he walked her to her car and kissed her. She told him that had been a lovely kiss, she hadn't been kissed for a long time, and she kissed him back. He told her it had been a lovely evening with her and he would like to do it again if she accepted.

She did, and she added that since he was new to the area she would like to show him more than just the town, perhaps over the weekend. He said he would be delighted.

The next morning at the conference Dr Morgan just glared at Lenny who smiled pleasantly and greeted the other staff members as they walked in.

Few comments were made about the first three patients discussed. No new patients had been admitted, but when it came to the fourth patient that Valentina, one of the psychologists had been working with, Danny Goldman had asked why Valentina was suggesting medication for a man who seemed to have formed a positive working relationship with her.

"I just thought it might be a boost to help him get better more quickly."

"But is there any good evidence that such medications really work in that way?" asked Danny.

Dr Trombollo, one of the junior doctors said, "even if there is just a placebo effect doesn't that count?"

"Good point," said Danny. "But if it were to be a placebo effect, how long would we want the patient to stay on it? Wouldn't they become dependent upon a placebo that might no longer have any real therapeutic benefit but could have other harmful effects?"

"Nonsense," intervened Dr Morgan. These medications effectively correct chemical imbalances in the brain. That's how they work."

It was time for Lenny to speak up.

"Actually there is no evidence to support that notion. It's a theory, which may be proven to be correct, but hasn't yet been proven"

"No," said Dr Morgan. "You don't know what you are talking about. There are many articles on Chemical imbalances."

"Yes, there are indeed," said Lenny, "so let me explain to those of you who may not know what happens when you send in an article to a journal based upon your own research.

Let us say you have studied twenty or fifty or even five hundred patients with certain conditions and you have produced data, nicely summarized statistically. The editor will then write back suggesting either as an editor or on the basis of the reviewers - and you will receive copies of the reviews - asking you to add your ideas of what you think your data means, and where to go from where you are at now.

Your reply to that now is speculation. You presented your data. That was it for where the science is concerned. What you might add are your speculations as to why the data turned out this way, and where you want to go in terms of further research.

When the researchers on aspects of brain chemistry and psychiatric disorders produced data, none of it so far has proven to actually conclusively demonstrate chemical imbalances in the brain as a cause of depression or any other psychological disorder, but many researchers have indeed speculated that chemical imbalances might be a cause.

But it is important to understand the differences between scientific proof and speculation, no matter who the person is who has speculated.

Speculation is still speculation even if the person is the head of such-and-such prestigious institution or has published 5000 papers."

"So, if I understand correctly what you have been saying, then perhaps if I have a good working relationship with this patient that I should continue without adding an unnecessary placebo, and only if he was getting worse should I consider asking for him to be prescribed a placebo."

"Excellent, Valentina."

"I've never heard so much nonsense. Chemical Imbalances are the cause of Depression, that's been accepted by all reputable psychiatrists. You'll put this patient on an anti-depressant from this morning - " interrupted Dr Morgan.

"No, she won't," said Lenny. "She's handling this patient well, there is no indication to introduce an ineffective medication. I don't know which reputable psychiatrists you are referring to, Dr Morgan, whom you claim believe that Chemical Imbalances cause Depression, because there is no current literature that views the notion of Chemical Imbalance as anything other than speculative. The goals of this unit - as of any other unit - must primarily be to do what is in the patient's best interest to help the patient get as well as possible, not to pander to your unsupported notions, Dr Morgan."

"Shut your fucking mouth, you moron," yelled Dr Morgan. "Get out of here. I run this unit, not you."

"I'm not leaving. I was asked to come here specifically to help raise the quality of the services offered here, and I won't let your ignorance or rudeness interfere with that."

"We'll see about that." Dr Morgan was seething.

Lenny turned to the group. "I think we should stop this meeting now. We've reached a certain impasse that needs to be sorted out. I think you are all doing good work. Please continue and we'll resume tomorrow."

"To my office. Now," yelled Dr Morgan.

Lenny turned to him. "No. You demonstrated yesterday and you've repeated it today that you have little control over your own behaviour. I'm not going to have you behaving rudely to me or throwing a chair at me again."

Lenny and the staff went to the different wards and clinics and continued their day's work.

At about 11 in the morning, Liz called Lenny and told him that he had a call. Lenny took the call.

"Dr Pressburg, I'm Gerald Morton, I'm chairman of the hospital board. The board would like to meet with you again. Can you make Friday evening, at 6, say?"

"Certainly. Can you tell me what it is about?"

"I'd prefer to tell you when we meet in person. So 6 on Friday in the boardroom?"

"I shall be there."

Dr Morgan did not come to the morning conference the next day, nor the next few days after.

Lenny took the lead, the meetings went well. There was a greater atmosphere of ease, people smiled, complimented each other and made comments and suggestions more freely than had been the case at the unit for a long time. Both Danny and Majar expressed this to Lenny.

Lenny came to the board room at the agreed time. Mr Morton and six other board members were. Two were women, Lenny estimated that they were in their late fifties or early sixties. The other four men included one much younger man and three others also in the late fifty to early sixty age group. Mr Morton sat at the head of the table. He introduced himself and then asked the other board members to introduce themselves, which they did.

"The reason we've asked you to meet with us, Dr Pressburg, is that Dr Morgan called us asking us to dismiss you. Before we do that we'd like to hear from you your version of what has been happening."

"Thank you, Mr Morton, members of the board. Unfortunately, you have currently as chief a person who is ignorant and incompetent, and only barely in control of his own rage and anger. The primary goal of any unit in a hospital must always be to put patient care first. When a person like Dr Morgan somehow slips into the role of being a chief of a unit, then major errors in diagnosis are made, which of course will lead to incorrect or inappropriate treatments being offered.

You have a good staff, with some fine younger psychiatrists and other staff members, and you have an obstacle in the person of a fool who tries to cover up his grotesque ignorance by bluster and intimidation. He has to go."

One of the women spoke up. "Dr Morgan has been with us for some years. He is licensed and qualified. What makes you the judge of his knowledge and capabilities?"

"Madam, have you looked at my record, my experience? Is that not why I was asked to come here? I repeat, Dr Moran is ignorant and incompetent, and quite unable to learn from someone like me. He is intellectually and emotionally blocked to any new understandings. I suspect that if past patients and families really knew the errors I am sure he has made - because in the short time I have been here he would have made some gross errors had I not intervened - the hospital could potentially be liable for lawsuits."

One of the men, Henry Jacksmith, a local banker, spoke up. "I believe you said that we should dismiss Dr Morgan rather than dismiss you. Why should he go and not you? Was there not peace before you came?"

"I believe that there was an absence of fighting, because Dr Morgan had intimidated the staff of the unit into following his orders. But the consequence of that was primarily failing many patients, and secondarily interfering with the positive educational development of some fine young staff members. I ask you again to look at my record compared to his. If you wish you can call a number of leading psychiatrists, heads of prominent departments, to ask about my record and abilities as a clinician and as a teacher. Dr

Morgan has very little. I suspect he was hired when there were few people interested in such a position, and you have felt grateful having someone to handle the unit, even though the work may have been very much sub-standard from him."

Another board member, Richard Pennington, a land surveyor, spoke up. "What Dr Pressburg has been saying is true. I did call some leading psychiatrists, here and in the US, and I also looked at Dr Morgan's background and Dr Pressburg's. There is just no comparison. Colleagues speak of Dr Pressburg as one of the finest clinicians and teachers they have come across. That he has an enormous and very well-deserved reputation as a person of excellence, very honest and very principled in his behaviour and dealing with people.

I also called some physicians in the community asking about their experience with Dr Morgan. The answers were not good. They described him as being aloof, unhelpful, arrogant, not interested in what any family had to say."

Mr Morton stood up. "There is another person that I would like the board to hear from now. Excuse me a moment," and Gerald Morton ushered in Liz Hendrickson.

"Dr Pressburg, I don't know if you have yet had the opportunity to meet Ms Hendrickson."

"Oh yes. Ms Hendrickson was the first person who greeted me when I arrived on Monday. She welcomed me, took me around and introduced me to the other members of the staff and then showed me around the hospital. I have been very impressed with her. She is the sort of staff member that I was saying earlier who is very capable and could be given even greater responsibilities."

Morton spoke. "After hearing Dr Morgan's complaints, I asked Ms Hendrickson to survey as many of the other staff members as she could. I'd like us to hear what she has to say. I haven't heard it yet myself. Ms Hendrickson."

"Thank you Mr Morton. I was able to speak with seven staff members. Their reports were pretty much unanimous. They said such things as, 'Dr Pressburg has been like a breath of fresh air,' or 'For the first time here I have felt as if I can express myself and that I am being listened to,' or from another person, 'I feel respected as a qualified professional,' or 'I am actually for the first time starting to learn something in our morning conferences or on the wards, and not just being used as a sort of rubber stamp to repeat what others elsewhere have done.' None of them had anything good to say about Dr Morgan. Most of them think that Dr Morgan is having some sort of a personal crisis. I think that summarizes the general opinion."

She left the room. Gerald Morton turned to the other board members. "Is there anything more anyone would like to ask or say?"

The youngest member indicated his interest in speaking. "Mr Brimley?"

The \young man, Mr Brimley, spoke.

"Dr Pressburg is homophobic. He should be dismissed."

Lenny smiled. "Two things. Number one, I have no idea on what basis you make such an allegation. Number Two, what does that have to do in any way with what you have been hearing around this table over the past half hour?"

"I just know it. You Jews say you have a nose for anti-semitism, well we gays have a nose for homophobia. And I would rather keep the incompetent Dr Morgan until we can find a non-homophobic replacement."

Lenny spoke again. "I'm wondering how Mr Brimley came to be on this board. Was he invited as a representative of the gay and lesbian community, or did he demand to be on the board because of his concerns in those areas?"

Gerald Morton responded, "No, I don't think that was the case - " but he was interrupted by Richard Pennington.

"Oh come on Gerry, you know very well that the gay lesbian lobby made many demands on us to have someone on the board to 'protect their interests' as they said.

I think Dr Pressburg is owed an apology for Mr Brimley's unfortunate and inappropriate comments, including what I take to be his offensive remark toward a distinguished expert who happens to be Jewish."

"Thank you Richard," said Gerald Morton. "I agree with you. If that is the sort of contribution you are going to make Mr Brimley then I think you might be better directing your efforts elsewhere, not here. We don't need that sort of divisive provocative behaviour. We can have enough of that from the patients and families our staff are trying to deal with."

"But he hasn't responded to my statement that he is homophobic," complained Mr Brimley.

"I think he did quite adequately, and in a more courteous manner than you really deserved."

Morton then turned to Lenny, "thank you for meeting with us Dr Pressburg. I think we are all - o'k with one exception - delighted to hear that you have made such a positive impression on the staff and that everyone thinks so highly of you. We shall have to deal with the problem of Dr Morgan, but in the meantime clearly you should continue the good work you are doing and the leadership you are showing."

"Thank you," replied Lenny, and stood up, went around the room and shook hands with all the board members, even Brimley.

He went out and to the main office and gave Liz Hendrickson a big hug.

"Thank you - "he started,

"No, no, "she said. "Thank you for those very nice things you said about me to the board. I was just quoting what others said about you. You said nice things about me directly from yourself. Actually I think that means I should be giving you the hug."

"Accepted, with pleasure," Lenny laughed.

Over the next few weeks the morning meetings became better and better. The working atmosphere was pleasant, there was a sense of fuller exploration and of learning and growth. There was also a greater sense of warmth and friendship and respect between the staff members.

Lenny and Liz became closer. That first weekend Liz had driven Lenny on Saturday around the county and on Sunday they had gone walking in the hills.

They liked each other's company, they enjoyed each other, found each other easy to talk to and to listen to. They were very comfortable with each other.

They started a sexual relationship that was a little awkward at first as they struggled to adjust to each other and to each other's preferences.

The first time they undressed he told her she had a beautiful body. She said to him, "Thank you. I know I'm overweight, but I'm trying hard to lose some. I've lost about ten pounds so far.

She then told him that she had started putting on the weight soon after Dr Morgan came. "You may find it hard to believe but I used to be around 135 to 140 pounds." She told him about the various diet schemes she had tried, but never really felt really appreciated for her efforts.

She told him about her fears of making another big mistake. He told her that he thought she was a really lovely woman, a very bright, very thoughtful, very sensible woman, who must have learned a lot from her previous experiences.

When a Bank Holiday weekend came with an extra day off, they decided to go away together, and drove to the Scottish Highlands. They had discovered that both liked mountain walking, they had driven to the Lake District and Lenny had become enthralled with the beauty of the scenery.

In the quiet of the Highlands, they had felt very close to each other. Not feeling rushed to get up early and prepare for work had enabled them to increase their intimacy. Love-making had become mutually pleasurable and delightful. He never failed to praise and admire what he told her was her beautiful body.

At the hospital Lenny had requested that Liz be given the official title of Administrator, with an appropriate increase in salary. He had also seen to her moving into what had been Dr Morgan's office, which she had refurbished into a much more comfortable and inviting office with armchairs and a settee for visitors to sit.

Four months later.

Dr Morgan walked into the conference room. He was wearing a suit, a white shirt and tie, and carrying his briefcase. He sat down. The staff looked around, quite puzzled.

"O'k, let's start. Who's presenting?"
Lenny, Danny and Majar walked in, saw Dr Morgan sitting and behaving as if he was in charge again.

"I believe you are leading the discussion today, Danny," said Lenny.

"Sit down. We've already started," Dr Morgan uttered in a very curt voice.

Lenny murmured to Danny, "ignore him, just carry on."

Danny stood and commenced, "who has a new patient, or a patient for discussion?"

One of the social workers, Janet Kizmarac, started describing a patient.

After she finished her description Danny asked her for her opinion.

"Excuse me. I'll decide what to ask. You, just sit down and shut up," from Dr Morgan. Danny continued as if Dr Morgan hadn't spoken.

Dr Morgan interrupted again, this time yelling. "I said sit down and shut up."

Danny looked at Lenny, "could I have a brief word with you outside?"

"Come back here, sit down, shut up, and maybe you'll learn something."

Danny went out with Lenny. "I'm sorry. I'm a bit uncomfortable. In my culture we don't talk back to older people, even if they are disturbed. I'm not sure how you want me to handle this."

"It is difficult," said Lenny. "Let me try and see if we can all learn something from this."

They came back in. "Please continue, Dr Goldman," said Lenny.

"I said that I'm in charge here and you should sit down," seethed Dr Morgan.

Lenny stood. "Dr Morgan, I don't know what you are doing here, but if you don't let us continue with our work then I am going to have to ask you to leave."

"I'm in charge here - "

No, Dr Morgan. You are not in charge any more. You haven't been for four months. Now please let Dr Goldman continue or I shall ask security to remove you."

Dr Morgan continued ranting and raving about how he was the chief and was in charge of the unit and Danny and Lenny should sit down and shut up. Lenny asked him twice more to stop. Dr Morgan refused, and finally Lenny called security and asked them to come.

When two guards came Lenny explained that Dr Morgan had been a senior psychiatrist who seemed to have developed some mental problems and that he should be treated respectfully. Lenny asked that Dr Morgan be taken to the Emergency Room at the leading teaching hospital in Manchester, and Lenny called the chief of psychiatry there and explained the situation.

Lenny then returned to the conference room.

"As you saw, Dr Morgan seems to have suffered some sort of mental relapse. Have any of you heard of fugue states?"

Danny and Majar both spoke up and described fugue states. Lenny then asked the staff to consider whether what Dr Morgan had demonstrated might be possibly a fugue state, and if so what might be the appropriate treatment?

A very lively discussion followed, including some other diagnostic possibilities that were put on the table. Lenny reminded them that as Dr Morgan was not a patient of any of them, they didn't really know what had been happening in Dr Morgan's life over the past four months. But as a number of them pointed out, Dr Morgan had appeared to be under great mental strain when he had left, and his manner of leaving and the reasons for it must have been extremely psychologically disturbing to him.

As they were leaving the staff room a number of staff members came up to Lenny and thanked him for turning what had been a very emotionally uncomfortable situation into a significant learning experience.

A week later Liz came to him in his office. She had brought a pile of papers with her.

"These are six applications from young potential psychiatrists who want to come and work and train here. These are their applications. When I had received letters of inquiry from them, I drew up an application form asking about them and their educational and experience records, and these are the replies."

"Now why am I not surprised that you would take such a brilliant initiative? But I am thrilled that so many people want to come here."

"Don't be surprised. You'll see when you read their letters. They've heard about you and this place and they want to come."

She left him with the letters and applications. He read them through. He then went to Liz's office and sat down in one of the armchairs.

"You realize what this means? We shall have to create a proper teaching and supervisory programme for them."

"You have two very good people whom you could appoint as deputy teachers and supervisors, Danny and Majar."

"I agree with you."

They continued talking. She suggested he appoint a committee to explore their needs and expectations, because - Liz said - they would probably have to go to the board to ask for more money.

Lenny called Danny and Majar into his office, showed them the applications that Liz had made copies of and gave them each copies of the applications.

Lenny asked them to rank the applications in order of whom they would like to see working and studying on the unit. He then explained to them his intention to appoint them both as senior teachers, and that they would be responsible for some aspects of the teaching and supervision of the incoming trainees, if they accepted that role.

Danny said that he was astonished with the offer. That he had hoped one day to become a teacher because he really liked to teach but hadn't imagined an opportunity would come so soon. Certainly not when Dr Morgan had been head. Majar echoed similar sentiments.

They chose four of the applicants. As the academic year came to an end, people at the unit started talking about having some sort of celebration. Lenny heard about it, and told Liz that he wanted to sponsor a lunch at the best hotel and restaurant in town. Liz made the arrangements.

The evening before, Lenny suggested to Liz that they go out to eat because they had a lot to talk about before the lunch the next day.

It was a pretext.

"I actually wanted just the two of us to be together because you have made this the most fantastic few months, far better than I could ever have imagined. I like being with you so much. You've really made me come alive again. I enjoy every moment of being with you. So I would like to make it permanent. I would very much like to marry you. Beautiful, wonderful, Elizabeth, will you please marry me?"

She looked at him, and tears came to her eyes. "You have made me so happy. I'd also not imagined that I was really going to find true happiness again. That I was going to become so comfortable with a man. You are such an amazing guy. I would be honoured to become your wife, and I'll try my hardest to be the best wife in the world."

He produced a ring. "I bought this ring in the hope that you would say yes. Since you've said yes, then I want to take you to the jeweller who can help you choose a setting and make sure the size is right."

"The diamond is beautiful. Thank you so much, Lenny dear."

The wedding was informal. Liz had her parents and sister and sister's husband and children, as well as her own children and three friends with whom she had been best friends since school days. She wore a very light blue jacket and skirt, she had lost more weight, was down to 150 pounds, everyone told her she looked fabulous.

Lenny had his children, it was too far for his elderly parents to come. Three colleagues from the US that he considered very special friends came with their partners, and most of the staff from work. It was a match that all agreed seemed to be a very good combination, a couple who radiated happiness.

HE WAS ONLY TEN YEARS OLD

He was only ten years old, but he was wise, smart, good in school and a good athlete. He played on the school soccer team, and was one of the best runners in the school.

He knew that some of his friends had left with their parents, he didn't really know what he and his parents were going to do.

A few days later, after dinner, his parents sat him down and spoke with him.

You have been a wonderful son to us - but the time has to come to send you far away from home. We have to stay here, and it is not going to be very good for us. But we want you to have a good life and to be free.

Your uncle Freddy, mummy's brother, in America, is sponsoring you. That means that he will make sure that you have a home to live in for the next few years, and school to go to.

We hope that we shall see you again, when the government lets us come out. But it won't be for a while.

Our neighbours, the Horvaths, are able to go, and they have agreed to take you with them until you arrive in America where Freddy will meet you and take you.

It is very nice that the Horvaths have agreed to do this, and you must be very thankful to them."

"I don't really understand why this is happening. I have seen that people are being taken away and put in prison and they don't seem to have done anything wrong, and I have been hearing people say not nice things about Jews. But I don't understand why I have to go, and you can't come with me like the Horvath's daughters are going with their parents."

"It is a very good question, and many families are asking the same question, that their neighbours can all go, and their children can go, but they have to stay. But governments often decide on things that we ordinary people can't control and have no choice and we have to do it."

"When will I go? What will I take with me?"
"You have to go tomorrow morning. We shall pack a suitcase for you, as much as you will be allowed to take. You can choose some of your favourite things, and we shall see how much will fit into a suitcase."

He cried, they hugged him and kissed him, and then went with him to his room to pack.

"Ugh, is he coming with us?" Greta, the Horvath's younger daughter who was eleven, expressed her displeasure seeing Laszlo join them at the train station.

"Laszlo is very nice, I like him, and I'm glad he is coming with us.
Laszlo, we have some time until the train goes, let's walk around the station."
Chava, the Horvath's older daughter who was fifteen, took Laszlo's hand and started walking with him.
Laszlo had always thought that Chava was the much nicer of the two sisters, and he was thrilled and relieved when she took him away from Greta. Chava chatted with him as they walked, trying to make him feel less anxious and upset and about leaving his parents. He had just said goodbye to them.

They came to a place in the station and Chava stopped and said, "would you like an ice cream?" She knew that Laszlo liked ice cream. Very shyly Laszlo said "yes, but I only have a small amount of money that I have to look after very carefully."

"When I suggested the ice cream I meant that I was going to pay for it. You just choose which favour you like."

The look on Laszlo's face when Chava told him she would pay for it made Chava feel very warm inside. It gave her a great sense of pleasure, seeing him so happy at such a difficult time.

Of course he chose a chocolate ice cream, and sat eating it happily until he finished it, and it was time to go to the train.

That was not the end of Chava's caring for the young Laszlo, it was just the beginning.

The train took them to the Italian city of Genoa where they boarded a large boat, which would take them all the way to America.

Laszlo was put in the cabin with the Horvath family, he was considered for the trip as one of them.

"I'm not sleeping in the same bed with him," announced Greta angrily. "You don't have to," said Chava. "He can share my bed." The beds were very simple bunks, for adults as well as children, and people had to make the best of the situation, even overweight families had to squeeze into small spaces.

There were no individual washrooms, toilets, or showers, just communal men's and women's facilities, that after a few days at sea were no longer clean. But people knew they had to put up with the conditions, it would only be for a few more days.

The food was also very modest. Bread, jams, and milk for breakfast, soup and fish for supper, and cookies for during the day or after supper. Nobody starved, but many people felt hungry.

The boat arrived at the port of Fort Lauderdale on a sunny morning. The passengers had to line up with their luggage and then be processed by the immigration authorities, and that took a very long time.

The Horvaths were met by members of their family, and Laszlo said goodbye to them. He thanked them very much for looking after him during the long journey, and Rachel gave him a very big hug.

He asked Chava if he would ever see her again, he knew they were going to a different part of the country than where he was going, and that America was very big.

"I certainly hope so. I like you very much Laszlo, you are a lovely young man, and you have made this journey for me much easier by being such good company."

"I have?"

"Yes, you have. So don't forget me, and we shall try to find a way to keep in contact."

But it was not to be. His uncle Freddy was a nice cheerful man who greeted him warmly after Laszlo had been processed and received his admission visa, and Freddy took him to the airport where they were going to fly to Phoenix, Arizona, where Freddy lived with his family.

Laszlo had heard that the Horvaths were going to New Jersey, and that was in the north of the country, a long way from Arizona.

Freddy had a nice wife, Banas, and two older sons who were in high school. Johnny was sixteen and George was fifteen. They didn't speak much Hungarian and Laszlo didn't speak any English, but they seemed friendly.

They showed Laszlo around the house and which would be his room. They showed him the television sets - there was more than one in the house - and the telephones.

The next day, Banas took Laszlo to the junior school that he would attend for the next few years. She introduced him to the principal, explained that he was a new immigrant who knew no English but she had heard from his parents that he was very bright. She added that he was also supposed to be a good soccer player and runner.

The principal explained and Banas translated, that it might be difficult at first coming to school in a new language, but she was sure that if he tried hard he would pick it up quickly.

Laszlo was taken into a classroom for his grade and introduced to the teacher and the students, who again were told that he was a new immigrant who didn't speak English. The teacher asked if any of the students spoke Hungarian - she knew that some did but she wanted them to identify themselves, she would see who was more welcoming and who wanted to keep a distance.

Two girls and a boy put their hands up. The teacher asked them to introduce themselves to Laszlo, they did, and he responded very politely and gracefully. The teacher was impressed.

The teacher asked them to help Laszlo at the beginning until he could understand more of what was going on. Laszlo could see that these students seemed to be comfortable with that, perhaps a little proud that they were able to do something that the rest of the class couldn't do.

The school day did not seem much different from what he had been used to. The three Hungarian speakers seemed to have decided themselves to share in a rotation the classes where one would sit next to Lazlo and help him understand what they were doing in that subject.

When it came to mathematics it was apparent right from the start that Laszlo was very good. He told the girl sitting next to him the answers to the questions before the teacher had even finished reading them out. The student, whose name was Aggie, would put her hand up, the teacher would ask for the answer, and Aggie would say "Laszlo says it should be..."

After the third time that this happened, the teacher asked Aggie to ask Laszlo if he had been in the regular class for his age or had he been with older students. Through Aggie, Laszlo told the teacher and the other students that he had been in a regular class but that mathematics was his best subject.

At the end of the day, the teacher asked Laszlo to wait behind, together with the Hungarian speakers, and the teacher asked them to tell Laszlo that she was giving him some mathematics questions to answer at home and bring back the next day.

The questions were one and two grades higher. When he brought back the answers all correct, she thanked him and then called his aunt in the evening. She told Banas that Laszlo was quite exceptional in mathematics and she didn't want him to be bored in that class while he still had to learn English to be able to follow in all the other subjects. So she was going to give him much harder work to do in the classroom during the math period.

Laszlo felt very pleased that his ability in one subject was appreciated, because he had felt very intimidated not being able to follow very much in some of the other subjects. He could see maps in Geography, and a few diagrams in Physics and Chemistry that looked familiar, but English and History and Civic Structure were truly foreign territory to him.

He was a quick learner, and each day he seemed to progress. But it was outside, on the soccer field, that the other students came to admire him and see him as an asset to the school and not a handicap.

Freddy and Banas had bought him soccer shoes and he had a top and shorts, and he had asked himself - with the help of his translators - if he could try out for the school team.

Once on the field there was no stopping him. His speed and his ball control skills were way ahead of the other players, and he was immediately put on the team by the coach and given a school top and shorts and socks.

He was told when the next game was and where, and was told to ask his uncle and aunt if they could take him, if not another family might.

It turned out that Freddy's older son already drove and he offered to take Laszlo.

It was a bonus for Laszlo's cousin Johnny, because the sisters of some of the other players came and Johnny had liked some of them and had a chance to talk with them and arrange dates.

Laszlo's team won, with Laszlo scoring three goals and creating two more. His team-mates were overjoyed. It was their biggest win over the past year.

Gradually, actually quite quickly, Laszlo picked up English and started catching up in the other subjects. He was a very good student, and he was well liked because he treated others nicely, and because of his outstanding ability on the soccer field.

In the summer term there was a sports day with running events. Laszlo won all that he entered. This won a lot of attention from the girls, and Laszlo tried not to make the other boys jealous.

The years went by. He would occasionally hear from his parents, Freddy was able to telephone his sister once a month.

Both she and Laszlo's father were in what they described as house arrest. They could go out to work during the day but not at night. Their work was limited to menial work. Laszlo's father was a school cleaner, his mother a cook in the school cafeteria. Laszlo's father had been a Professor of Biochemistry at the University, and his mother a Mathematics teacher at the senior high school, but in the great social drive towards equality they had been thrown out of their positions, as had all Jews who were not permitted to leave.

Laszlo could talk to his mother for a few minutes. At first he would cry. Gradually he stopped crying. Once a year on his birthday his father was allowed to talk to him.

Laszlo was invited to try out for the state junior soccer team and he was invited to play. He was asked to try out for the national team, but by then he was looking at taking the SAT university qualifying exams and he concentrated on studying for those.

He was very eager to obtain scholarships to university. Freddy and Banas had been very generous with him but he knew they had paid a lot to help their sons go to university and he didn't want to burden them more. So he was trying very hard at school to obtain very good marks and for the SAT, and he was willing to give up the chance to play for the national team.

When he received his school marks and then his SAT scores, and was awarded very valuable scholarships, he believed it had been worth giving up the soccer. He was sure he could take it up again later.

It was time for the school prom. He had come to understand what a big event this was. He heard the talking going on among the boys and girls of his graduating class who was going to go with whom.

Laszlo surprised many people. He asked Larissa, a girl he had been very friendly with, who was also very good at Mathematics and Physics and they had studied together.

Larissa was a tall, overweight young woman, but Laszlo liked her very much. He also thought that because she was very smart and rather big, most other guys wouldn't ask her, but he wanted to.

She was delighted, she was thrilled. She told her very good friend Heather who had been asked by four different guys.

Heather also knew that Larissa had a single mother, and they weren't very well off.

"You have to have something nice to wear, and it needn't be something expensive, so I'm going to consult the best fashion expert I know to help you choose. So come around to my house tomorrow evening and I'll get the expert to help us."

Larissa had an idea whom the 'expert' might be, but didn't say anything, and went the next evening to Larissa's house.

"Mum, you remember my friend Larissa. The class genius Laszlo has asked her to the prom, so we've got to find something that is just her, perfect for her."

"H'mm, I see. Ok, well first I am going to ask you to take off your top and jeans so I can have a better look at your real figure. I hope you're not embarrassed."

"Of course I'm embarrassed, you're going to see just how fat I am." There was silence. Larissa looked at Heather and her mother, and slowly took off her sweater, and then her jeans, standing in her bra and panties.

"Yes, I see your problem, Larissa. You have no self-confidence in yourself as a woman. You have a distorted self-image, and so you don't see what an attractive young woman you are. You have a lovely shapely figure, with curves that men will rave about, if you give them a chance to get to know you."
 Larissa was quiet. Heather could see tears forming in Larissa's eyes and Heather gave her a hug.

"You've never heard anybody say that to you, have you?"

"Well, I have. Laszlo says it sometimes. I just don't believe him. I think he's just being very nice, which we all know he is."

"Larsissa, we also all know that Lazlo is the most honest person. It's unbelievable sometimes just how honest and straight-forward he is, yet still is very nice."

"O'k, o'k girls. Let's get on with the important job of finding something nice for Larissa. We'll take my car."

They drove to the large mall and went into three dress stores, Heather's mother each time choosing some dresses, holding them up against Larissa, asking her what she thought of them, and trying on a few.

Then they went to the store that Heather had guessed her mother would eventually go to. A store that sold very nice teenage dresses that weren't too expensive.

By then it hadn't been too difficult to choose a colour and style that brought out the best in Larissa's hair, eye, and skin colours and her shapes. Larissa tried it on, it must have been at least the fifteenth she had tried that evening, and it was perfect for her, they all agreed.

Heather went into the changing room with Larissa, and when Larissa took off the dress Heather took it out to her mother who took it to the cash desk and paid for it, and when Larissa came out of the changing room she saw Heather's mother paying for the dress.

"No, Ms Solomon, I can pay for the dress myself."

"I know you can my dear. But you've been a wonderful friend for Heather for years, and it's my gift of appreciation to you. All I ask is that you have some pictures taken to show me how good you really look in it on prom night."

Larissa threw her arms around Heather's mother and gave her a big hug. "Thank you so much. Heather's been a really great friend, a lot of the other girls weren't very friendly to me sometimes but Heather has always stood up for me, and she has been a role model in clothes and many other things."

The big evening came. The boys rented tuxedos and a very smart Laszlo came to pick up Larissa in the car Freddy's son had lent him for the evening. He brought Larissa flowers and said hello to her mother.

"You look really lovely in that dress, Larissa," he told her. She blushed. "And you look very handsome in that tuxedo."

"Well thank you, young lady." and he said good evening to Larissa's mother.

Larissa's mother gave Larissa a big hug, and said to Laszlo, "thank you very much for taking her. It means a lot to her."

"She has been a great friend, and there's no-one else I would even have considered." Larissa blushed hearing this, and they left.

When they came into the prom together, some of their classmates cheered, which Larissa found very touching.

Both of them had practised dancing a little, so they weren't too awkward, and Laszlo was known for his athleticism. But he was delighted that Larissa proved to be a much better dancer than he had expected, and also more athletic than he had thought.

He told her he was very impressed. "Since you asked me to the prom, I have made an effort to start exercising and take better care of myself. I hope I'll keep it up."

"Since I've known you, if you make up your mind to do something, you do it. You don't give up."

"Thank you, coming from you, that's a very nice compliment."

They had spent some time discussing some of the prom and post-prom traditions, and agreed that some of the events or activities that were important to others were not for them.

They weren't going to get drunk, he wasn't going to try to rape her, they weren't even going to try serious narcotics.

But at the end of the prom, after they had danced a few slow dances together that had led to some very pleasant and increasingly longer kisses, they did find a couch in the outside area where they sat for a while, continuing the kissing.

They told each other how enjoyable it had been, and how much they liked each other and appreciated the friendship.

They knew they were going to different universities in the fall. Larissa would be working to save money towards her college expenses, even though she also had been smart enough to obtain some good scholarships. Laszlo was going to be doing an unpaid internship in a hospital in Kansas. He was still trying to choose between medicine and dentistry.

They continued going out until Laszlo left. When he dropped at her house for the last time, her mother came out as he was leaving.

She took him in her arms and gave him a big hug. "I can't thank you enough. You have done so much for her self-esteem. She used to be so down on herself, and you have helped her like herself and see herself as the lovely young woman she is. I wish you were both old enough to get married now, but I know that is not real life. So I thank you Laszlo, and I wish you all the very best, you really deserve it."

"You brought her up, and she is indeed a truly lovely woman, and I have felt very proud being with her these last few months. She has made me a much better person. So I wish both of you the very best."

They met again during the winter break, and they kept up their very easy and comfortable friendship that eventually became sexual, with Laszlo raving about the beauty of her body, lavishing kisses on every part of her, and her telling him how much she liked his masculinity.

After their first degrees, she went to Columbia to do a MBA and that led to her staying in New York to progress in the financial field, while he went to California to study dentistry.

He received an invitation to her wedding. It was to another financial analyst whom she had met while consulting.

He flew to the wedding and congratulated her. Her new husband seemed nice enough, he wished them well. He had met some of her single friends at the wedding, briefly dated two of them. They were very attractive as well as being very smart, but there was an aggressive quality about them that he wasn't comfortable with.

Laszlo graduated, and started a practice with three other classmates, two women and another man. They opened a new office in an expanding suburb in Scottsdale, Arizona, not far from where Freddy and Banas lived. Their sons had married and left home and were living in Oregon. They had gone into business together, and according to Freddy and Banas they were doing well and had married very nice women.

Johnny already had one child, and George's wife was pregnant with their first.

"And who is this very handsome young man?"

There was something very familiar about the beautiful woman who had approached him.

"Chava?" He looked at her name tag. It read Chava Horvath Cameron.

"You are not sure who I am Laczy?"

She was using the diminutive that close friends usually used for a person named Laszlo.

"I'm so surprised to see you after all these years. You have a different name. But you look absolutely fabulous."

"Well thank you. So I see that you are Dr Schwartz now. You are a dentist?"

"Yes. I qualified two years ago and started a practice with three other classmates in Scottsdale, it's a suburb of Phoenix. And I see you are also Dr, so you are also a dentist?"

"No. I am actually a research scientist, and my research is in dental materials and teeth protection. That's why I've come to this conference. But I'm very happy to see you again, and I'm very impressed that you've become a dentist."

"Do you have some free time, so we could sit down together and talk about what we have been doing with our lives since we came to this country years ago?"

"Yes. I'd love to do that. Would you like to have dinner together?"

"Definitely. Where are you staying?"

"I'm at the Hilton. And you?"

"I'm at the Marriott. Have you heard of a nice restaurant here, or been to one yet?"

"I only came today, so I haven't been to one but I've been given some recommendations."

"So let me pick you up at your hotel. What time would be good for you?"

"I like to exercise at the end of the day. So if I finish here at 5, go back to the hotel, go for a run, I should be ready about 6.30."

"I'll see you then. Will your husband mind if I give you a big hug?"

"My husband won't mind because there isn't a husband. I'll tell you about it over dinner, but I'm not married. Are you?"

"No. And I'm not in a relationship at the moment either."

She laughed, and put her arms around him and gave him a big hug, which he reciprocated.

"I remember the hug you gave me when we last saw each other after arriving in this country. I've always treasured that memory. There is something very special about your hugs. It touches me very deeply."

"You were a very sweet young boy. I have the sense that you've become an ever sweeter grown up man. I'll see you later."

He was supposed to go to a three o'clock lecture on new implant techniques, but he found he wasn't concentrating. He left, went back to his hotel and went for a long run himself, then spent time in the hotel gym, returned to his room, showered, and rested. And all the time his thoughts revolved around Chava.

"Now we have a little time together again, can you tell me what happened in your marriage? You don't mind me asking?"

"I'm pleased you are asking. It's not easy to talk about, but I need to tell you."

He wasn't sure why, but he did want to hear, and sensed it was important for her to talk about it.

"Do you remember that when we talked while we were coming to this country I told you about how girls may come on to you very sweetly, and you get sucked in, and then they take advantage of you. Well, as they say, physician heal thyself. I should have taken my own advice.

My husband seemed very nice at first, dressed nicely, treated me nicely, he had a university degree, and he came from a very good family, and after just a few months we married. It was a nice wedding, and we had a very nice honeymoon in South America.

We came back, and he said he wasn't sure what he wanted to do. He tried at first working in a bank. He passed the interviews easily. He was nice looking, dressed well, had a degree. But the job didn't last long. After four weeks he stayed at home, saying he hadn't liked the work after all, it was boring.

He wasn't sure what to do next, so he applied to work as a manager in a large store. Again passed the interview easily, but after three weeks again stopped. It wasn't for him after all.

I still thought he was genuinely lost, uncertain what suited him, so I started looking in newspapers and magazines and on-line with him to see what might interest him.

This time he thought the world of high-tech might be the place, even though he had no advanced engineering or computer studies background. After about four weeks I had a sense something wasn't right. He was dressing, going to work, yet didn't seem enthusiastic, didn't talk about the work, didn't seem quite focused.

I was at home going through the mail, and I saw something on a bill that I didn't recognize and so I called where I thought he was working.

A young woman answered the phone and asked me to hold while she transferred my call. I thought she was looking for him, but another woman came on the line and asked me who I was, and I said I'm his wife.

She then said, "You don't have to answer this, but I would appreciate it if you did. How long have you been married?"

I said four months. The woman then suggested that I sit down, because she had some things to tell me.

He wasn't working there any more. They had let him go two weeks earlier. He had been coming in late regularly, and when he came in seemed to be not fully focused, and some of our young employees said they were sure he was on drugs.

But that wasn't all. Some of our young women who are very bright computer wizards, said that he was a bit loose with his hands, specifically that he was patting and caressing their bums.

I spoke with him about this, he tried to laugh it off, and to tell me that every woman wanted it and that's why they wore tight pants or skirts. I told him that even if he were in a relationship with any one of them it would still be inappropriate at work, and he should take this as a serious caution.

Three days later he tried it with me. I told him it was totally inappropriate, and this was the very last warning. His comment was "aren't you getting enough from your husband?"

I was pretty much at the end of my patience, but didn't send him home that day. But the next day he came in over an hour late and with a glazed look, and I sent him home and told him that he was dismissed.

Mrs Cameron, I think your husband needs help."

When he came home I asked him where he had been, he told me at work. I asked where, and he gave the name of the company I had called. I told him I had called the company, what he had told me was untrue. He admitted he hadn't been working, that he really had no interest in working, there was nothing he really wanted to do, and he admitted taking drugs.

I told him that he knew that some of these were absolute no-no's for me, drugs, lying, not working. I told him I couldn't stay married to him and I hoped he wouldn't give me a hard time about divorce.

Maybe that is one of the side benefits of the marihuana or whatever he was taking, that it makes some people so passive that they don't get angry and fight. The divorce was quick and peaceful, and I continued my research, got my Ph.D and then positions, and research grants, and started publishing and teaching. And for the most part I haven't become too involved with many men. I've had some dates, and some relationships that have lasted for a few weeks or months, but nothing very serious. That early failure, disappointment, has really made me hold back."

Laszlo stood, went over to her and gave her a big hug. "Thank you for sharing that with me. I wonder if that man had the slightest idea what a treasure he was letting go."

"I think he did. But I think that he genuinely felt incapable of being a grown up responsible adult."

He looked at his watch. "Do you know that it is already eleven thirty?" She confirmed the time. "It has been so nice talking with you, being with you again, I haven't wanted it to stop."

"Nor have I. Can we do it again?"

"Of course. I still have to hear your story. How long more are you staying?"

"Tomorrow was going to be my last day, and I have a plane tomorrow evening."

"So we can get together again tomorrow afternoon?"

"Yes. I'd love to do that."

He knew he would soon have to take a cab to the airport, so he told her that he wanted to see her again, and that he would be delighted if she would come to Scottsdale, but he would be happy to go to Philadelphia if she preferred that.

"Yes, I'd like to get together again with you, and I think I'd prefer to do it first in my home territory."

"O'k. Then when we both get back to our homes I'll call you to set up when it would be convenient for you for me to come, and you can tell me which hotels are near you for me to stay at."

There was no way in which she was going to let him stay at a hotel, but she wouldn't tell him yet. For now they exchanged telephone numbers and e-mails, and parted.

She kissed him first, he responded, and they continued kissing until she said to him that much as she would like to continue to enjoy this pleasure, she didn't want him to miss his plane and struggle to make alternative arrangements.

She waited for his call. It didn't come. She was very disappointed. For over a week she found herself sad, felt hurt, wasn't really sure why it upset her so much.

And then she received an e-mail.

"I am so sorry that I have not been in touch with you for more than a week. When I returned I found that some very special goods were waiting for me, and I had to make some very complicated arrangements to pick them up. I even have to leave the country to do this. I still very much want to get together with you, and I hope you will forgive me for this delay."

She called him straight away. The first call was to his home number. It was an answering machine. She then tried his office, was told by a secretary that he was busy. She asked the secretary to ask him to call her back as soon as he had a free moment.

When he called back she didn't hesitate. "If I understood correctly, based on things I've read in the newspapers the last few days, I have an idea about the very special goods you are going to collect, and I think that you could do with having someone with you. The procedures might be difficult, and you might also benefit from having some emotional support while you are doing this."

He was quiet. He was stunned. He didn't know what to say.

"Laczy, are you still there?"

"I'm not sure if I'm still here. I think I'm in some sort of a dream world. You would take time off from your work to come with me to do this?"

"I think that was what I offered and why I'm calling you."

"You're incredible. You're just amazing."

She asked him and he outlined the travel plans he had made, and she told him she would make her own inquiries how she could coordinate her flights with his, and where they would meet.

They agreed that they would meet at JFK airport in New York at around four in the afternoon on the next day. They would both keep their phones on so they could tell each other where they were.

He hadn't told her yet where he was supposed to travel to, but he booked two seats on the plane. He would tell her when they met.

But she had guessed, based upon his urgency and what she had read in the newspapers, that his parents were among one thousand former prisoners who were being released to go to relatives in other countries, and that Laszlo was sponsoring his parents to bring them to the US, and the formalities might take some time. She packed a travelling bag with her most important necessities, and hoped that wherever they had to go she could buy anything more that she might need.

They met the next day at the airport, he almost cried when he saw her, he still couldn't believe that she wanted to come with him.

He told her that they were going to Genoa. He repeated what she had already read about the one thousand people being released and he told her that his uncle had heard from his mother that his mother and father were among those, but it could change at the last moment. It wasn't absolutely certain. Chava couldn't imagine how hurt Laszlo would be if his parents were not among those being released, and she was aware that being there for him emotionally, if that happened, would more than justify the trip.

"I see you've bought tickets for both of us. How would you like me to pay you?"

"Do you remember what you bought for me when we were waiting for the train to leave all those years ago?"

"Of course I remember."

"Well, that's how I want you to pay me. Varieties of chocolate only." She laughed. "I love your laugh," he said. "When I was feeling so sad your laugh brightened me up for a while."

The plane ride took nine hours. At some time during the night she rested her head on his shoulder and then his chest, it felt very comfortable to him. He gently stroked her hair.

He had been given the location of the huge convention centre where the former prisoners had been assembled, and where booths of the major countries ready to receive the people had been set up.

She was the first to see his parents. She brought him to where they were. They stood. They saw her first and recognized her, she had been a teenager, a grown young woman when she left. He had still been a very young boy.

His parents had aged, they were thin, they obviously had not eaten well over the years, but they did not seem to be unhealthy. He hoped not.

Chava and Laszlo then took his parents to the American area and began the long process of registering them, processing them, applying to sponsor them to become immigrants.

They were asked who they were and to produce identification. Laszlo introduced himself as her son, and introduced Chava as his partner. She squeezed his hand and smiled at him.

It took a long time, but eventually his parents were released and given identity cards.

Laszlo and Chava thanked the officials, and hugged his parents. Laszlo then explained that they were going to take his parents to his home in Scottsdale.

"You've been wonderful, coming with me, but I don't want to take you away more from your work."

"I would like to fly with you and your parents, if you don't mind. And it will give me a chance to see how you live, and your office."

All four went first to Fort Lauderdale where the plane landed, and Chava suggested that before they fly on to Scottsdale they could spend a weekend in South Florida, and she suggested they drive a short distance north to the town of Boca Raton.

Boca is a very pleasant quiet town, it is on the sea, has many fine hotels and restaurants, and broad streets that make driving easy. They rented a car, Chava drove and Laszlo pointed out aspects of American life to his parents.

They had contacted a hotel from the airport and drove there. Laszlo took his parents and their suitcases to their very nice room. He pointed out the amenities, they were fascinated by the large bathroom which they said was bigger than the home they had been allowed to live in for the past three years, when after Laszlo's father had been released from prison, they still lived under house arrest, unable to go out from night until morning.

It was Friday afternoon, and Laszlo's father surprised him. He told him that one thing that had kept up his courage over the years was that he had still tried to pray, and as much as possible Laszlo's mother had still lit candles on Friday evening to welcome Shabbat, the day of rest.

Laszlo went to the front desk and made inquiries. He was given the address of a synagogue not too far away, and he was told that people couldn't light candles in the room but the concierge was sure that at the synagogue his mother would be able to.

But before that they had to do some preliminary shopping for Laszlo's parents.

They took them to a mall and to a clothes store, and bought some simple starter clothes. Pants and shirts for Laszlo's father, and pants, skirts, blouses and sweaters for his mother, and underwear for both.

They also bought good sturdy suitcases to replace the very cheap, crumbling ancient cases they had come with.

Chava also bought some replacement clothes for herself.

They drove to the synagogue, and Laszlo and Chava asked about lighting candles and his mother was able to do that. It stirred up memories in Laszlo's mind.

Chava admitted that when her family had come to America they had mostly given up observance. They did go to a reform temple on Rosh Hashanah and Yom Kippur, but Chava had not found it very meaningful.

The rabbi of the synagogue came over to them and welcomed them, Laszlo introduced himself, Chava, and his parents.

At the end of the service the rabbi came over to them again. "I have the impression from seeing your father that he might be more comfortable with the orthodox synagogue not too far from here. You can't actually park there on Shabbat, but you can park very near and walk the rest.

Laszlo took his advice. When they arrived back at the hotel, they had supper, and then helped his parents to make some tea for themselves, and then took his parents to their room.

It had been a long journey for them, and a long and quite emotional day. They were overjoyed to be with their son, but also tired.

"Do I have to ask what you reserved in terms of rooms?" Laszlo asked Chava.

"I would really hope that you wouldn't have to ask," she said with a smile

Their room was also large and comfortable. They took time talking with each other, exchanging their feelings about seeing his parents again, and then kissing and caressing each other.

After a while Chava suggested they take a shower. "Together?" asked Laszlo, "of course," said Chava.

He let her use the bathroom first, then he used it. She was in her underwear when he came out.

"You're even more beautiful than I imagined," he said seeing her. He took his clothes off as she started the shower and set it at a comfortable temperature, and then took off her bra and panties.

"Your body is...absolutely fantastic, sensational. I've never been so close to such a beautiful woman," he told her.

She ran her hands over his body. "You're in pretty good shape yourself."

They spent a long time in the shower, soaping and caressing each other, and then made their way to the room, towelling each other, and then fell on the bed kissing and caressing.

The next day they drove to the synagogue the rabbi had suggested the night before. A man came over to Laszlo and a woman to Chava and asked them about themselves, and both Laszlo and Chava explained that his parents were among those just released from Hungarian prisons.

The rabbi came over to Laszlo's father and talked to him in Yiddish, which astonished and pleased Laszlo's father.

At the end of the service, the rabbi again came to them and invited them to lunch at his house. They were reluctant, they thought it was an imposition, but the rabbi explained that in congregations like these it is very traditional for the rabbi to invite visitors, and a rabbi and his wife usually prepare to host a large number of people at their table.

It was an unusual experience for Chava, sitting in a synagogue in a women's only section.

At the rabbi's house, the rabbi spent a long time talking with Laszlo's father in yiddish, and Laszlo's father told him afterwards that the rabbi had asked him to tell the rabbi their stories.

Laszlo was impressed with the attentiveness that both the rabbi and his wife showed to Laszlo's parents. He could see that his parents were deeply touched that after their many years away from anything related to their background and tradition, in a completely different country people were reaching out to them and really interested in them.

Laszlo's parents also told him that the rabbi had said that there were a number of people of their country of origin in the synagogue, though they had been here many years and hadn't gone through the very traumatic experiences Laszlo's mother and father had suffered.

The lunch would be a turning point, for Laszlo and Chava, and for Laszlo's parents.

After lunch, the rabbi suggested that Laszlo's parents might like to rest. They had been through a lot with their travel and this adjusting to a new life and country, and after they rested the rabbi would take Laszlo's father to shool for the afternoon service and at the end of Shabbat the rabbi could drive them back to the hotel or Laszlo and Chava could pick them up.

"The area around here is very nice," said Chava, I think Laszlo and I would like to go for a walk and see more of it, and then we can all go back together after Shabbat."

Laszlo wasn't sure what Chava had in mind, but he trusted her implicitly, and agreed.

When they walked, Chava thanked him for agreeing, for giving her that degree of trust.

"This weekend, so far, has had quite an effect on me." Chava started. "As I told you, my family drifted away from being religious after we settled in this country. It soon became just Rosh Hashanah and Yom Kippur that we would go to shool, and that was to a big reform shool that just didn't give me any sense of meaning or purpose. The man I married also had no interest in anything traditional.

In the past two years particularly, I have had a growing sense of missing some things in my life. One was obvious, not having one person, one man to love me and me to love.

What I didn't quite realize was the other thing that was missing, and I have felt it last night and especially today. That is this special day that is Shabbat. I used to enjoy it. We would go to shool, we would eat, often together with friends, and then I would go to a youth group.

I see how it has already brought your parents to life in such a short time, and I feel this extra sense of calm, being together with you and sharing this Shabbat experience.

And I realize that I'd like us to continue this. I'd like us to find a place to live together that has a community like this, because I think it would also be a very good atmosphere to bring up children.

And, and this may sound presumptuous on my part, I'd like to think seriously of us together finding a place here for your parents to live. I think they'd be very happy here, and would have a support system.

We haven't decided yet where we are going to live, but wherever we choose, we can still arrange to come every second or third weekend to be with your parents."

"You are absolutely amazing," Laszlo replied.

"I am in awe of your kindness, your decency, your wonderful heart, and since it all comes with such great beauty, I feel very privileged that you want me to be with you."

"I see very similar qualities in you, and you know now that I think you are also physically gorgeous. What we have to do as a couple is always appreciate and love each other as much as we do now," Chava reciprocated.

Laszlo had his parents, his uncle, aunt, and cousins and their families, his partners and their families and the assistants who had been with them since the practice opened, to the wedding.

He also invited Larissa and her family and her mother, and they all came.

Chava's parents came, as did her now married sister, whom to Laszlo seemed to have not changed at all. She was grumpy, complaining, constantly pushing and pulling her son and daughter's hair and clothes that in her perfectionist mind weren't quite right.

Greta's husband was a big man, with a large pot-belly, but very much in his wife's shadow.

The wedding was in the synagogue in Boca that his parents had liked so much and become attached to.

Chava spoke first at the reception after the ceremony. She said that she had always loved Laszlo, that he had been a delightful boy who had grown into a wonderful, caring man. She had visited his practice and met his partners, and saw how well they worked together and had so much respect and admiration for each other.

She acknowledged that she had made a poor choice when she was younger, and was very glad that she had waited until the love of her life had come along.

Laszlo was very touched by her speech. When it was his turn to speak, he told the guests the story of his parents having to send him away and how after leaving them a beautiful angel had come from heaven and immediately taken his hand and looked after him. How this angel had been to him the most beautiful, loveliest, kindest woman in the world.

But then he had lost touch with her as they both made their way in the new country.

He had been taken in by his wonderful uncle and aunt and he thanked them and praised them and his cousins. He had been fortunate to make many good friends such as Larissa, and the people that he opened practice with.

And then he had met Chava again, now an adult woman, more beautiful than ever, and how he had thought he might have lost her when the news came through that his parents might have been released, and that when he did contact Chava to apologize for not following through on his promise to arrange to meet with her again she had immediately understood why, and insisted on coming with him to meet his parents and help them through the admission process. That she had just dropped everything else to join him, and his admiration for who and what she was as a human being had awed him.

After the wedding, they went to her home in Philadelphia for two days and talked there.

He suggested that they buy a place together in a different place from where each of them had been living before they married, and Chava acknowledged that he really wanted to be near his parents and help them adjust to a new life, in a different country, speaking a language they didn't understand. They were bright, smart people, who had been dragged down by the empty uselessness of the persecution they had endured.

So they bought a home in Boca together, not far from the small home that Laszlo had bought for his parents. Chava had wanted to contribute, but Laszlo insisted that had to be his responsibility, what he wanted her to share with was buying their own home together.

Laszlo started off commuting. Flying to Phoenix early Monday morning, and working in his practice until Thursday evening, then flying back to be with his family for the weekend.

Chava looked for a new department to work in the day after they returned. Her field was small and limited, but that also meant that most of the important people in her field knew her and had a good opinion of her. She was offered three positions, at the University of Central Florida near Orlando, at the University of Florida in Gainesville, and in a large manufacturing company that knew her work and wanted her to work with them to develop their existing and new products.

The third offer was very tempting. Financially it was excellent, and she had examined the facilities and had been very impressed.

Laszlo had come to realize that when Chava was looking for his opinion on a difficult choice, she usually had made her own mind up but was giving him the respect and recognition that as her partner he had an equal say. His response would be to tell her that he had suspected what her decision was likely to be and that her decisions were usually very smart, but that he appreciated deeply being asked for his opinion.

They were a good couple. Other people saw them as genuinely liking and admiring each other and warmed to them.

They had been married four months. He was spending his three days in the practice in Scottsdale, and Chava hadn't sounded her usual self on the phone.

He phoned again later that evening and could barely understand Chava who seemed to just groan into the phone.

He phoned his mother, who to his surprise didn't tell him much. Just that she had been around to see Chava and made some soup for Chava.

But when he arrived home on Thursday evening, he was greeted with a huge hug by a very happy Chava who had a big smile on her face.

"I'm pregnant."

FIGHT TO DEATH

"Welcome to "Fight to Death". I am going to explain the rules to you even though you have all read them in your application package. But this is your opportunity to drop out if you change your mind, and we want you to hear the rules out aloud, in case any of you didn't understand what you were reading.

We call it "Fight to Death" because people can die. You fight inside an enclosed cage, and the winner is the person who is still standing, and the other person has either given up, or is completely unable to fight.

Some people want so much to win that they keep trying to fight even when they are being knocked senseless, and those are the times when people may even die.

You only fight with your fists. We did away with the kicking years ago because we found the crowds really didn't like it.

There are no rounds, no breaks, you fight continuously until one person can no longer respond.

We made a big change from that old sport boxing; there is no holding on to the other fighter while you take a rest. If the judges see one person holding on to the other they will call out "stop holding" and you have three seconds to stop, otherwise you are disqualified.

Someone who is disqualified may get one chance to fight again. Two disqualifications and you are out.

So what are the rewards? You start off at 1 gold bar for one win, two for your second, three for your third, and so on until 10.

Then from 11 to 20 you get 2 gold bars for each fight you have won, so for your 12th win you would receive 24 gold bars. From 21 to 30 you get 3 gold bars for each victory, so for your 25th win you would receive 75 gold bars. Then from 31 to 40 it jumps to 5 gold bars for each victory, so for your 32nd win you would receive 160 gold bars. Then from 41 it jumps to 10 gold bars for all your victories, which means for your 45th win that is 450 gold bars, then for each fight more add one more up to 50 when you get 20, or 1000 gold bars, and then after that from 51 on it is 40, then 45, then 50, and so on.

There are a lot of you here in this room just starting, and as you know this is being held all over the world. You could be sent to any other country to fight, and to start off all of you will be fighting people at the same level. For your first fight you will fight someone else having their first fight. If you win, your next fight will be against someone else who has won one fight. In your early fights, for those of you that keep winning, there will be enough people at exactly the same level for you to fight.

But if you become very successful, then the higher you get, there will be fewer people at the same level, and people who have won twenty fights or more are usually fighting someone who has won either more or less, but very rarely exactly the same.

But we try very hard not to let the level of experience between two fighters be too great.

We have a very small number of people who have won 50 or more fights. We have a few more but still not a lot who have won 40 or more. Some more who have won more than 30, a fair number who have won 20 or more, and a lot who have won 10 or more.

The more fights you win, the better and stronger the opponents that you will have to fight afterwards, and that's why very few make it past 40. Even those who have won 40 or more have become very worn out. And that's when it becomes dangerous, when they are tired out and someone younger and faster comes along.

You will all start with a three month training period to get you into peak condition to be able to fight continuously, and put up with the barrage of pressure from other sources.

At the end of these three months you will have your last chance to back out, but remember that if you back out during the training, you can't come back.

There is another reward that some of you may really like. You get to sire children with many women who want you to sire their babies.

As you all know, you all had blood taken from you when you were born and it was put in a stem cell bank for later use, and also your gene code was determined. On the basis of that gene code everyone is given a list of eligible partners, partners that the computer has matched to be the best match for each person, and you have to choose from those eligible partners.

But because you are warriors, the best of the best, many women request that you sire them, and that is a special privilege that you have as warriors. Most of these women are the most beautiful from your country and from other countries also, and they demand the strongest and best warriors.

Some of our outstanding warriors have sired thirty or forty or even more children. But you cannot have that privilege until you have completed the training programme and won at least fifteen fights.

I shall now take questions for a few minutes, and then your first trainers will come in and tell you about the training and conditioning programme."

"Yes, that is a very good question that I should have dealt with. We do provide living accommodation. You don't have to take it, but we won't pay for you if you live outside, and you will still be expected to follow the training schedule wherever you live, and that includes very early morning runs."

"Are referees inside the cages? No, the referees are outside. But as I said, failure to obey the referee's instruction to pull away or to stop, results in disqualification.

There is no punching someone when they are down on the floor. You wait to see if they can get up. If they can, you can continue to hit them until they stay down or signal that they have had enough."

"How many fights is the most anyone has won? Fifty three."

"What happened to that person? He lost his last fight to a younger person. He is now in a nursing home, brain damaged."

"Has anyone retired undefeated after winning a large number of fights? No."

"Another very important question that I should have dealt with. Are there different weight categories? Yes. We have four divisions. 130 pounds or less. 131-165 pounds. 165-200 pounds. 201 pounds and more. Height doesn't make a difference."

"Are we being evaluated during the training programme? Officially no. The trainers of course are observing you and making their guesses as to who is going to be good and who won't make it very far, but they don't report this officially.

They only report someone who is really performing so poorly that the person should be told they are not suitable before they get really badly hurt. As I said, at the end of the programme those who have finished will all be considered trained and ready for your first fight."

"I think that is all for now. I'll finish off by telling you all that we are now the third most popular sport in this country, after football and baseball. We have overtaken basketball, hockey, soccer, and we have definitely put out of business that nonsense that people called wrestling. So you are joining a very active and dynamic organization and we hope that all of you have your dreams fulfilled."

Rodrigo had always been curious about people. Who were they? where did they come from? what sort of homes and families had they grown up in? what lives did they lead? did they have any love in their lives? did they feel fulfilled or unfulfilled?

He had looked around the large room while the introductory session was going on and he had the same curiosity about his fellow warriors-to-be. He saw some big and sturdy. Others with angry frowns and scowls as if they had joined to get rid of some of the rage they felt at their lot in life. Others appeared slighter in build. Were these the fast and clever fighters, he wondered?

Rodrigo left the building. He had decided to live outside because he wanted to have the freedom to live other aspects or his life.

He went to his usual table in the library and was surprised to see a bag on one of the chairs at the table and some opened books at that place. He usually had the table to himself. He wondered who the person might be, but first he went to the shelves to retrieve the volumes he had been working on. When he returned to the table he saw the long dark hair of a woman on a head that was poring over the books that had been left there. As he sat down with his books she glanced up, then looked back at her books, then perhaps realizing that she was possibly behaving in a socially unfriendly manner she looked up again and said, "I usually have this table to myself."

That didn't sound very nice, she thought. But the student who had brought his books to the same table rescued her with his comment, "I was about to say the same thing. So we must both consider this our own special table - just at different times."

"I think I've seen you before, haven't I, in a philosophy class?"

"Yes. You are the young lady who makes some very interesting observations on the position of women in Greek society," he said with a smile. She blushed.

He introduced himself, "I'm Rodrigo."

"I'm Astania. Are you taking philosophy as your major?"

"No. I am actually intending to do law and I thought philosophy would offer me an interesting opportunity to understand some of the fundamental ideas upon which our legal system was developed, and how it might be improved."

She had noticed him in the class. She had thought him at the time good looking. He hadn't said much. She was pleased that he had noticed her. She liked the way he expressed himself.

He had enjoyed her comments in the classes. Close up now, he became more aware of just how beautiful she was.

"What are you working on now?"

"I am preparing a class discussion comparing women in Greek society and in early Roman society, and trying to see which aspects have remained influential still today, and which have faded, and which of the two societies would we say today has left the strongest impression. What about you?"

"I am one of a team in a mock trial debate. One side is the prosecution and one side is the defence, and each of us has to contribute something to presenting our side of the case."

"What is the case?" she asked.

"It's a case of a poor person stealing. Not only do we have to make a case for the person actually having done it or not, but we also have to be careful to balance the subjective aspect of the person being poor, with the objective aspects of what actually are the facts of the case. How much can both sides allow emotion, and how much can emotion be excluded."

"Sounds very interesting. Which year are you in?"

"I am half way through my second year at the university, but I am still taking some first year courses because I have also been working at various things to earn money to be able to pay to study and have enough to live."

This startled her for a moment. She had not had to worry about money to live and to study. Her parents had been able to support her. She was very grateful for their support, but she needed reminding from time to time that others had to struggle to pursue the education that interested them.

He liked listening to her speak, and as she talked and he looked at her he became aware of a sensation of an arousal that was not so much sexual in nature as deeply intimate. He felt the closeness and warmth of her femininity. It provoked within him feelings of wanting to be totally immersed in her, more than just his penis inside her but wanting to be as one with her, a sensation that he had never before experienced in his relationships with women.

She also sensed that she was feeling something different being close to him and talking with him, as if they already shared something together even though they had only just met and spoken with each other for the first time.

"I don't want to rush you if you have a lot of work to do, but if at some time you would like to take a short break maybe we could have a drink or something to eat together," he suggested

"Yes, I'd like that," she agreed. "I want to finish this chapter and then I'll be glad to take a break."

They both continued poring over their books and making notes for some minutes and then Astania announced that she had finished her chapter and if he was ready they could leave for a while.

He suggested a juice bar across the road from the library which suited her. "I prefer juice myself," she told him. "Cranberry, Raspberry, anything like that. How about you?"

"All the above, and many of the newer flavours as well."

They sat for two hours together, talking easily about themselves and their courses. He was thinking to himself that she was a delight to be with. She thought that he was the nicest man she had met in all the time she had been at the university so far.

"We've been here for two hours. I think we should head back to the books."

"Gosh, has it been that long? It seems like just a few minutes."

"You are great company."

"Well thank you sir, and so are you."

"Perhaps we could do this again for a longer time, maybe not during school hours?"

"Are you suggesting we go out together, even without checking our genetic compatibility?" she asked, with a big smile on her face.

"I do believe that I'm suggesting exactly that, even though I sense that we might be genetically compatible. But I am enjoying your company so much that I don't want to worry about those rules for now."

"A very daring man." Now it was his turn to laugh. "I don't know if I am so daring, I just know that I really find you very attractive and very very, interesting and I want to spend more time with you. What do you usually like to do over the weekend?"

"I didn't grow up here and so I have tried to go somewhere different each Day 7 or Day 1 and explore a new area."

"That sounds wonderful. Did you have any areas planned for the next few weekends?"

"Yes. There are three that are next on my list. Do you think you would be interested in joining me?"

"Absolutely. I love the outdoors and walking, hiking, and climbing in mountain areas? Do you do that?"

"I love it."

"Great. So which day is best for you?"

They talked more and agreed that they would meet Day 7, Saturday as it used to be called, mid-day. She told him that she shopped for her food for the week on Saturday morning, and also did the main cleaning and tidying of her home that morning.

Rodrigo trained seriously, and started fighting. His speed was too much for his early opponents, and he won his first eight fights while hardly being touched.

After that, he was assured that his winnings were being deposited, and that future fighters would be at higher levels.

He was surprised at first by the appearance of his next opponent, Yari Slevanian. Where was he from? Finland perhaps, thought Rodrigo? Very tall and very thin. He didn't look as if he could take many hard punches. But if he had already won sixteen then he must have some special ability. Rodrigo could see that Slevanian had very long arms. Perhaps those arms had kept other fighters at a distance, not being able to land many blows on him while he wore them down with his punches? Perhaps also he was very fast?

They came into the cage, touched gloves, and the start signal was given.

As Rodrigo had expected Slevanian moved well, took up the centre of the cage, and sent out those long arms of his trying to hit Rodrigo. As Rodrigo moved away and tried to move in under Slevanian's long arms he quickly realized that Slevanian was also quite skillful, that he moved gracefully out of reach.

Rodrigo found himself on the defensive, having to cover himself to ward off those long raking tentacles sent out by Slevanian. He had to think quickly to decide how he was going to handle a person who must have had a very good boxing career.

Rodrigo took his time to observe Slevanian more closely and he started to see a pattern emerging. Slevanian would send out a right hand, would attempt to follow it with five quick blows to the abdomen, and then would gracefully step back and sway out of the way.

Rodrigo started counting. At the same time he had to protect himself from not getting hit too hard and too often. He started to feel Slevanian's rhythm. One, two, three, four, five, back, sway. He let the sequence happen twice more and then just as Slevanian stepped back Rodrigo put his head down and fired three quick blows to Slevanian's mouth and face.

Slevanian was shaken, surprised, but quickly regrouped and this time led with his left. But Rodrigo waited patiently, counted, and saw the pattern was the same.

Rodrigo let Slevanian carry out the manoeuvre a few more times, perhaps thinking that Rodriogo's attack was just a lucky foray, not a well-thought-out counter-move. Rodrigo defended himself against those attacks. Then Rodrigo counted again, waited for the back sway, and this time launched himself into a fast and ferocious attack on Slevanian's midriff. This time he could hear Slevanian gasping with the speed, the surprise, and the force of the attack. On the next series Rodrigo attacked Slevanian's upper body and face and Rodrigo swung round-arm movements to hit Slevanian on the face, by-passing those long raking arms of Slevanian.

Two more series from Slevanian and then Rodrigo launched another powerful assault on Slevanian's abdomen, and for the first time now Slevanian visibly wilted, bent forward, damaged by the blows to his midsection.

Rodrigo took up the initiative. Now Slevanian was using his long arms to try to defend himself against Rodrigo's assault, and Rodrigo was rapidly alternating from the head to the body, back to the head, and again back to the body, and Slevanian became more and more defensive. He stopped throwing any punches himself, just trying to remain upright. As he held his hands to his face and head Rodrigo pummeled his abdomen, and then launched a vertical uppercut, catching Slevanian flush on the chin. Slevanian's head snapped back and Rodrigo delivered another crushing blow to the middle of his abdomen that sent Slevanian reeling to the canvas. The seconds went by, Slevanian was obviously very much still alive, but he seemed hardly able to get up, and after a long time waiting for him to stand the judges awarded the victory to Rodrigo.

Rodrigo had won, and he had not killed. He felt pleased and relieved.

Rodrigo decided that he would take the opportunity to look at some of his potential opponents, some of the fighters who had won 40 or more fights. He looked up the schedules for the next few weeks, and started calculating which countries and cities he could visit in a two week period. No classes at university were scheduled, but he would have to keep up his training if he was going to fight more of the best.

He asked Astania if she would like to come with him.
"During the day we can tour the cities and the areas around the city, and in the evening I can go to the fights and you can study if you want, if you have work to keep up with. Or you can do something else if you want to."

Astania was delighted that Rodrigo had asked her to go with him. She was becoming very used to his presence in her life and the thought of him being away for a few weeks wasn't very comfortable. Also, the idea of visiting some places that she had never been to was exciting, especially with his company.

"I'd love to. Thank you for asking me," she said.

The next day Rodrigo told her that he had planned a trip that would take him to five different countries where some leading fighters were due to fight, and that also sounded interesting places to visit. Airline schedules would allow them plenty of time between the fights to be tourists for a few days in each place.

"The fights are in Athens, in Wellington in New Zealand, in Tokyo, in Gotenburg, and in Dublin."

"I haven't been to any of those cities. That sounds very exciting. When would we go?"

"We would leave this Thursday to be in Athens for Saturday. Stay there until next Wednesday. Then to New Zealand. Five days there and then to Tokyo. Four days in Japan and then Sweden. Four days in Sweden and then Ireland. Three days in Ireland and then back here. We would be away just over three weeks."

"I can stay in contact with my classes. Will we be staying in nice hotels that have business facilities that I can print any articles I need?"

"I shall make sure that they have, I believe that any good hotel today will have that."

"Do you know what every woman asks?"

They chimed together, "what will I wear, what is the weather in those places, what do I have to pack to wear?"

"How did you know that?" laughed Astania. "I didn't know you had been away with so many women before?"

"I haven't. But I've heard people say it and make a joke of it so often, that I know the words."

"That doesn't stop it being true."

But Astania was ready with one large bag and one smaller bag on Thursday morning when Rodrigo came to her home to take her to the airport. "I'm so excited."

"When you are excited you have a lovely look on your face. Your eyes are wide open, you have a huge smile, you almost bounce along you are so eager to go."

"I'm just so happy to be with you going away, doing something different, adventurous, spending time together away from our homes and our studies and our work."

They enjoyed their time together. Their love relationship developed very naturally. They liked each other, they asked each other what each wanted, how and where to be kissed and caressed.

They had a respect for each other from the start. They both knew the other person was smart, intelligent, thoughtful.

They also delighted in each other's bodies. Astania had not wanted to see him fight, she did not want to see him hurt.

It had provoked mixed feelings in him. He felt a bit let down, that she wouldn't be there for him, yet he could also empathize with her fear of not wanting to see him being hit and hurt.

So although she had seen him mostly undressed while training, he had not seen her fully undressed until they were together, and he expressed his admiration for her beauty.

As she had hoped, it was adventurous, so many new and different places, flying to different parts of the world, different hotels, different foods, different people, atmospheres, stores, they both loved what they did - and being with each other.

When they came back, they talked about making their relationship permanent. She asked him whether it was true that successful fighters were offered different women to sire, that many attractive women wanted to be sired, and he was an extremely attractive man.

"They want me for my body, my physical strength, I suppose they want the genes that contributed to that. But I want a partner, a woman to share life with who is intelligent, smart, interesting, who loves me for more than my body or what my sperm may carry."

"And do you think I might be that woman?"

"I know that you are that woman for me. The question would be do you feel the same way about me? Or do you think that with all your wonderful attributes you could do even better?" he asked.

"I don't know what even better is. I know that when we are together I feel very close to you, as if we are one person together rather than two. Do any young couple in their twenties know how they are going to feel in their forties or fifties? Do two people meeting in their forties or fifties think that they would have married the same person when they were in their twenties? They might have become very different people over twenty or thirty years, and have very different ideas, interests, preferences. What I know now is I want to be with no-one else other than you. For me, you are the very best."

They made arrangements to marry. He still had at least one big upcoming fight.

It was against a huge Russian, who had won twenty six fights, which was more than Rodrigo who had won twenty one.

The Russian had killed seven people, and eleven were severely brain damaged as a result of fighting him.

He looked at the Russian at the weigh-in, he thought the Russian was at least two metres tall, the official conducting the weighing-in announced his height as two hundred and three centimetres. Rodrigo was one hundred and seventy eight centimetres.

They were supposed to be in the same weight class, the Russian weighed-in at one hundred and sixty eight pounds, seventy six kilograms.   Rodrigo couldn't believe it. The

Russian was taller, much more muscular, Rodrigo himself weighed one hundred and seventy two pounds, and he was nowhere near as muscular as the Russian.

One of Rodrigo's trainers also could not believe the readings. He had an idea. The trainer approached the officials.

"I don't believe the accuracy of these readings -"

An official interrupted him, "You've been right here observing everything. What are you objecting to?"

"I'd like the fighters to take their shorts off and be weighed without any clothes on. I am sure Rodrigo will agree, even if there are women here."

Rodrigo nodded his agreement. "And don't think I want to show off my cock. I don't claim anything special about it. It's average. My only concern is that the woman I am with likes it. Not it's size."

That brought about some laughter and eased the tension.

The Russian team had a dilemma. Were they going to allow their fighter to be exposed in this way? And if they said no, would that raise suspicions?

The chief referee stepped in. There had been concerns before about the discrepancies between the huge Russian and his opponents, and the severe, even fatal damage he had caused.

The Russian team were asked whether the women should be asked to leave, Rodrigo's team disagreed. They were willing to be embarrassed, for the sake of honesty and accuracy. His coach said afterwards that if there had been cheating, then the presence of the women might have prevented any over-reaction by the Russians.

Rodrigo slipped off his shorts, the scale showed less than half a kilo difference from with his shorts on.

With the greatest reluctance, with an air of heavy resentment, radiating nasty looks, the Russian slipped off his shorts. The scale read two hundred and thirty two pounds, one hundred and five kilos.

Everyone gasped.

While people were stunned, shocked, someone from Rodrigo's team had picked up the Russian's shorts and felt the waist band.

He offered it to the chief judge. The judge felt the waist band, and asked for a pair of scissors.

The elastic was cut open, and revealed a magnet sewn into the seam, set at a reading of one hundred and sixty eight pounds, seventy six kilos.

The Russians left immediately. Not only were they immediately disqualified, but their whole team, every competitor, was disqualified.

Their organization would now be vulnerable for huge lawsuits from the killed and brain damaged fighters who had been misled, having to fight someone very much bigger and heavier than them.

Ultimately, the bill would come back to the Russians, but that would be a lengthy legal and political process, getting them to pay - with the alternative of being thrown out of every sports federation.

For Rodrigo, it had saved him from possible severe injury.

His relationship with Astania was so open that reluctantly, he told her the whole story. It strengthened her wish that he give up the fighting, finish his studies, and perhaps they might try to start a family together.

It took him a while to decide, which made her more tense. He realized her tension was her disappointment that he was so reluctant to give it up, that he didn't immediately see the good sense of stopping.

And then something happened that solidified his decision. He hadn't made public his uncertainty whether to continue or stop. It was assumed by the organization that he was continuing and another fight was being lined up. But walking one evening in the park near their home, he was attacked. Astania was grabbed from behind as Rodrigo was hit with lead pipes by three men.

Dazed, he tried to fight back, and landed some good punches that stopped two of the men, and then he smashed his fist into the size of the head of the man holding Astania.

The man collapsed, and Rodrigo told Astania to run and call for help while he tried to fight the three men still flailing away with their lead pipes.

He broke two noses, punches to the abdomens of the men caused them to double over groaning, but three against one with the three carrying and using powerful weapons was too much.

Eventually police sirens were heard, and the three men ran away.

Rodrigo was taken to hospital. He had a concussion, some broken bones, but he was alive.

He spent some days in hospital recuperating, and then went into a lengthy rehabilitation programme. Astania devoted herself to being with him and helping as much as she could.

When he had improved sufficiently to start exercising again, he told her that the attack had made up his mind to retire. She was delighted.

She might have been a little less delighted to hear what happened at the interview when he announced to the board his intention to retire.

"We understand. You might be convinced that you will never recover the speed and agility you had before the attack.

It's very unfortunate, you have been one of our outstanding fighters and also a very articulate person to be interviewed. You probably could have a very good career as a pundit, a commentator.

What you are eligible for, of course, is to be a sire to many women who would desire you to sire them.

We can bring you details with photographs, videos, of the most beautiful desirous women, and you can choose at your leisure."

He had thanked them, but told them that he was already married and hoped to start a family with his lovely wife who had saved his life, and whom he felt very attached to.

Astania understood some Russian, and she had heard the attackers speaking so she knew who had sent them. They blamed Rodrigo for their loss of the profits from the fighting arena, the profits they made from their giant's easy victories, and possibly their cheating at other weight levels.

And of course they were aware that eventually a very big bill was going to come to them for the deaths and damage they had caused.

So pulverizing Rodrigo was no surprise. They were very sore losers.

Astania insisted to Rodrigo that in fact he had saved her life. That if they had succeeded in their attempt to very seriously damage Rodrigo, they would have been unable to leave her alive as a witness and would have killed her.

Her only reservation was that to demonstrate the Russian cheating, he had let some other women appreciate the beauty of his manhood that she thought was her own very special privilege.

AUTHOR BIO

Joseph Berger graduated as a doctor from the University of London, England, trained as a Psychiatrist in the United States, and practised for more than forty years in Canada.

He taught students at the University of Toronto, and has published two books and many articles on medical topics.

His second book "Life's Lessons: How We Cope With Life's Challenges" published by Amazon in 2018, was based upon his years of work with patients, and provided the inspiration to write dramatic stories with psychological themes.

This series is the first of a series of short-stories, that will be published in the future.

He and his wife now live in Israel, they have four fantastic married daughters and a number of amazing grandchildren.

He has run five marathons, enjoys his family, travelling, soccer, and chocolate desserts.

Look out for his next book "**Wrongful Imprisonment**" that will be published soon.

He welcomes reviews, and comments can be sent to him at jbstories27@gmail.com.

BACK COVER

Psychological dramas are about people and their lives. An international crisis, fighting nasty bullies, a young child growing up without his parents in a new country, an older person trying to look after a much loved but now limited partner, an experienced professional opposed by an assertive, angry, but incompetent predecessor, a young man using his skill in a futuristic competition, but is the prize money worth what he might lose? The characters in these stories are people you can see, hear, and feel. They will touch you emotionally.